INSATIABLE APPETITES

HOW SWEET IT IS, BOOK 3

FIONA ZEDDE

To Kat

Thanks (?) for always challenging me.

2018

Photo credit: © Shutterstock/Conrado

Design: Red Raven Design and Publishing

ISBN: 978-1975600891

ALSO BY THE AUTHOR

Bliss
Broken in Soft Places
Dangerous Pleasures
Les Tales (novella collection with Skyy and Nikki Rashan)
Nightshade (novella)
Rise of the Rain Queen
The Power of Mercy
To Italy with Love (novella and stories)
When She Says Yes (stories)

Every Dark Desire (Vampire Desire #1)
Desire at Dawn (Vampire Desire #2)

A Taste of Sin (How Sweet It Is #1)
Hungry for It (How Sweet It Is #2)
Return to Me (How Sweet It Is #2.5)

CRITICAL ACCLAIM FOR FIONA ZEDDE'S WORK

"[Fiona Zedde's] sex scenes are lusty and make the book into a pleasurable poolside quickie."

- *Girlfriends Magazine*

"Fiona Zedde is a culinary artist with words, cooking up spicy, flavorful tales that she hopes will satisfy the appetite of a malnourished audience."

- *Washington Blade/Southern Voice*

"Fiona Zedde conveys the helter-skelter speed of this chic life-style with sharp prose, fast-moving actions, and erotic interludes that are intense, shocking and arousing."

- *Erotica-readers.com*

"Fiona Zedde's portrayal of a black lesbian love affair is exquisitely written and described." (about short story, *Love, Zora.*) - *femininezone.com*

"As the title implies, A Taste of Sin is chock full of the delicious sex scenes one would expect from Ms. Zedde. After all, she gave us the debut novel Bliss, a tour de force in black lesbian literature."

– *Sistahs on the Shelf*

"Fiona Zedde has done many remarkable things with *Bliss*, but one stands out more than all the others. She presents a credible heroine, despicable antagonists, and a plot that moves with fluid and exciting twists and turns."

– *Erotica-readers.com*

"This is a torrid sizzler of a novel [that] morphs into a nuanced story about reconnecting with the past, finding solace in the present, and learning that there is a future filled with true love. In addition, Jamaican-born Zedde writes about her native land with an honest affection that adds travelogue heft to her light fiction."

- *Richard Labonte (BookMarks/Q Syndicate)*

"Fiona Zedde [...] has created an excellent summer read. The landscape and people of both New York and Jamaica are vividly described, and the reader is bathed in the warmth of a colourful, sometimes dangerous, vista, and the excitement and heat of an erotic awakening – or is it love? Great stuff."

– *DIVA Magazine*

"*Bliss* [...] gets the positive critical attention that it deserves. [*Bliss*] is well written and filled with passion and culture, telling a compelling story of self-discovery in an exotic locale."

– *Terry W. Benjamin, nHouse Publishing*

"Kudos [...] for bringing out another novel filled with dykes of color, living and loving boldly, under the talented pen of Ms. Zedde."

– *AfterEllen.com*

"The sensuality of the narrative style, the intensity of the characters' emotions, and the complexity of the plot are all satisfying. [...] This book stands out from the red sea of current vampire erotica and casts its own powerful spell." (about *Every Dark Desire*)

– *Erotica-readers.com*

"Zedde's explicit erotic scenes keep no secrets, and her tender, masterful storytelling will keep readers spellbound and squirming."

– *Publishers Weekly*

CHAPTER ONE

Sage thought she'd be first to arrive at the restaurant but Nuria, the sexy femme already sitting at her table, looked like she'd been there for a good ten minutes. That was her fault for trying to fit in a quickie before she left the house.

Nuria had her drink in hand and was idly looking around the place when Sage walked up.

"Hey, *macha*." Nuria lifted her cheek for a kiss as Sage slid into the chair beside her at the round table prepped for four. She smelled dizzyingly of a dark and sweet perfume. "How's the happy, dysfunctional couple today?" Nuria asked with a grin.

"We're good, as always." Sage pinched her friend's ass as payback for her rude comment about her and her girlfriend, Phil. "No thanks to your bad-mind."

"Bitch..." Nuria laughed and playfully scraped her long nails over Sage's head, barely disturbing the low fade on the side and much longer, tight curls on top.

Seductively dressed in a white dress that contrasted with the even cocoa dream of her skin, Nuria took up far more room than her average sized body should have. Even seated and quiet, her larger-than-life personality surrounded her like the throbbing corona of the sun.

Along with Rémi and Dez, Nuria was one of her closest friends. These women were the only ones who knew Sage at her gayest. Her most free. "Why are you here so early?" Sage barely glanced at the slim drink menu near her place setting, already knowing what she was in the mood for.

"I was already in the neighborhood," Nuria said.

"What, you're fucking somebody on this side of town?"

"Not every aspect of my life is about fucking, you know," she said, although her whiskey and dark chocolate eyes sparkled with a tease.

Nuria was well aware of her reputation within their circle of friends and out in the larger world, but she didn't do anything to tame it. She fucked who she wanted to, male or female, could drink any of their friends under the table and, although firmly in her thirties like the rest of their posse, seemed in no hurry to settle down. She was just as wild at thirty-three as she had been at twenty-three, hell, probably even at thirteen.

Sage motioned the waitress over, ready to start the party. "Are you saying you weren't rolling around in somebody's sheets a couple of hours ago?"

Her friend snickered. "It was *one* hour ago, thank you very much."

The waitress appeared, a pretty and very young thing with a septum piercing. She eyed Nuria with a curiosity Sage had long grown used to.

"What can I get for you tonight?" the waitress asked once she'd torn herself from the shameless eye fuck Nuria treated her to.

"Appleton Estate white rum," Sage said. "The whole bottle, with a bottle of pineapple juice."

The girl nodded but didn't scribble anything down. "And

you?" She turned to Nuria and Sage got an eyeful of her ass, tastefully displayed in black slacks, the pretty curve of her back, and her thick fall of black hair down to the middle of her back.

Sage fully expected Nuria to ask for the girl's number because she did shit like that, but her friend only asked for a seven and seven, smiling up at the girl with her whole body.

"Of course." The girl's voice was a little breathless. "I like your thing, by the way." She pointed at Nuria's piercing, a silver stud between her dark purple lower lip and the tip of her pointed chin. "Very retro."

Nuria blinked. "Uh...thanks?" she muttered, frowning.

The girl smiled then sashayed off.

Sage laughed. "You gotta leave these young things alone, my girl. They're fresh out the cradle out here these days."

Nuria made a dismissive gesture then touched her piercing. "Is this played out?"

"The fact that you said 'played out' instead of whatever the fetuses are saying these days should tell you plenty." Sage settled back in her chair to take in the newly open restaurant-bar that had been a suggestion of their friend, Dez.

It was cool enough, though not in the same league as the A-listed jazz bar Rémi owned. Wilde's Bar and Grille was a typical Miami rooftop set-up overlooking Biscayne Bay and the city's glittering lights. The Yelp review Sage read promised half-naked bartenders twerking on the bar while making some of the most lethal cocktails in Miami.

She swept the place with her gaze again. So far, the crowd was subdued, the bartenders' feet firmly on the floor, and the lighting dim. Maybe all that raucous fun was supposed to happen later. Although she didn't know when since Wilde's closed at two in the morning.

"I think I should be insulted," Nuria said, still apparently stuck on the piercing thing.

"I don't know why, babe. We're the same age, you know. I'm too old to be saying shit is 'lit' or whatever, too."

"Oh my God..." Nuria rolled her eyes. "Speak for yourself, *macha*. I have plenty of fire in me yet. Whether they call it lit, happening, or *gostoso*." She drew out the last word like she was talking about food. Or the last really good porn she saw.

"*Gostoso*?"

Nuria tipped up a shoulder. "Something this Brazilian chick I hung out with last week was saying."

"Are you sure she was talking about you and not the flan or whatever you were feeding her at the time?" Sage asked.

Nuria was a phenomenal cook, although only her friends and the rare fuck buddy knew it. Despite her new gig as a talent agent, she still found time to make elaborate and criminally tasty dishes she invited her friends over to share.

"Fuck you," Nuria growled around a smile.

"Is that invitation open to everyone at the table?" Rémi, resident beautiful badass, appeared out of nowhere and leaned down to give Nuria European cheek kisses.

Rémi's curls gleamed in the dim overhead lights, cut low and highlighting her model-pretty face that was all smiles. Her black on black outfit—button-down shirt rolled up at the elbows, jeans, cowboy boots—skimmed her tall and muscular form in a way even Sage envied, although she knew she didn't look half bad in her own black jeans and tight white T.

"As if you'd ever take me up on it." Nuria patted the chair beside her and Rémi took it after exchanging a hug and back slap with Sage.

"Stranger things have gone on around here." Rémi put her motorcycle helmet in the middle of the table and draped her leather jacket over the back of the chair.

"Not that damn strange." Nuria tossed her head and sent the thick mass of curled dreadlocks slithering halfway down her back. They all knew Rémi wouldn't touch her with another dyke's clit.

Rémi was in love and monogamously—ecstatically, ridiculously, enviably—involved with a woman nearly twice her age. A woman who just also happened to be her best friend Dez's mother.

The whole start of that relationship had been a butt-load of trouble, but everybody was past it now.

"What's up, Sage?" Rémi settled into her chair. "Out solo tonight? Where's Phil?"

"She's at some kind of lecture thing with her science geek friends."

"Cool." A look flickered over Rémi's face, and she shared a brief glance with Nuria who hitched up a narrow shoulder in a shrug. "Who's our waitress?"

"I don't know," Sage said the same time Nuria offered, "Her name is Crystal."

Rémi flashed Nuria a look. "Working her already?"

"Not at all, darling. I'm just observant."

Sage had no idea how Nuria had "observed" the girl's name when she wasn't even wearing a name tag, but whatever.

"Here she comes." Sage waved toward the slim girl who wove through the crowd carrying their drinks on a small round tray.

She had to admit the young waitress was cute. But there was no way she'd fuck her. Technically, if Sage had started pumping out babies early, she was old enough to be Crystal's mother. Hell, on her last trip to Jamaica, she'd met some women her age who were damn *grandmothers*.

Her body rippled with a shudder of horror.

This was new for her. Five years ago, she would've thought nothing of sleeping with a girl as young as eighteen. Then again, five years ago, she'd barely been twenty-five, nothing close to the boring ass thirty-year-old she was now.

Crystal the Waitress gave out the drinks and took Rémi's order, her eager eyes bouncing between Rémi and Nuria, probably wondering which one she could entice into bed or the nearest unoccupied bathroom. The look was obvious to Sage who'd seen it on countless men and women over the years. It took someone with a strong ego to hang out with all these pretty bitches and not get a complex about her own looks.

And Sage was that someone.

At an average height of 5 feet 6, her looks were anything but. Square-jawed face, narrow and direct eyes, straight nose, even the gap between her pearly whites. Separately, those features belonged to a runway model, but together they had a different effect.

Sage knew there was something a little off about her looks, maybe it was her resting smug-asshole face, it could even have been her oversized Rihanna forehead. She could never be pretty, or even handsome. Called "striking" more than anything, she liked to think her looks, like cocaine, became more addictive with each exposure.

Her body, though, made an immediate and powerful impression. Having skipped the awkward, pimply phase as a kid, her deep brown skin was smooth and flawless, only a shade or three lighter than the black tribal tattoos covering both arms, her back, one thigh and flowing all the way down to wrap around the top of her foot like abstract fingers. Add to that the fact that she could sing like Tracy Chapman and had a new, but successful, career recording songs for movies and performing at decent-sized venues around town, Sage was basically lesbian catnip.

"Thank you, Crystal." Rémi showed the waitress how grateful she was with a smile and a twenty-dollar bill, a tip nearly twice the cost of the drink.

"Okay, high-roller." Nuria teased Rémi with a flutter of her fingers then snagged her martini glass to steal a sip of the hot pink drink. "Hmm. That tastes good. Maybe I should get one."

"It would go well with the pink lips you just flashed me from under your skirt," Rémi said with a grin.

Nuria leaned in, upper lips pursed in a kiss and glistening red. "Aw...you noticed."

"Seriously, guys?" Sage was never in the mood when they played around with each other like that. It seemed almost like incest.

"Don't get your panties in a wad, babe," Nuria said. "You can have a look too." She swiveled in her seat, her thighs already moving apart under the skirt. Sage looked away with a yelp, covering her eyes for good measure.

"I'm just in time for the show, I see."

The last one of their group, Dez Nichols, sauntered over. She moved around the table giving and receiving hugs from most, but a kiss from Nuria.

"Hey, baby." Nuria's enticing purr was aimed strictly at Dez.

Her pretty eyes smoldering with playful heat, Dez buried her hand in Nuria's thickly curled dreadlocks while their kiss lingered a little too long to be truly platonic. But that wasn't going anywhere either. Dez had her own woman and didn't entertain any others in her bed these days. Not even ones who looked like Nuria.

A shame. Sage used to love watching Dez and Rémi work over a woman together. At the peak of their power as The Good Time Twins, they'd been *ridiculous* to watch. Endlessly greedy and feeding off each other in ways the woman between them always enjoyed. Now though, they were living less eventful lives, both paired off and shackled to the women they'd fallen in love with.

Sage and Phil had their own thing. Completely committed to each other but free from the burden of artificial restrictions like monogamy or even wedding rings. They were faithful to each other where it really counted—in their hearts and minds.

She wouldn't say it was better than what her friends had, but even if she didn't say it, it was better.

Thinking about what she and Phil had led Sage's mind back to their interlude on the living room floor just before she left, the memory of Phil's mouth and hands and the teeth-clenching pleasure that had arched her back off the floor and damn near blew out her vocal cords. Maybe after her lab thing, Phil would come home and they—

"I can see all over your face what you're thinking." Fingers pinched Sage's side and she squawked, flinching away from Nuria.

"What?"

"You were thinking of some disgusting thing you and Phil got up to earlier. I know that look." Nuria giggled. She obviously approved.

"It wasn't anywhere near disgusting," Sage said, helpless to the smile that tugged at her mouth. "And I'm sure you've done a lot more."

"She got you there, love," Rémi said with a grin.

Nuria rolled her eyes. "You two are just so gross. All of you are. So in love and lording it over the rest of us..." She looked around the table. "And by that, I mean me." Since she was the only single one at the table.

"It's not my fault Phil is perfect for me," Sage said.

"Shit, I still can't believe you two have been together for this long." Dez lifted her drink, newly delivered by the young and lovely Crystal, toward Sage. "It's freakin' crazy."

Rémi nodded, though she looked more pleased than amazed.

Her relationship with Phil was the single miracle in Sage's life, one that she was so damn thankful for. Even with the growing feeling that something was going on with Phil, she was still happy to be with her woman.

Whatever was going on, it probably had nothing to do with them as a couple. Phil had family issues of her own that were coming to a head. Parents on the verge of divorce even though their constant fighting since she was young often made her wish out loud they would break up and spare everyone the daily trauma.

The Howards' rocky relationship made Sage grateful for her own parents' stability, even though Trevor and Vivian Bennett didn't know her as completely as she sometimes wished they did.

At times she wondered if they knew.

Then she dismissed it. If her mother knew about them, there was no way she would keep her mouth shut about it. Sage would have gotten a phone call within moments and couldn't imagine she would have been so easily welcomed back home.

"The cat and dog fighting you two get into sometimes is a little much, though." Nuria watched Sage with that inscrutable look of hers. "As much as you two fight, I thought you'd have given up on being together years ago."

"But they make up as intensely as they fight." Rémi's mouth twisted. "I've seen it. And believe me, it's not something I want to see ever again. Especially not live and direct from the floor of my office."

A flush of heat moved under Sage's cheeks, and she was very grateful for the darkness of her skin that disguised her blush. More than once, she and Phil had ended up at Rémi's club, Gillespie's, locked in one of their massive fight and fuck fests.

Although they'd calmed down in the last year or so, she and Phil had gotten into some nasty shouting matches in unfortunately public places. Usually over somebody one or the other was fucking. But as fast and hot as their tempers burned, their lust for each other burned hotter and easily canceled out whatever anger or resentment each felt. Their make-up sex was fucking *epic*.

Sometimes Sage worried that they only fought so they could fuck each other with the unrestrained savagery of animals in heat. "We're not that bad," she protested anyway.

Groans echoed around the table.

"Whatever you say, honey."

"I can't believe you'd say that shit with a straight face."

"Okay, next topic of conversation..."

"Yes, please..."

THEY SPENT about four hours in the restaurant. Talking shit, eating too much food, catching up on what they'd missed out on in each other's lives since the last few days they all saw each other. Good times.

But like some prick once pointed out, all good things had to come to an end.

Rémi was the first one to call it a night. The restaurant, which had been growing steadily emptier in the last hour, was giving them the side-eye anyway.

"I gotta get going," Rémi tossed some cash into the middle of the table. "Claudia is meeting me soon."

Across the table from her, Dez didn't even flinch at the mention of her mother. Things had changed a lot in the last couple of years.

"Yeah, the place looks about ready to kick us out anyway," Sage agreed.

They settled up the bill and headed on their way.

Outside the restaurant, Nuria and Dez drifted off to their separate cars. Sage kept Rémi company at the edge of the emptying parking lot while Rémi waited for Claudia to show up in the cab. What a college professor and middle-aged fox-like

Claudia was doing playing with Rémi out so late on a school night, Sage had no idea. But whatever it was must be one of the things keeping their relationship fresh and passionate.

"Things going good with you and Phil?" Rémi pulled on her riding gloves and glanced at Rémi from under her lush eyebrows. "You seemed distracted when we were talking earlier."

Sage shrugged. "Yeah. Me and the old lady are still doing our thing, you know."

A smile lifted the corner of Rémi's mouth. "I know."

Sage thought she saw a hint of judgment there. Or maybe she imagined it. She knew that except for an incident or two back when they first got together, Rémi and Claudia's bed only had room for the two of them. Although her friend never went into detail, Sage knew from just the way Rémi swaggered around that the sex between her and Claudia still burned up the sheets. Rémi was just too much of a horn-dog to be in something where she couldn't get her rocks off on the regular and spectacularly on top of that.

"There's nothing wrong with how me and Phil do our thing," Sage said defensively. But right after she said it, she could've bitten her tongue.

"Hey, I don't think there's anything wrong with whatever you guys are doing." Rémi curled her fingers in the tight leather gloves to make sure they fit right, then swept a gaze around the parking lot, obviously checking for her woman. "Do it 'til you're satisfied, that's what the song says and that's how you should live. When and if that open thing stops working for you guys, that's when you stop. If it keeps being sweet, keep it going." Rémi shrugged like it was nothing to her either way.

Rémi wasn't saying anything Sage didn't know, but unease had been burrowing under her skin for the past few weeks making her defensive. No point in taking it out on her friends though.

"Sorry," Sage said.

"No big."

Just then, a taxi cruised into the parking lot and pulled up near Rémi's motorcycle. The door opened, and Claudia stepped out.

Just... Damn.

Sage blanked her face to make it look like she *didn't* just swallow her own tongue.

Rémi's woman looked like a billion dollars. Cash.

At fifty-two, Claudia was slim yet curvy, her ass high and yoga-tight under dark jeans. A white, sheer blouse glowed under the high-collared, black leather jacket and low-heeled motorcycle boots hugged her small and delicate-looking feet.

On most days, she was easily the most beautiful woman in Miami who wasn't Phil. Her short, snow-white curls showed off the smooth darkness of her face and made her look a little bit like a pixie, especially with that pointed chin and slightly tilted eyes that crinkled with rays of sunshine at the corners. And she had the kindest mouth Sage had ever seen.

The door of the cab thudded shut, and Claudia stepped away from it and toward Rémi with a soft look. Her kind mouth became all lush sensuality and Sage felt a little dirty looking at her. Like she was watching her parents about to fuck.

"Here she is." Rémi raised her fist for a bump from Sage. "See you later in the week."

"Cool," Sage said as Rémi loped off to get her woman.

Smiling wide, Rémi stepped up to Claudia like she was the only being who existed in the entire world.

The two of them were far enough away from where Sage stood that she didn't hear what they said to each other. But the way Rémi planted both hands on Claudia's narrow waist and drew her in for a kiss was unmistakable.

There was passion there, yes. Mouths opened to devour,

bodies plastered together. But the spread of Rémi's hand in the middle of Claudia's back was a sweet tenderness. Like she was holding her lover close and allowing her to feel every ounce of her passion. But she also held onto Claudia like she was precious. Not delicate but valued in a way beyond words. Beyond price. Beyond anything.

When was the last time she and Phil had been together like that?

Sage couldn't remember.

She swallowed and took out her phone as an excuse not to look at her friend and her lover. While she fiddled with the call function on the phone, the bike rumbled to life. She found Phil's name under "favorites" and, by the time she looked up, Rémi's bike along its precious cargo was already cruising out of the parking lot.

From the back of the bike, Claudia clung to Rémi's waist, looking both regal and sexy. The two of them were gorgeous together. Perfectly paired in a way most people could only dream.

Sage hovered her finger over Phil's name on the phone but did not connect. Instead, she stared down the brightly lit road long after the two lovers disappeared.

CHAPTER TWO

One night, nearly a year ago, Sage almost asked Phil to marry her. She didn't know where the impulse came from, only that it rolled over her like the intoxication from a fruity drink, unexpected but not entirely unwelcome.

They'd stayed in, just the two of them. Netflix on the TV. Phil's favorite popcorn in a bowl between them. Their bare feet stretched out on the ottoman.

Chewing Gum played on the screen and Phil was cracking up every five seconds at the main character's antics.

"Oh my God, she's hilarious!" Phil poked Sage with her salty, popcorn fingers and collapsed against Sage's side with an attack of the giggles.

Just then, the light from the television turned her into a stunning, gray-tinged portrait. Sage lost her breath. That moment, her woman's laughter, the incredible contentment glowing inside her. She wanted to keep it all forever.

Will you marry me?

The question burst onto Sage's tongue and hovered there all night.

One question. Four words.

But she'd had zero courage, so the question had remained unformed in her mouth. Weighted down by fear. Ultimately unsaid.

CHAPTER THREE

Her woman was hiding something.

Sage didn't know what it was, but her clit was involved now, couldn't fully care.

"That's it, baby..." She groaned long and deep, arching up into the mouth riding her clit.

They'd been together long enough that Phillida knew exactly what felt good. Just how Sage liked it. How hard, how fast, how— "Fuck, baby!" Pleasure rushed through her in one hot slide, gathering in her hips, in her pussy that was soaking wet and dripping all over Phil's mouth. She was a breath away from coming... Just one more— Phil pulled away.

"You bitch..." Sage groaned out her frustration as her woman's laughing mouth withdrew, shiny wet, from her pussy.

"Yeah, but you love me." Phil shook her hair back from her face, the soft strands falling around her shoulders and face, highlighting the early morning sex look Sage loved so much. But there was something she would love even more right now.

"Are you going to eat me out or what?"

Hands grasped her thighs and slid between them to stroke

her clit, her slit, and lower to dart briefly to her asshole. "At this rate, you're lucky to get a damn good morning kiss." Phil teased her with a stinging bite on the thigh, and Sage hissed from the pain. And pleasure.

"I thought that's what you gave me already." Sage knew she wore a cocky smile. But it was Phil's fault. She was the reason Sage woke up happy and sexually voracious every morning for the last twelve or so years. Her mornings were so good because Phil was there. Fucking her. Eating her. Loving her.

Phil laughed, the odd dimple just below and to the right of her mouth making an indentation in the pretty tea biscuit skin. "You're spoiled," Phil murmured with her teasing smile. "I should make you wait."

But she didn't. Sage groaned from the stroke of knowing fingers on her clit. The touch fired pleasure all through her pussy and hardened her clit even more against the titanium barbell through her clitoral hood. She gasped, and the sound ricocheted through their bedroom and out the door they never bothered to close.

"Fuck me, baby." Sage groaned the plea, writhing under the skillful fingers, aching to be filled.

"For you, anything." And Phil bent her head.

The hot mouth covered her clit, sucked on the hard metal through her tender flesh, and licked a moan all the way from Sage's core. Her back arched into the sweet sting of lust, the sheets brushing under her heated skin, warming with early morning sweat. Another stroke of tongue and then—

"Ah!" Fingers slid deep inside Sage, "Fuck...just like that."

Slick pleasure. Phil's pierced tongue on her clit, her fingers sliding deeply inside Sage, stroking the weeping walls of her pussy while the knowing tongue turned her inside out.

She gripped the sheets and twisted her hips against her

woman's face, gasped Phil's name with each stroke of those knowing fingers, each sucking bliss of her tongue.

So good, so fucking—

Then pleasure stole the rest of her thoughts. The fingers curled inside her to find that place that made her scream.

"God—goddamn!" And just like that, she was done.

Her vision went icy white as pleasure shot through her entire body, obliterating everything else. The morning sun, the sound of the radio blaring through the house, the smell of morning coffee from the timed machine that told her it was way past time for her to get out of bed. The cum erased everything but Phil. Everything except the woman she adored.

"Phillida..." Sage panted, as she floated back down to earth, her skin slick with sweat, her heart racing past the finish line. She licked her dry lips.

Her woman laughed. "I love it when you call my name." She lifted her head from between Sage's legs, her mouth and chin wet, strands of her hair sticking to her damp cheeks.

"Oh yeah...?" Sage reached down, swimming up from the lethargy of her morning cum to cup the back of Phil's neck and tug her up to connect their mouths in a sloppy kiss.

The salt of her pleasure was perfect on Phil's lips. She tasted the flavor, chased it, leisurely stroking her woman's tongue with her own, sucking on the titanium piercing through the slick and agile muscle, feeding some of the pleasure she felt back to Phillida.

She pulled Phil up her body, their breasts and stomachs pressed together, kissing, turning them in the bed until Phil was under her, her thigh between Phil's and they were grinding together, moving sinuously in the bed, the sparks of fresh arousal and desire licking through Sage's body.

She was more than ready to go again.

It was damn near supernatural how horny this woman could

make her, even after twelve years of sharing the same bed—or whatever semi-private place they could wrangle to fuck each other's brains out. She never got tired of touching Phil, of loving her.

"I love you so much," she groaned into Phil's mouth.

Phil's pussy was soaked. It easily took Sage's two fingers, then three. Phil groaned, gasped into Sage's mouth, her hips moving faster to chase the satisfaction Sage offered.

Phil groaned her name, circling her hips in the bed. The whimpering sounds of desire at the back of her throat pulled Sage in deeper, made her want to hear more, feel more. She stroked the wet flesh, fucking into her with her fingers, swallowing the soft noises of helpless desire with her devouring mouth. A faster stroke, a flick of her thumb against Phil's clit, a curl of her fingers.

Phil tore her mouth away from Sage's with a long and desperate sounding gasp for breath. At the same time, her pussy clenched around Sage's fingers, gushing and squeezing her completion into the sheets.

Her pleasure came quietly, in soft and kittenish sounds that Sage had never heard from another woman. Phil wasn't a screamer. Had never been. And when they'd first gotten together, that had worried Sage, made her wonder if she was doing everything right. But over the years, she learned to read the more subtle signs of her delectation—and the not so subtle ones—to know what was working, what was turning her on, what made her lose her mind.

Grinning with triumph, she fucked into Phil's pussy, slowing the strokes as the tight contractions grew fewer and lighter, less desperate. Her wrist hurt but she kept fucking until she knew Phil had had enough.

Almost.

Phil's slick juices dribbled down Sage's fingers and her wrist.

"Baby..." Phil whimpered. Her lower lip trembled and tears of pleasure leaked from the corners of her eyes.

But not yet.

Sleek and electric, she twisted under Sage, her body hot and slick with sweat, hips fucking up, pussy wetly sucking on Sage's three fingers. Tiny lightning strikes of pleasure darted between Sage's legs, but she controlled them with the tight press of her thighs. This wasn't about her right now. She fucked into her woman, gentle and sweet.

So close.

"Yes, baby, yes." Sage groaned her encouragement.

Then Phil shivered one last time and Sage, quivering inside from sympathetic pleasure, fell between the sprawl of Phil's legs as she collapsed into the sheets panting from her release.

Perfect.

Phil's hair fanned out over the pillow. Her eyes fluttered closed and her breath came quickly. The sweat from their sex glowed all over her beautiful face, throat, and heaving breasts.

"I think you fucked me back to sleep," she said without opening her eyes.

"I doubt that." Sage laughed softly. Her love was about as sleepy as she was. Which was not at all.

Making a lie of Phil's claim of being asleep, her thighs tightened around Sage and she bucked, shuddering ecstatically.

Yeah, her woman was far from asleep, and besides it was only one orgasm.

She made a low sound of contentment and slowly pulled her fingers out, sighing when the pussy clenched around her fingers and Phil made a soft whimpering sound.

"One of your friends from the lab called," Sage said, suddenly remembering the earlier message. She lightly stroked Phil's clit in apology. "He said something about needing you there right this morning."

"Not fair," Phil said. "It's Saturday." But she opened her eyes. Her gaze felt like sunshine on Sage's face, warm and precious.

"Today just isn't your day. It's your turn to make breakfast." Sage tapped Phil's thigh with a grin and got up from the bed. "I'd like a veggie smoothie and egg white omelet," she called from the open door of the bathroom.

"I should tell you to go fuck yourself," Phil muttered.

Sage slid open the door to the shower. "But you already took care of that so..."

Behind her, Phil gurgled with laughter. "You're such a pain in the ass."

"But I'm your pain in the ass."

"So true."

Sage felt her grin grow wide enough to give her Joker face. She pulled the glass door closed and turned on the water. Today was going to be a damn good day.

An hour later, Sage walked out of the bathroom to the chime of a message notification on her cell.

No texts. But she'd a missed call.

She tapped the play button and put the message on speaker, leaving the phone on the bed while she lotioned her skin.

"Sage. It's Mummy and Daddy."

Bending to smooth the citrus-scented lotion over her muscled calves and thighs, she frowned at the breezy tone in her mother's voice.

A naturally tense woman, her mother was at her happiest when she was about to get into some shit.

"Why don't you pick up the phone?" Her mother paused like she was talking to an old-fashioned answering machine and could somehow get the person listening to answer the call. Then, after she didn't get the interruption she was clearly expecting, she went on. "We're coming up to Miami soon for Errol's graduation. I hope you didn't forget. One week we're staying."

Another pause that only gave Sage silence enough to hear her own suddenly out of control heartbeat thundering in her ears. "Okay, call us back so I can give you the details. Your daddy is very excited to see Miami again. Bye now."

"Was that your mother?" Phil came from the other attached bathroom dressed in her geeky-sexy clothes.

Dark slacks that hugged her perfect ass, a black shirt that clung to the curve of her breasts. She'd showered and wet her blow-out until it sprung back into elastic curls and coils around her face.

A heavy thud of her heart, a tightening low in her belly—both normal reactions to seeing the woman she loved and adored—stopped Sage in her tracks for a moment. She stared her fill until her woman lifted a teasing eyebrow to get her to answer the question. After twelve years, she still had it bad.

"Your mother is coming?" Phil asked. "Here? With your father?"

"They are, yes." Then Sage's brain caught up. Her parents. Visiting. "Oh, shit."

"That's one way to put it." Phil's smile looked tired around the edges. They both knew what this visit meant.

In the years since her parents "retired"—or whatever you called it when two people who'd never had to work a day in their lives moved back to an island they left when they were young—Vivian and Trevor Bennett had only set foot in Miami a handful of times. Maybe three or four.

And each time, Sage pretended Phil was just her friend.

Her parents were Jamaican. She was Jamaican. No way Sage could let them truly see and know her in all her "big bad dyke" glory. They'd never accept it. They'd never accept *her*. Already, she'd seen up close and personal what a homophobic family was capable of doing to someone they supposedly loved. She was scared to death that the same thing would happen to her.

Her friends sometimes teased her for still being in the closet, laughingly wondering out loud how her parents could be blind to her—a pants-wearing stud half-covered in tattoos and who never had a boyfriend—being gay.

But it just never came up between her and her parents. At least that's what Sage told herself. Now the boy they'd half-way adopted since then, some kid named Errol Sage had never met, was graduating from high school and they were coming up for the big event.

"Shit..." Sage muttered again, and her stomach sickened with anxiety.

"It'll be fine, babe." Not meeting her eyes, Phil dropped a dry kiss on Sage's cheek and headed for the bedroom door. "We'll handle it just like we did the other times."

The sound of her stilettoed footsteps rang out as she stepped off the thick, Turkish rug and onto the golden Travertine tile. Without once looking back, she disappeared down the long hall-way, on her way out the front door. She left Sage in the lingering trail of her subtle, floral perfume. The scent of it was an accusa-tion, a sweetness she didn't deserve.

Sage cursed again. She knew Phil was sick of being shoved back in the closet every time her parents came to visit. It was fucked up and inconvenient as hell, and not just because Sage had to sleep apart from the woman she loved. Twelve damn years. This had gone on for far too long.

The house rang with an empty silence in the wake of Phil's exit. Sage groaned out loud. The bed sank under her naked ass as she sat down, her arms locked tight, her eyes staring, dry and unseeing, at the rug between her feet.

This closet she'd barricaded herself into was hurting the woman she loved, but did she have the balls to change things now?

CHAPTER FOUR

As a kid in Jamaica, Sage had been scared shitless of her sexuality. Not about what it meant to be gay or whatever. But about what everyone else would do if they found out she liked pussy instead of dick.

She hadn't been living under a rock, even as a kid, so she knew some rabid Jamaicans got all up in their bullshit, macho feelings and had killed the head of the island's only gay and lesbian organization. That terrified her.

People in school, at her parents' church, even in their neighborhood said the man deserved it. Shit, they had a fucking parade celebrating his murder. Just for loving someone they didn't approve of.

The man's killing carved grief and fear deep into her bones.

So, she'd kept to herself, ignoring the boys who asked to go into the woods with her and play "show me." And she definitely ignored the girls who wanted to play at kissing at her exclusive boarding school, practicing at getting their mouths and bodies to do the right thing in preparation for the boys they would eventually fuck and marry. Sage kept herself locked up tighter than Fort

Knox. And then her parents decided they would move to America.

The move had nothing to do with money. They had money, inherited some of it and made the rest by investing and using their considerable financial brilliance. Her parents were so alike in their outlook on the world, on their backgrounds—they had been neighbors growing up—that Sage would have suspected them of being siblings. Three things dominated her parents' time: Church. Making money. Travel.

Her father had gotten the chance to sit on the board for a company in Miami, thriving and massive, that insisted on their board members living in America. He made the move with his family, and why not? It wasn't like he was doing anything in Jamaica aside from playing polo and showing off to the locals how rich he was.

Sage had never been so grateful for anything in her life.

In high school, she quickly made friends with other out gay people and began to slowly transform herself. The self that left the house was hardly the same one who showed up for school - she changed clothes as soon as the house was barely a mile behind her - and got tattoos in secret, wore her white T's and baggy jeans, then button-down shirts and tailored slacks. Kissed girls and went to parties, got to know Dez, Rémi, and a few other girls in school who were unashamedly themselves. She never invited them to her house. They never knew she was in the closet at home. And when her father had quit the board and moved back to Jamaica at her mother's insistence, she knew even greater relief and snatched at that last piece of freedom.

They'd asked if she wanted them to stay with her while she was in college. But she gave them all the permission they needed. And she lived her life.

And now, they were coming back to blow that life she'd built straight to hell.

CHAPTER FIVE

Later in the week, when Dez called to invite her and Phil out on a double date, Sage latched onto the invitation with an embarrassing amount of desperation. At that point, she was ready for pretty much anything to avoid thinking about her parents' pending visit.

Dez and her pretty wife, Victoria, picked them up in their red Porsche SUV and took them to the movies.

"What are we seeing anyway?" Sage asked from the front passenger seat.

"That Taraji movie where she plays a bad ass assassin," Phil answered. At Victoria's insistence, both femmes lounged in the back while Sage and Dez sat up front.

"Good, I've wanted to see it forever," Victoria said, fluffing the loose curls that spilled down around her face and to her shoulders. "Good choice, baby." She reached between the seats with red-tipped fingers and rubbed her wife's shoulder.

Dez grunted but any fool could see how pleased she was by just that little bit of praise from her wife. After three years together, they were still disgusting to be around sometimes.

Less than half an hour later, they ended up at the open-air theater in the park. It was the perfect place to see a movie, especially on dry, fall evenings. After the film, they grabbed coffees and beef patties from a food truck and went for a stroll along the park's well-lit, winding paths.

The evening was cool and perfect, at least by Miami standards. Which just meant they weren't sweating their clits off outside. They started off walking side by side but ended up with Victoria and Phil up ahead while Sage and Dez slowly brought up the rear.

"Well, that wasn't as bad as I thought it was going to be," Sage said, sipping her coffee.

The movie was okay, not great. But it had been damn good to see a black woman as the lead in a film that wasn't leaning heavily on all the usual stereotypes.

"It was pretty good," Dez said with a grin. "Gimme a movie with a chick in high heels and nice tits and I'm in heaven."

Sage barked out a laugh. "If only everybody was that easy to satisfy."

Dez's smile drifted away. She looked up ahead to where Phil and Victoria were laughing together about something. "Everything okay with you and Phil?"

"Yeah, yeah. We're cool." She didn't mention the nagging feeling she had that something was off with Phillida. Sometimes it seemed like Phil turned to her with words just waiting to fall out of her mouth, then her lips would tighten and a laugh, joke, or invitation would flood out at Sage instead. "My parents are coming into town again, that's all."

"Right, right..." Dez nodded with her listening face on. "So, is it the same game plan for you guys as usual?"

"Yeah, why wouldn't it be?"

Dez shrugged. "I thought Phil would've gotten tired of that crap by now. You've been together twelve years, not twelve days. Getting hidden away like a dirty secret can't feel good to her."

Sage had been thinking about the same thing, but she couldn't do anything about it. The life she had was the life she had. She never asked for Jamaican parents or to be from a country that would stone her to death for loving the way she did.

"It's not like I can do anything about it," Sage muttered. "Things are what they are."

"I guess if that's what you're willing to accept..." Dez shrugged again.

But Dez could never understand. She'd been raised by relatively liberal parents who mostly embraced her whole gay self—okay, her father was an asshole and a cheat. Sage never had that life. She never had that acceptance.

A low squeal of excitement drew her eyes to Phil and Victoria. The women had stopped walking and now chatted with a lesbian couple, long-haired femmes in designer dresses and sensible but sexy shoes. They were gorgeous.

One of them had a hand perched on a massive stroller.

"She's getting so big!" The words drifted back to Sage a moment before Phil reached into the stroller and plucked out a sleepy-looking baby.

The smile on her woman's face was absolutely smitten as she held the child on her hip and said something Sage couldn't hear. Phil and Victoria cooed over the kid while the hot lesbian moms looked proud as hell. Like they'd done something amazing together.

By unspoken agreement, Sage and Dez slowed their steps until they were practically standing still. The two strangers looked like women both of them would've banged back in the day. At least it was back in the day for Dez with her married and monogamous self. If they didn't have their kid with them, Sage would invite them back to the house with her and Phil for a hot foursome.

"You're such an animal," Dez muttered.

"What?"

"I know what you're thinking and it's not even a little bit cute."

"As if going home with two hot chicks and fucking them blind isn't some shit you've already done." Sage made a dismissive sound. "More than once."

Dez blinked, then flicked her gaze up to the women. Both were curvy, sophisticated and poised, but something about them hinted that they got down and dirty in the freakiest of ways between the sheets. "You're not wrong," Dez said.

Sage drained the last of her coffee and veered toward a garbage can along the path. Dez did the same. Phil and Victoria were still in baby admiration mode, so she left them to it. Nighttime hovered on the other side of the sunset currently burning up the skies above them, but nobody was in a rush.

Sage shoved her hands in the pockets of her skinny jeans. It was easier to watch Phil than to go up there and pretend to make a fuss over some random kid. If she had one of her own, she'd love it unconditionally, but she wasn't just a general admirer of babies.

One of the women looked past Victoria and Phil, her intrigued gaze landing where Sage and Dez stood. Lust practically dripped out of her eye sockets as she watched Dez. But Dez plainly wasn't interested.

"Do you ever miss it?" Sage asked.

"What?"

Sage quirked the corner of her mouth at her friend. Dez wasn't fooling her at all, and her friend finally gave a reluctant laugh.

"Are you trying to get me in trouble here?" Dez asked.

"You know me better than that."

Deliberately turning her back to the thirsty baby mama, Dez shrugged. "I'm not sure if 'miss it' is the right way to say what I feel sometimes." She looked over her shoulder, and Sage knew she wasn't taking a peek at the baby mama but at her own wife. "Sometimes I just wonder how the hell I ended up here. With low-key weekends, a wife, and nobody else in the bed with us." She made a sound of amazement. "It's a whole different life from the one I used to have. And sometimes I feel like another person. Like, did I give up my real self for this woman?" Her eyes tracked back to Sage like it was a real question.

"Damn, really?" Sage swallowed as thick unease rose in her throat. Dez loved her wife more than...more than just about anything. If she was having doubts, what did that mean for Sage?

With a flashing smile, Dez continued. "Then I realize that I'd rather have this woman than all the anonymous fucks in the world." She jerked her chin toward where her wife stood. "Victoria doesn't bitch and moan when I kick my shoes off in the foyer and just leave them there. She supports my good ideas and calls me on my bad ones. And I fuck her like a god because she's the one and only goddess in my world." Dez waggled her eyebrows and grinned, then abruptly turned serious.

"Anyway, change is necessary," she continued. "If we run away from it, we're also running away from our own happiness, and from knowing who we really are. Plus, I didn't want to be that old ass, perverted dyke in the bar still trying to strap down the young thangs born the same decade I got my first leather jacket."

Sage had to laugh. "Word." She'd never do some dumb shit like that. The young ones were completely off-limits.

"Are you two over here hiding from the big, bad baby in the stroller?" Victoria appeared behind Dez with Phil at her side. She looped her arm around her wife's waist and leaned in for a quick kiss.

"Nope," Sage said. "We're just talking about the old days."

Victoria pursed her lips and gave her and Dez the side eye. "I can only imagine..."

Wearing an absent-minded smile, Phil threw a look over her shoulder at the couple continuing down the path with their baby. The look on her face was soft. Longing mixed with...resignation?

Worry throbbed in Sage's belly. She reached for Phil's hand and drew her close, murmuring indistinct words of comfort, relieved when her woman managed a faint smile in response.

"That stuff is all in the past, love." Dez nuzzled her wife's throat with a flirtatious grin and a loaded look at Sage. "We're all moving toward the future now."

CHAPTER SIX

Sage stepped from the SUV, handed the valet her keys, and walked around to the passenger side to help Phil from the car.

"This is much nicer than I thought," she tipped her head up to whisper in Phil's ear.

Phil, dangerous in high heels and a brilliant yellow dress—plunging neckline, a triple string of fine gold chains raining down her cleavage—that made her look like an incarnation of Oshun, grinned and wrapped an arm around Sage's waist.

"I love it already," she said.

Around them, cameras clicked and flashbulbs sent lightning through the throng of photographers. A long line of cars and valets rushing to help out drivers and passengers wound behind them.

Sage hadn't been to a movie premiere in ages, and it was only boredom and Phil's unexpected desire for a night on the town that had dragged her from a date she'd made with a pair of Black Russian gymnasts. The premiere tickets came courtesy of Nuria, who was now some sort of agent to the stars.

She'd invited them out before but none of them, not even Rémi who still modeled every now and again, were particularly inclined to mingle with the rich and over-exposed. But Phil wanted to see the movie and the actress (and actor) who played a post- and pre-op transwoman. Sage had been shocked enough when Nuria announced they were bringing such an overtly queer story to Hollywood.

Rémi had only twisted her mouth with cynicism. "Don't worry. I'm sure they'll mess it up."

So here they were.

And Sage had to admit, it wasn't half bad. She shifted her shoulders under the tuxedo jacket and damn near floated at Phil's side while the cameras flashed and clicked. Photographers had no idea who they were, she was sure. They were just taking shots of them just in case they were important.

"I hope there's food," she said.

"There better be." Phil tightened her arm around Sage's waist and grinned. "I wore my stretchy dress just in case."

As if any extra weight dared stick to her. In the twelve years they'd been together, Phil hadn't gained a pound. Sage met her at five feet ten of perfect, and she still was that and not an ounce more.

The escorts in dark suits swept them up the red carpet and into the massive theater. It was an open space of classic lines, lush marble, and high ceilings. The acoustics were incredible. With a grin, Sage imagined it would make an ideal venue for an orgy. Moans and grunts and meaty slaps rolling one after the other and in stereo, the sounds echoing and amplified by the high ceilings and wide halls.

"This place is amazing!" Phil spun around, and the brilliant yellow dress swirled around her long legs.

The place was already more than half full. Women in designer dresses and tuxes, men in suits and tuxes themselves.

Sage noticed a few people she'd seen on her television screen. An actress she'd briefly had a crush on in her teens, his wife who was much younger than him and a current rising pop star. Wall to wall movie and TV stars, and them. Sage chuckled at the thought.

"You're here!" Nuria appeared out of the crush of bodies with a smile and a hug for each, the dark and edible scent of her perfume tugging at Sage's senses as they briefly pressed together.

"We said we'd come, now here we are."

"Help yourself to anything you want." Nuria gestured around them to the waiters in white uniforms flitting between the beautiful and rich carrying trays of hors-d'oeuvres and drinks. She could be talking about the waiters or the food or both. "The movie will start in about thirty minutes or so. The lights will dim when it's time to go in. Just mingle and have fun in the meantime and text me if you need anything."

Then she was gone again.

"When she decides to do a job, she goes all in, huh?" Phil smiled as she watched Nuria's back disappear into the crowd.

"You know she does. She's an all or nothing kind of girl, and that's one of the things I love about her."

"Yeah." A wistful look settled into Phil's face. "I wish I could live like that."

"You don't?"

"No, not really." Then her face cleared, the dimple coming out to play, her white teeth flashing. She tugged Sage toward what a sign advertised as a Whiskey Station. "Let's go check that out."

Sage allowed the distraction but made a mental note to ask Phil what she meant. None of this meant anything if they weren't living the lives they wanted. But for now, whiskey.

They sidled up to the glorified bar to taste the selection of whiskeys from Scotland and other places in the world. By the time they left the whiskey station, each with a tumbler of something smoky and delicious in their hands and the flavor of two of three whiskeys they'd tried still slick on their tongues, Sage felt *good*.

From her pocket, her cell phone buzzed with a phone call.

"Where are you?"

"Near the front of the theater." Rémi's voice, laced with annoyance, came loudly through the phone. "There's some guy near me dressed like Jack Sparrow."

Sage craned her neck and looked toward the front, caught sight of gold teeth and long dreadlocks on a white guy. "I think I see who you're talking about." She turned to Phil. "Raise your hand, babe, so Rémi can see you." She was well aware that her modest height—aka being short as fuck—made it nearly impossible for anyone who knew to spot her in this crowd of high heels and six foot plus leading men and wanna-be movie stars.

Phil raised her hand, using her bright yellow handbag to draw even more attention, then did one better with a piercing whistle. The sound came back to her through the phone.

"You hear that?"

Rémi laughed. "I think everybody did. I see you. Heading that way now."

A few moments later, she emerged from the crowd, pretty and elegant in simple slacks and a blazer, her girlfriend's hand tucked into the crook of her elbow.

"Hey, girls!" Claudia waved at them, a queenly movement of her hand that made Sage smile.

Like Rémi, she wore pants, but hers were slim-fitting black capris, elegant and classic, that hugged the lines of her hips, thighs, and legs. A high collared blouse in rose-red reflected the color of her lips.

"This place is packed." Rémi tucked her phone in the inside pocket of her jacket and tugged a smiling Claudia out of the way of a passing trio of starlets waving their claw-like manicures around.

"Tell me about it," Sage muttered. "I didn't think people in Miami were into movie premieres this much."

"Maybe not, but we love our movie stars." Phil cheek-kissed Rémi and hugged Claudia, her body a little on the stiff side even after two years of trying to get used to her and Rémi together.

Sage knew Phil was still having a hard time adjusting to dealing with Claudia Nichols as a peer. Or at least someone Sage and the rest of the other women hung out with when they were doing "couple-y things."

"There are plenty of them out tonight," Claudia said.

She looked around appreciatively, eyes bouncing from one beautiful face and form to another before landing back on Rémi. Sage imagined her thinking that no one at this party was as gorgeous as her lover.

"This movie is a great project," Phil said. "I was really surprised to hear that the book was optioned by such a big studio. It has the potential of being the trans-Brokeback Mountain."

"I'm not sure if that's necessarily a good thing," Claudia said with a soft laugh.

"You know what I mean. At least have the conversation about and experiences of LGBT people be the focus of a movie, and not in a stereotypical way either."

"I guess we'll see once we get in there."

A flash of curled dreadlocks and pale green caught Sage's eye. Nuria waving them over. She nudged Rémi. "I think Hollywood's latest power agent wants us to join her."

They slipped through the scented and richly dressed crowd until they were at Nuria's side.

"Hey, loves!" She slipped one arm around Rémi and the other around Claudia. "You know my client, Collette." She introduced them again to Collette Victor, already a star in France and a rising talent in America. "And meet Zachary and Zoe Baxter." She tilted her head toward a man and woman, obviously siblings, both with ink-black hair down to the middle of their backs and model high cheekbones. "The stars of the movie."

"A pleasure." Phil extended her hand to the male Baxter before Sage or any of the others did, her smile small but genuine. "I'm really looking forward to the movie."

Introductions went around in a circle.

They were interesting enough as people, but it wasn't long before Sage was bored. Being a member of them, the idle rich were never that interesting to her, but Phil stayed close to both siblings, asking questions about the movie and how they'd gotten their roles. After a quick touch at the bottom of Phil's spine to let her girlfriend know she was wandering off, Sage left to find more interesting things to do.

The lights flashed, announcing the imminent start of the movie, and interrupted a forgettable conversation Sage was having with a closeted Hollywood starlet with a plunging neckline and memorable tits. Would it be worth it to invite her to the hotel across the street for a quick fuck? Probably not. Pretty tits were a dime a pair in this town.

"Maybe we could role-play or something," the starlet said with a lick of her bright red lips. "I'm real good at that."

Uh huh...

The warning lights flashed again, and Sage looked around for her friends, much preferring to sit with Phil and her girls than chase after some woman who may or may not drop to her knees for Sage later.

It wasn't much of a decision.

"I guess it's that time," she said with faked regret and pulled away from the woman who had her cleavage practically on Sage's shoulder.

The starlet bit her lip. Then, after a sharp breath of decision, slipped her card into Sage's front pocket, fingers stroking a hip during the transfer. "I'm at the Ritz in Coconut Grove." Then the woman was gone.

Always good to have options.

Sage made her way through the crowd, most of the people moving toward the arched entranceway into the screening room. She skimmed the crowd, looking for that flash of yellow, that explosion of hair that belonged to Phil. But she saw Rémi first, leaning against a column, hands in her pockets as she talked with Claudia. A smile played around her mouth as she listened to whatever her woman as saying, then she laughed, fingers floating up to coast along Claudia's jawline then back to her pockets as if she couldn't help but touch. Despite how they'd began—in secret and at the risk to the long-standing friendship Rémi had with Dez—they were beautiful to look at, sometimes painful with their obvious love and lust for each other.

"Hey, you guys see Phil or Nuria?"

"Nuria's probably going to be babysitting her client, but I already have the seats she reserved for us." Rémi pulled out a set of tickets and passed a pair to Sage. "We have them all in a row. I sent a pic of the tickets to everyone earlier today." Rémi had gotten the tickets from Nuria a few days before but hadn't gotten the chance to give them out in person.

"Cool. I'll just wait a few more minutes here for Phil then I'll come in."

"All right." Rémi slipped her arm around Claudia. "See you in there."

Sage went to look for Phil. Just as she was about to give up and head into the screening room, a familiar shade of yellow moved into her field of vision. Phil walked with Zoe Baxter, their steps in sync, their bodies brushing in places and in ways Sage was more than familiar with. She opened her mouth to call out to her girlfriend. But something made her pause.

Phil was in game mode. That zone where she was flirting with the intention to fuck. And it looked like she was going to score if the way the other woman leaned into Phil was any clue.

Something distracted Zoe Baxter and made her turn toward Sage. And Sage drew in a sharp breath. Phil wasn't flirting with Zoe, she was flirting with *Zachary*, the brother. The bottom dropped out of her stomach and she swallowed hard.

Maybe she hadn't seen what she thought. But another look at Phil with the *man* only confirmed what she already knew. Her girlfriend's eyes, her lips parted in a predatory smile, ate up the trim figure of the man in his dark suit. She touched his arm to bring his attention back to her, fingers lingering against the black material of his suit jacket, then her neck tilting back to laugh at something he said.

Was this some kind of joke?

The lights flashed again, a glowing red this time, and Sage made a split decision, whirling around to go into the theater instead of waiting on Phil. She navigated her way into the theater and to their row of seats. By the time she got one of the empty chairs, Dez and Victoria were already there, sitting next to Rémi and Claudia. Nuria sat just in front of them with her client, occasionally looking over her shoulder and making comments to their friends that sounded garbled to Sage's ears.

A hand squeezed her shoulder. "You okay, baby?" Phil sat in the chair next to her that had just been empty.

Sage nodded, not quite able to use her vocal cords. Her skin flushed with heat then cold, and she shivered. Was she overreacting? With a faintly worried smile, Phil touched her thigh then, after peering into Sage's face to search for whatever she didn't find, settled back in the velvet-lined seats.

Someone made an announcement and introduced the film. The film started. The credits rolled. But Sage didn't see or register any of it.

When the house lights came back up, she blinked into the sudden brightness. Applause erupted around her and the crowd stood up, clapping still for what had apparently been a film worthy of such a reaction. Sage didn't remember a single that happened on the screen.

Nuria turned to them. "I'll meet you guys at the after-party. I have to wrap up a few things here first." Her client muttered something and Nuria patted the girl's back, her hand wandering lower than strictly necessary.

"Let's wait until most of these people get out of here," Dez said, peering around at the crowd swarming toward all the exits. She kept her hands on Claudia's hips.

Awareness of the things around her was coming back to Sage. With the sounds of the movie being over, the lights, her friends moving around, a sense of normalcy was reasserting itself. These were the same people she'd always known. Phil was the same woman she'd always known. They loved each other. What she thought she saw earlier didn't make sense. Maybe she'd just been too tense over her parents' planned visit.

"Sure. That's a good idea," she co-signed Rémi's suggestion.

"Where is the after-party?"

"It's here," Nuria said. "Just in a bigger ballroom than the one they had us in from earlier."

Soon enough, the flow of people slowed down enough for them to leave the auditorium and head for the ballroom. Sage was more than aware of Phil just in front of her, even had enough presence of mind to grip the hand Phil extended behind her for Sage to take. The slender hand was warm and dry. The grip firm.

Whatever she thought she saw earlier, she obviously made it up.

The ballroom was massive. Much bigger than the one they'd all been corralled into earlier with food and liquor stations along each wall, waiters in more festive clothes, dance music flowing from an open door from which flashing strobe lights beckoned. It was just the kind of place Sage would've normally been into. Liquor and gorgeous women. Hype music and the space to enjoy it all without feeling cramped.

"I'm going to dance," Dez said, then she whispered something in Victoria's ear that made her wife giggle.

"I want to dance too," Phil said. "This music is on point." She turned to follow Dez and Victoria to the dance floor, but Sage grabbed her hand.

"Hey." She didn't even know what she was going to say.

Were you seriously thinking about fucking that guy? That wasn't a question she thought she'd ever ask her girlfriend.

Years ago, when Dez had a fling with a bisexual boy from college, Phil nearly lost her shit. Talking about how Dez was straight now and wondering if she'd ever been a dyke at all. She'd calmed down since those first volatile days, especially once everyone understood her anger was from being unceremoniously friend-dumped by Dez, no goodbye, no "I need time to sort myself," no nothing. They'd all been hurt and got it out of their systems in various ways. Especially after Dez came back and shared how she'd felt about her boyfriend, and what she now felt for her wife.

"What's up, baby?" Phil spun into her arms with a smile, casually towering over Sage in that way they'd both become used to, an easy pose that pressed Sage's face into Phil's throat, or put her breasts at a convenient height. She raked her nails down Sage's back.

"What was that back there?" Sage asked.

"Back where?" A frown settled between Phil's eyes.

Maybe this wasn't the place for a conversation.

"Phillida."

They both turned at the sound of the masculine voice, Sage

tensing with the suspicion she knew exactly who had just called her girlfriend's name. She wasn't wrong.

Zachary Baxter moved through the crowd toward them, then paused to accept what Sage assumed were congratulations on making a good movie. The tuxedoed man who'd stopped Zachary looked happy as fuck to be talking to the actor, but Zachary kept looking over the man's shoulder at Phil. Phil who pulled slightly back from Sage, leaving aside the intimate caress to drape a casual hand across Sage's shoulders. It felt like a slap in the face. She clenched her teeth.

"Back there, with him," Sage said.

"What—?!" But they'd been together too long for that pretend confusion to work.

"Are you telling me you don't want to fuck him?" Sage kept her voice low, but she could feel her temper bubbling up under her breastbone, a threatened implosion.

By then Zachary had escaped his well-wisher and was only steps away from them.

"Sage!" Phil leaned close and dropped her voice.

"Is everything okay?"

"I'd suggest you mind your own fucking business," Sage snapped.

Phil put a hand on her shoulder. "Baby, don't make a scene." Her voice was low compared to Sage's nearly full-throated shout.

Sage temperature surged higher. After all the public fights they'd had over the years, now Phil wanted to be discreet, now that this asshole was involved? Movie star or not, fuck him!

"We're fine, Zachary." Phil turned a pleading look to the actor before she gave her full attention to Sage. Attention she damn well deserved. But Zachary didn't move off. He wasn't the important part of this though.

"Are you going to tell me what's going on?" The anger surged in her hot enough to scorch away the last of her common sense. "Are you trying to fuck him?"

Faces toward them, a flurry of whispers started around them. Fuck. But despite knowing she was seriously fucking up, knowing that there were cameras around, that there were at the place where Nuria was doing her damn job, Sage was livid and wanted Phil to know it.

Phil stepped away, misery all over her face. She crossed her arms over her chest, suddenly looking cold in her summer yellow. "I'm not right now, but I want to." The words were quiet. A low whisper that Sage wanted to pretend she never heard.

"Fuck!" She took a deep breath, then another. "I need—"

Strong hands clasped her shoulders from behind. She growled and spun around, or at least tried to.

"Calm down, Sage." Rémi's voice rumbled in her ear. "You need to take this someplace else. Someplace private."

Rémi squeezed her shoulders again, an edge of command to the touch that no one else could have managed with Sage. Dez cut through the staring crowd with her wife and mother following close by. More strangers crowded around them in a not-so-subtle attempt to see what was going on, some lifting their cell phones to capture Sage's stupidity.

Zachary Baxter watched Sage like she was a rabid dog needing to be put down, worry for Phil all over his stupidly pretty face. As if she would hurt her own damn girlfriend.

Dez slipped close, looped her arm around Phil's waist. She jerked her head toward the door. "We should head out." She exchanged a look with Rémi and they both turned toward the entrance of the theater, somehow corralling Sage and Phil between them. Sage's vision blurred at the edges, aware of the people watching them with their excited whispers and not so low laughter.

They made it to the front of the theater and one of their cars was already there, Rémi's big SUV, with Claudia moving into the driver's seat and the valet stepping back with a curious glance at their growing party.

"Get in," Rémi ordered.

Phil was just behind her. She could smell the perfume she had put on before they left, a light and flowery scent they'd gotten together on their last trip to Milan. The scent was now overly sweet and the thought of being trapped with it, with Phil, in the car for any length of time was unbearable.

Sage shook her head and stopped in the open door of the black SUV. "I can't."

"Just for now," Rémi said. "After we leave this circus behind, you can do whatever you want. People are looking and if you stay, they'll probably follow you around with a camera or something equally stupid. I'm not sure you want that."

"She doesn't want to be in the car with me," Phil said from just behind her. "Take her and I'll get our car."

Even in the middle of turning Sage's world upside down, knowing that Phil could read her mind eased some of the tension from her shoulders. She got into the SUV and felt Phil step back. Her scent faded away.

"Okay," Dez said.

After a whispered conversation with Victoria, she climbed into the backseat with Sage and closed the door, leaving Victoria standing with a stunned-looking Phil on the sidewalk.

After Rémi got into the front passenger seat of the SUV, they pulled off.

"What the fuck is going on with you two?" Rémi asked. "Is this more of the same shit?"

Her head thudded back against the leather seat. God, she wished things were the same. "No...Phillida..." More words failed her. Any other words stuttered behind the lump in her throat. What was going on? What was she going to do?

"I'll drive home and you all can take the car," Claudia said quietly.

"Babe..." Rémi began.

"No, it's okay. This looks intense and I'm sure she'd rather talk about it privately than have me here."

Rémi didn't protest any further. Both she and Sage knew Claudia was right. Although she wasn't sure that once she got that privacy, she could say anything. A weight of sadness and betrayal pressed down on her chest.

"Thank you, Claudia." Despite the shards of agony rattling inside her, Sage reached over to squeeze the woman's arm.

"You're welcome, honey. I hope this can be fixed, whatever it is."

The car drove in silence for not long enough, the big and damn near silent engine taking them away from the theater through downtown Miami, into Coconut Grove. Claudia climbed out of the car, her purse in hand, and Rémi got out of the car, closed them both outside in relative privacy for a few seconds before Rémi climbed in the driver's seat and pulled back out of the driveway. She heaved a sigh.

"So, tell us. What's going on with you two now?"

Sage's heart knocked in her throat, stopping any words. Was she just being completely stupid?

"Apparently, Phil is straight now."

"What?" Rémi turned all the way around in her seat. It was a miracle the SUV didn't jerk into another lane.

"That doesn't even make sense," Dez said. "Start from the beginning."

"This *is* the beginning." Or the end. "I saw her about to toss her panties at that guy from the movie. Then I called her on it. She didn't deny wanting to fuck him."

"That doesn't mean she's straight," Dez said.

"If she's into dick now, it doesn't matter what else she fucking calls herself."

"Don't you think you're being a little unreasonable?"

"Seriously?" Sage opened her eyes to peer at Rémi.

"Yes. Claudia is bi, you don't see me having a damn coronary over it." She jerked her head in Dez's direction. "You remember Dez went off with that Ruben dude a few years ago. So, what?"

"So what?" Sage sat up, looking at both her friends like they lost their minds. "You're not in a damn open relationship, that's what. You don't have to eat your girl's pussy knowing that you might suck too hard and end up with some guy's jizz in your mouth."

Dez rolled her eyes. "Don't you two practice safe sex with the randoms you hook up with?" Her look said she was well-prepared to judge Sage if the answer was 'no.'

"We do, but that's not the point."

Rémi muttered some choice curse words from the front seat.

Silence fell into the SUV and it rambled on. It felt like most of Miami passed by the windows—Little Haiti, Miami Gardens, North Miami Beach. The darkness flared with the lights of the city they passed, the little strip malls, other cars, people still waiting on buses, bicycles laboring by illegally on the sidewalks. Sage felt drained. Empty.

Days before, she'd been thinking again about marriage, something Phil had never mentioned but Sage knew she wanted. At least she'd talked about having a baby and what that would mean for the kind of life they now had.

As a child of parents who'd loved her but pretty much left her to her own devices, Sage was apathetic about being a parent herself. She didn't have any particular desire for a child and definitely had no gift at child-rearing either. But after the initial shock of finding out that Phil did want kids, she was willing to change their lives to nurture one. She was willing and ready to get married.

Not now though.

"I was going to ask her to marry me," Sage said.

Dez squeezed her thigh. "You still can."

Sage damn near shook her head off. "The hell I can." The cloak of bravado she wore felt heavy and unwelcome—this was *Phil* they were talking about, for God's sake! —but she couldn't shrug it off. It was all that held her shattered insides together. She clenched her fist hard enough for it to hurt.

Rémi made a sound like steam again, the breath leaking from between her teeth in a long hiss. "You're being really stupid right now."

"Yeah, you are," Dez naturally agreed.

Now Sage rolled her eyes. Of course, they were agreeing with each other. The two of them had always been close, even after the fiasco that led to Rémi falling in love with Dez's mother. They had repaired that rift and were tighter than ever.

If it had been Sage in that position, it would have been a forever kind of loss. Something beyond repair. Her mother had always accused her, rightly so, of being unforgiving. The girl who'd stolen Sage's jacks when she was barely six years old was still on her shit list. On visits to Jamaica, she barely tolerated the girl's presence, preferring to go and walk down the lane with tick-ridden dogs than pretend she wasn't still pissed at something the girl did when she still had baby teeth. It was a flaw. But one Sage wasn't about to correct. She probably wouldn't even know how.

The car hummed beneath them. From beneath her half-closed lashes, the world came at her in glittering, barely discernible circles. Nothing clear. Everything beautiful. She wanted things to stay just like that.

"What are you going to do?"

Her eyes fully opened to Dez's grim look. Mouth tight,

cheekbones sharp, the light from outside the window alternately shadowing and revealing the glittering intensity of her eyes.

"They'll do what they always do," Rémi said, her voice rough with impatience. "Fuck it out then talk it out." She'd seen enough of Phil and Sage's fights to know exactly how something like this usually went.

"If the thought of her fucking a guy is what's got your boxers in a bunch, then close your damn relationship. Didn't you mention suggesting that to her one time?"

A while ago, Sage *had* said something about closing up their open relationship, but she'd been feeling sentimental after hanging out with her monogamously coupled friends at an evening picnic. Phil had been off meeting with some girl or other and the picnic had been a last-minute thing, arranged so the couples could have an easy evening together. Phil couldn't make it, so Nuria had been her replacement, showing up with her game face on, even dressing the part in a retro 1950's dress, complete with polka dots and a big red bow at the waist. She carried an old-fashioned picnic basket, swinging it cheekily as she walked over the grass to meet them. Nuria was a good sport about being the replacement. As always, she was great company, telling jokes and trying to scandalize them all with tales of her latest sexual adventure.

But, for Sage, it wasn't the same without Phil, her partner, the woman she could easily imagine being her wife.

"She and I can't have a closed relationship," Sage said now to Dez and Rémi. "That wasn't our agreement."

It was an agreement they made over ten years ago when Miami was just an endless buffet of pussy they both wanted to gorge themselves on.

"I don't know why you're being so stubborn," Dez said, finally dropping limply into the seat at Sage's side. She tapped her fingers on an upraised knee and exchanged a glance with Rémi in the rear-view mirror.

At that look, something inside Sage broke open.

Rémi and Dez were close. Partners. Not the closeness of lovers but something that nothing could crack in two. Unlike her and Phil.

Sage sat up, squeezed her eyes shut and opened them, blinking away an annoying and unwelcome onslaught of tears. "Let me out here."

"What?"

"I just need to walk. This little drive isn't helping. I can't stand to look at you right now, either of you." She reached for the door handle. "Stop the fucking car and let me out."

The worry on Dez's face split her in two. She grabbed the handle and squeezed. The door clicked open.

"Fuck!" Cursing, Rémi swung the car into the far-right lane with a squeal of tires then slammed on the brakes. Sage jerked forward in the seat, the seatbelt catching painfully across her chest. Next to her, Dez clutched at the "oh shit" bar and stared at Sage, shock and fear on her face.

"What the fuck are you doing?" She shouted. "Are you trying to kill yourself? Kill us?"

But this wasn't about them. Why couldn't they understand that?

The SUV was still, its engine running. Rémi twisted around to glare at Sage, eyes glittering. "What the fuck are you smoking? Are you high?"

A fury of car horns blasted behind them, more tires screeched against the pavement. Sage shoved open the car door and jumped out, ignoring the curses raining down at them from the dozen or so cars that had stopped just in time behind them, the onlookers from the sidewalk, people rubbernecking from other lanes.

Dez jumped out of the SUV behind her and followed, the

heels of her boots clicking furiously against the sidewalk. "One of these days your fucking temper is going to get you in trouble!"

"Not today!" Sage jammed her hands in her pockets. "Don't follow me. I have my phone. I'll find my own way home." She shouted the last over her shoulder and cut through the empty bank parking lot. Still, she heard the sound of her friend behind her, honking horns that told her Rémi hadn't put the SUV back in gear to drive away. "Fuck off! Both of you. I'm serious!"

Then she ran.

She didn't know where she was going. She just had to get away from their well-meaning stares. Their logic. Their fucking happiness.

Neither of them knew what she was going through. They probably never would.

Sage ran.

The breath huffed from her parted lips. Her dress shoes slapped hard against the pavement with every step and, already, her feet hurt. But that pain was nothing compared to what was happening inside her chest. She ran through another parking lot, her feet catching in the manicured shrubbery. She tripped and stumbled against a pine tree and the bark scraped her palms.

"Goddammit, Phil!"

She screamed and ran on and ran and screamed, mourning the loss of a future she hadn't even realized she'd been counting on.

CHAPTER SEVEN

Late, late that night, Sage knocked on a door across town. The walk there had been long, but she needed it. Unlike what her friends probably expected, she didn't rush home to confront Phil. She didn't get blind drunk and try to fuck her way through the bar either.

It was late. Well past the time any of her friends would've come back in from a night's debauchery.

The door opened.

"Come in, sweet." Nuria shoved her hands in the dark spill of curled dreadlocks and moved them out of her face. She tied the belt of the shimmery satin robe around her waist. She looked tired, worried. "I'm glad you came here."

It was obvious Nuria hadn't been sleeping. In her massive, sunken living room, the TV blared the lurid details of a murder gone wrong. A sign of her addiction to crime TV. The smell of coffee wove through the persistent scent of the fresh flowers she always kept in her condo. A bouquet of bright red roses sat on an antique side table. Without looking, Sage knew there was another bouquet of flowers in the middle of the kitchen table, just as red, just as beautiful.

She pulled off her jacket and shoes and left them by the door.

"Shouldn't you be sleeping or partying?" Sage asked.

Nuria made a noise of irritation. "How can I have a good time knowing you're running around Miami like a crazy person in God knows what kind of emotional state?" She ran her hands through her hair again and went into the kitchen. "What kind of friend do you take me for?" she muttered as she walked away.

When she came back, Sage was sitting on the couch, pretending to watch the saga unfolding on the onscreen. High school sweethearts involved in a torrid and apparently deadly three-way with a teacher from a nearby school.

Nuria pushed a hot cup of spicy hot chocolate into Sage's hands and curled up on the couch with a fresh cup of coffee.

"You want to talk about it?" Nuria asked.

"Not really."

"Okay." Nuria sipped her coffee and turned her attention to the TV.

The actors playing the high school sweethearts looked more thirty than eighteen, but they were putting their all into the performance, including the simulated sex scenes with the "teacher" who lured them away from their honor society lives into a world of sin.

"Phil told me she was bisexual today."

From the look on Nuria's face, the total lack of surprise, she must have already known. She pressed the coffee cup against her lower lip, giving Sage her full attention.

"You already know?"

Nuria shrugged. "I suspected when she started asking me these random questions about being bi about a year or so ago."

A year? Sage swallowed the surge of temper with a mouthful of the hot chocolate.

"Why didn't you tell me?"

Nuria gave her a look and she had to turn her own gaze away. Her friend had her own code of ethics, no matter how fucked up they may seem to other people. And she was a vault when it came to keeping secrets.

"Yeah, I know, I know," Sage muttered, holding up a defensive hand before Nuria could say anything. "But we're talking my relationship here."

"Yeah, but we're also talking about Phil's life. Her choices and her self-discovery. I figured she'd tell you when she was ready." Nuria sighed and made a regretful face. "I'm assuming the way it all came out in the open wasn't ideal."

Sage remembered that smug-ass actor with his long hair and Hollywood face, grinning at Phil like he was already imagining what she looked like in his bed. She clenched her jaw. Then told Nuria everything.

"So, no, it wasn't ideal." Sage ran her fingers over her short, tight curls. The headache that had exploded in her skull at the theater pounded even harder behind her eyes.

"This isn't what I want," Sage said. "She knows this."

"It's probably why she was worried about telling you." Nuria sounded so reasonable Sage wanted to spit. "So, what are you going to do?"

"What am I supposed to do?"

"Act like an adult?" Nuria raised an eyebrow.

Sage bristled. "I'm already dealing with this shit like an adult."

"I'm not giving you adult points for not beating up a stranger in front of reporters if that's what you're after."

Sage *had* been proud of the fact that she hadn't swung on the pretty actor. Both their muscles came from the gym. She took kickboxing classes, but he undoubtedly had security. It might have been an even match.

Nuria snorted impatiently, put her coffee cup down. "I'm serious, you know. You have to do *something*. Running off into the night like a spoiled kid won't cut it."

"I really don't need your lecture, Nuria. That's not what I came here for."

"Then why did you come?"

Sage honestly didn't know. For a friendly ear? To talk with someone who was bisexual and gain some insight into what just happened to her relationship? To have a friend listen and take her side of things?

Nuria might be Sage's best friend—they were two island girls who formed a strong connection from the day they met—but she was also a friend to all of them. Phil included.

A frustrated breath huffed from Sage's mouth.

In the sofa, Nuria just draped the robe over her legs and blew at her coffee.

"How come I didn't know this about her?" Sage paced from one side of Nuria's living room to the other. She wanted to wail and scream like a kid having a tantrum. "She—we've been together for twelve years. I've seen her fuck. I know she likes women...at least I thought she did. Now I find out she's straight."

Nuria scrunched up her face. "How do you bypass the obvious choice—that she's bisexual—and go all the way to saying she's straight. No one fakes pussy-lovin' that much."

"But bi? For real?" Before she could stop herself, she made a sound of disgust.

"Excuse me?" Nuria didn't move but her face tightened and the hold on her coffee mug became far from relaxed. "Did you just forget who you're talking to?"

"That's not what I meant, and you know it."

"I have a lot of assumptions, apparently," Nuria said. Her voice was tight now. She got up from the couch with her coffee and left the living room in a swirl of blue and gold satin. The loud gush of the faucet came from the kitchen, then she came back with a glass of milk. No coffee.

She settled the slippery cloth more firmly over her shoulders and sat in the corner of the sofa to give Sage her complete attention. "Tell me what you meant. I don't want to assume anything."

"Nuria, you know I don't have any problems with you being bi."

But sitting between them was the awareness that despite having had an initial attraction to Nuria when they first met, Sage had never tried anything with her. Although Sage wasn't sure how she first formed the preference, she'd never willingly got involved with a bisexual woman. Whether it was for sex or anything with long-term potential. She flirted like crazy with bi girls, but that was as far as it went.

"But you're disgusted by Phil now? That's what I'm getting from this conversation." Nuria gripped the glass of milk more firmly between her hands but didn't drink from it. "She hasn't changed at all. She's the same woman you supposedly fell in love with, the same woman you damn near asked to marry you last spring, but now because she says she might like a little dick in her life, you're ready to write her off completely?"

Sage wouldn't put it that way exactly, but Nuria was relentless.

She continued, "If your so-called love can disappear that quickly, then you didn't call it by its right name."

"Don't bust my balls about this, Nuria," she muttered. "This isn't what I need from you right now." The headache was threatening to split her head open now. She squeezed her eyes shut and pressed both knuckles against her forehead.

Nuria's face turned hard. "Then what exactly do you need from your bisexual friend who you just told you're disgusted by your girlfriend's newly realized bisexuality? Tell me, what exactly do you need that I'm supposed to provide?"

Dammit! Everything was just coming out wrong. "Did I ever tell you what happened to me when I was fourteen?"

Nuria cut her eyes at Sage. "So, you're switching it up to story time now?"

"Come on, this is important..." Sage didn't like to beg, but the story was right on the edge of her tongue. The moment felt too important for her not to spit it out.

"Fine," Nuria muttered and crossed her arms over her chest. "Go for it."

Sage swallowed thickly, the memory rising up to choke her just like it always did when she allowed it to surface. "When I was a kid in Jamaica, I was really jealous of the other kids who got to move in America.

Jealous was a mild word for the acidic resentment that burned through her guts and into her eyes when someone she knew in the neighborhood got that chance at freedom she ached for.

"I wasn't out at home, and I was scared to death to have any friends that looked even a little bit queer. But for some reason, Clarence and I became friends anyway. He was maybe a year younger than me.

Her old friend's face appeared behind her half-closed eyes. Skin like brown rice, a big and sassy smile.

"Anyway, Clarence got the golden ticket when his parents moved to America for work. I was glad for him, but the jealousy just about ate me alive. Clarence and I knew that you could be as gay as you wanted to be in America—lesbian, queer, trans, any of it—and the whole country turned around and embraced you." At Nuria's disbelieving look Sage shrugged. "We were kids on an island. All we had to go by was TV. Anyway, Clarence left, and I was mostly happy for him.

"We kept in touch by email and all that, but then one day..."

The memory burned behind her eyes. "...one day, I got the news that he was dead.

"It wasn't just any dead, though. His uncles and cousins ganged up on him and beat him like a piñata. Busted his head wide open on the streets of New York. They...they even took a picture and circulated it online for a while." A stone ball lodged itself in Sage's throat and she shifted it around, so she could finish. "I never wanted to see that photo. But then I did." His face kicked to a pulpy mess. Teeth scattered on the ground. So much blood.

His own family had killed him because he was gay, even in this land of gay love and acceptance where he was supposed to be safe. Where they were *all* supposed to be safe.

"That's awful." Nuria slid across the couch to grip Sage's hand and lace their fingers together. "I'm sorry you had to deal with that as a kid, and I'm sorry for your friend."

"I know. It's... fucked up."

Nuria's fingers squeezed hers, a grounding and sympathetic touch. "I don't mean to be an ass, sugar, but what does this have to do with you and Phil now?"

Sage licked her dry lips and said the thing she'd been hiding from herself for far too long. "Sometimes," Sage clenched her jaw, "I feel like the thing that happened to Clarence, even though it didn't happen to me, fucked me up real good. I mean, obviously, it fucked up Clarence's life you know it's *over* but...his death...it left me so afraid of *everything*."

Because of this, she was scared of telling her parents the truth. And this thing with Phil... She just felt like she was losing someone she loved all over again.

"Look... Maybe coming here wasn't the best idea for me." Despite her still trembling legs, Sage stood up. She scraped a rough hand over her face. She was just so damn tired.

The milk glass clicked against a wooden coaster when Nuria

put it on the table. "Don't be stupid," she said. "Go in the guest room and rest." Exhaustion tugged at her voice. She plucked at one of the curled locks hanging below her chin. "We can talk more in the morning."

Sage glanced at the door, then Nuria's face. "Okay." A sigh rushed from her throat. "In the morning."

HOURS LATER, Sage woke up feeling like shit. Although she didn't drink any liquor the night before, her mouth tasted like something had crawled into it, taken a shit and died from a maggot infestation. At least her headache was gone, though.

A groan slipped past her lips as she slowly rolled onto her back in the queen-sized bed. Waking was slow and painful. The muscles in her legs ached from her long and mostly aimless walk and the bottoms of her feet felt like somebody went at them with a baseball bat.

Note to self: it is impossible to literally run from your feelings. Especially in Italian leather dress shoes.

She blinked blearily at the ceiling and strained to hear what was going on in the rest of the apartment. But everything was quiet.

After what she said last night, did she still have Nuria as a friend?

Sage winced, remembering the pain on Nuria's face when she'd spewed her frustration. The last thing Sage wanted to do was hurt her friend. In hindsight, she felt stupid saying those things to Nuria, a woman who accepted and loved all parts of herself, her bisexuality included.

Okay, enough of this.

Sage dragged her tired body from the bed, took a quick shower, and grabbed a change of clothes from the stash she kept there. Determined, she strode into the living room ready to talk everything out.

But the condo was empty. The spare key to Sage and Phil's place sat in the middle of the kitchen island. Next to it was a note written on a hot pink Post-it.

HAD to run off to work. My client is acting a fool today. We're not done talking.

Call me later. - N.

WHEN SHE STEPPED out of the cab and walked up to the home she shared with Phil, it was barely 9 o' clock in the morning. The garage doors were closed down tight. No cars were parked in the circular drive. Just like at Nuria's place, everything was quiet.

The long-limbed palms shielding the front yard from the street swayed in the breeze, and the half dozen crepe myrtle trees lining the drive shed their purple blossoms all over the green grass and gray pavement. A squirrel chattered and jumped between palm trees.

Inside the house, she dropped her keys into her pocket instead of the ceramic bowl by the door as she normally would. Nothing felt normal today.

During the last few months, she and Phil had been waking up together, having slow morning sex then sitting on the back verandah with their morning drinks, talking, or just sharing the quiet. A far cry from their usual drug-fueled fuck fest parties when they'd lived in Wynwood. The new house in Coral Gables with its quiet neighbors, fenced-in pool, and massive yard had been a sign of their changed lives, their willingness to change even more for the next step.

A baby. Marriage. Despair rolled over Sage in a chilling wave. All that was gone now.

She moved toward the bedroom.

"Phillida?" she called, her voice low.

No answer.

But the bedroom door was closed. She pushed it open with worry gnawing at her belly. The bed wasn't empty. And Phil wasn't alone.

CHAPTER EIGHT

The bedroom floor was a wreck of discarded clothes. A pair of high heels tumbled onto their sides near the door. Phil's yellow dress turned inside out. Her purse. Black tuxedo pants and a jacket also lay crumpled nearly. The bedroom itself was dark, shades pulled to keep out the disgustingly cheerful sunlight. But Sage didn't need light to see the couple entwined on the bed.

Phil looked ravaged, even in sleep. Her face, normally at its most peaceful while she slept, was swollen and tinged with gray. Her thick hair was still pulled up to the top of her head in a dark corona of coils and curls. She hadn't bothered to take off her makeup or her underwear. Mascara smudged around her eyes and the pillow under her cheek was dusted dark with her foundation. The remainder of tears stained Phil's face and, though trapped in sleep, she twitched like she was in pain. Guilt twisted in Sage's stomach as she watched. Along with a sick satisfaction.

Good, at least she wasn't the only one suffering.

Phil's underwear, a matching bra and panty set in deepest gold, showed off her body to perfection. But that perfection was easy to overlook with the grief that ravaged her face. She was a woman in pain, and it showed. Low on her belly, the platinum chain with its infinity charm winked mockingly at Sage. A present she'd given Phil years ago.

Proof that nothing was forever.

Phil lay facing her bed partner, who also only wore underwear. Their hands were loosely clasped while they slept.

Victoria. Dez's wife.

Her jungle of pale and dark curls tumbled across the pillow and around her face, hiding her expression.

Sage clenched her jaw so hard that it hurt.

Was this what she had done? Driven her woman into another's arms on the worse night of their lives as a couple?

You didn't do anything wrong.

But she ignored the voice trying to grant her absolution.

Outside the bedroom, she looked around in confusion. The familiar lines of the house she'd shared with Phil for the past year felt alien and hostile. The couch where they'd had moments of intimacy, sexual and not, dared her to walk away. While the scattering of Phil's science journal next to Sage's music magazines mocked her. Signs of their life together that was now...now what?

They felt like nothing.

Suddenly, Sage couldn't be in the house anymore. In the garage, she took the car they'd ridden in the day before—they'd held hands on the way to the movie premiere—swallowing thickly at the hints of Phil's scent still trapped in the leather seats.

She slapped the window controls, sending down all four windows with a symphony of electronic whines. Sage didn't know where she was going. But it didn't matter. Just like the night before, her friends had only provided her an escape from the scene of Phil's betrayal. Now, she just needed to be on the move. Needed to be away.

But every place she passed, everywhere she looked, reminded

her of Phil and the foundation they'd built together that was now crumbled to dust.

She wanted to howl like a grief-maddened wolf. Howl and tear things apart.

But she only drove on.

SHE ENDED up at the only place she could think of in the city that had no memories attached to Phil. Wilde's, the bar where she and her friends met up for their last dinner. Phil had never been there. Perfect.

It was early. A few minutes to ten on a Saturday morning. And there was a crowd. Brunch gays waiting to get seated. A nearly full patio with the sound of conversation and laughter raining down to where she stood waiting on the hostess to find a place for a singleton.

"You can sit at the bar," woman in the red blouse and black skirt chirped.

She slid onto the padded leather stood, leaned her elbows on the polished bar and ordered a Bloody Mary.

"Extra spicy, please."

"Sure thing, sugar."

The boy behind the bar reminded Sage of that boy Dez fucked their last year of college. Pretty and obviously gay. Clear, brown skin. A slim and supple body under clothes he wore very well.

Shit. Was *she* turning bi too? Checking out random dudes she didn't give a fuck about?

Sage spun around on the stool to check out the rest of the restaurant bar. It was *busy*, nearly as busy as their favorite brunch place, Novelette's, was on Sundays, a hurried collection of sights and sounds of professionals in uniform rushing between packed tables. Just about everyone in the restaurant gave off an air of carefree happiness Sage envied with a searing pain.

Stop being so fucking dramatic.

But even the harsh command from her own brain wasn't enough to turn off the internal faucet of tears.

"Here you go, honey..."

She jerked back around on her stool in time to catch her elbow on the edge of the glass the bartender put in front of her.

"Fuck!"

With a rattle of ice and a crack of glass against wood, the Bloody Mary spilled all over the bar, all over her shirt, splashing her red and dumping freezing cold into her lap. The glass tumbled to the floor but didn't break.

Sage cursed again and jumped up from the stool. Cold red dripped from her shirt, from her jeans.

"Oh, honey! I'm so sorry." The bartender rushed around the bar with a cloth, trying to dab away the full glass of red cocktail with a few sparse napkins.

She wanted to be pissed at him, but it was partially her fault, so lost in her own bullshit that she didn't hear him coming up behind her, spinning around fast enough that even the most attentive bartender would've been caught off-guard.

"It's cool." She moved back from his attempted clean-up. "Just point me to the nearest bathroom and I'll take care of it."

With a waving of hands and more apologies, he pointed then walked her halfway to a dark hallway where gendered signs for the restrooms dimly glowed. Walking bowlegged to stop the cold and wet from seeping any more into her crotch, she stumbled toward the bathroom.

"Oh, shit!" A slim shape coming in the opposite direction moved quickly out of her way then stopped. "You okay?" It was a woman, a young girl, who looked vaguely familiar although Sage couldn't think of how.

"It's cool," she said, still making her way toward the bathroom. "It looks worse than it is."

The girl followed her. "That's not blood, is it? I can call—"

"Nope, just the blood of a few tomatoes." Sage pushed the bathroom door open, looked over her shoulder in surprise at the girl following her. In the brighter light, she saw the girl wore a uniform with the name of the place stitched discreetly over the left breast.

"Oh, thank God!" She pressed a hand over her chest and blew out a breath of relief.

"Don't worry, I wouldn't sue your boss even if it was blood. This was all my fault."

She grabbed a fistful of napkins from the dispenser and scrubbed at the front of her jeans. When they were as dry as they were going to get, she yanked off her T-shirt and shoved the whole thing under the hot faucet. Tomato juice trailed in a swirl down the drain and she quickly washed it then wrung it out as much as she could, so she wouldn't look like a homicide victim walking out of the place.

Suddenly, she was aware of the complete silence behind her. She looked up in the mirror to see the girl staring, open-mouthed, at Sage's back and the reflection of her chest in the mirror.

When she realized Sage was looking, she snapped her mouth shut and took a few steps back. She stumbled into the wall and grunted, blushed, a subtle rise of color coming up under her pale brown skin. Not once did she take her eyes off Sage's body and the tattoos marking her flesh.

"Uh..."

Flattering as it was, Sage wasn't in the mood. She wrung out the shirt some more—fuck her stupid for putting on white on a day she was feeling this ruined—then pulled it back on. The wet shirt clung to her chest and arms, clearly showing off the sports bra underneath and the muscles she worked hard for in the gym.

"Do you want..." The girl's eyes roamed over just about every inch of skin on display. "...want a shirt to wear?"

"I'm already wearing one," Sage said, although she hadn't planned for a wet T-shirt contest when she left home. "I'm good."

The girl licked her lips then bit the corner of her mouth. "I have a shirt in my locker you can have."

Sage thought about her options. It wasn't like she could walk out of the restaurant without feeling self-conscious in the stained, wet T-shirt. She was too embarrassed to go back to Nuria's for more clothes and going back to her own place wasn't something she was ready to deal with.

"Sure. Why not?"

"Okay." The girl's eyes flickered down Sage's body again then she backed out of the bathroom, not looking away until the door blocked her view. The sound of her footsteps outside the door told Sage she was actually running to get whatever shirt she had.

This is a bad idea.

Sage stared in the mirror but dodged her own gaze, her hands curling around the cold edge of the sink. When the bathroom door opened, she turned, expecting the waitress. But instead, a trio of girls tumbled in on high heels, obviously tipsy.

They stopped when they saw Sage—which would have been funny if Sage had been in the mood for laughing—nearly tumbling down like dominoes as if they'd collectively run into a brick wall.

"Are you sure you're in the right bathroom?" One of them asked with a twist of her mouth.

One of her friends shoved her shoulder. "Stop it, Mandi." But she ruined the effect by giggling.

The last friend looked Sage up and down like she was the last piece of prime steak at an all-you-can-eat buffet. She pressed her lips together, staring with wide eyes while the other two disappeared into neighboring bathroom stalls.

The bathroom door swung open again. This time it was the young waitress. Breathless, she clutched a plaid button-down shirt to her heaving chest. Did she run the whole way there and back?

"Here." She shoved the shirt at Sage, and the staring drunk girl looked between the two of them with curiosity all over her face and made no attempt to get into one of the other three empty bathroom stalls. On any other day, Sage would've offered to rock her world. But...

She took the shirt and shrugged it on. "Thanks."

The pale blue plaid was a little tight around the shoulders and the bulk of her arms, but it covered the important parts and made her look decent enough to walk through the restaurant without attracting attention she wasn't in the mood for.

"You're welcome." The young waitress shifted the backpack she was carrying over one shoulder. "You want to...?" She hitched her shoulder toward the door.

"Sure."

Sometimes Sage didn't know why she did half the shit she did. Shit with doors clearly marked "do not enter." But she'd blundered with her eyes wide open and didn't see why this time was any different.

She followed the girl out the back door of the restaurant and out into the warm day. Sunlight immediately sank into Sage's skin, prickling up heat and sweat. *Thanks a lot, flannel.*

"I don't live too far from here if you want to shower and ... um...wash your clothes in the laundry room downstairs." Her brown eyes were big and hopeful.

Bambi, the sex kitten. Or was it sex deer?

Either way, taking the girl up on her clumsy offer was better than dwelling on the wreckage she'd left behind at home. "Okay," Sage said.

When the girl headed toward the street instead of the parking lot, she started to rethink her choices. Again. This chick didn't have a car?

Sage's reluctance must have shown plain as day on her face because the girl pointed up ahead. "My place is walking distance from here. Not far at all."

And the way she looked at Sage, her wide eyes bouncing from her face to her body, made her suddenly recall where she'd seen her face before. This was the young as hell waitress from Wilde's the night she and her friends went there for dinner. That night, the girl stared hard at both Rémi and Nuria, practically drooling every time she dropped by their table.

Back then, Sage hadn't paid the girl much attention other than to acknowledge that she was attractive enough, for a fetus. But with the sun burning down on her head and the rage rampaging through her at the loss of her life with Phil, her self-preservation and usually steady moral compass were on the fritz.

So, she very much noticed that the girl was like a younger Zoe Saldana, complete with long ponytail, wide mouth, and pointy chin. Not Sage's usual type of girl at all. But not one she'd turn down given the right set of motivations.

"Oh, I'm Crystal, by the way." She didn't offer her hand.

Sage gave her own name. "Do you remember me?" The heels of her boots thudded against the concrete.

Crystal scratched the tip of her nose and glanced briefly away. "Yeah. You came to Wilde's with your–friends that one time." Sage was pretty sure she had been about to say "your hot friends."

"That's right." At least they were starting whatever this was on somewhat of an even footing. She shoved her hands in her pockets, moving the damp material away from her crotch as possible. Wet jeans weren't the most comfortable thing to have pressed to your pussy, especially when you didn't have on any damn underwear.

A few minutes passed in semi-awkward silence. "So..." Crystal began, worrying at her bottom lip with her teeth. "Where are your friends?"

Did she think they'd pop out of the bushes rearing to go for a hot foursome?

"Probably at home," she said. "Two of them are married," Or as good as. "—and not fucking other people." Best to just get that out of the way in case she wanted to use Sage to get into Rémi or Dez's pants. It wouldn't have been the first time.

"Oh, okay."

They got to her building, a slightly run-down Art Deco spot that had been skipped in that neighborhood's renovation boom, and climbed the stairs to her small second-story apartment.

Crystal hung her backpack on a hook behind the door and shoved her keys, hanging from a green lanyard advertising a local university, into the bag's outer pocket.

"This is me."

The apartment looked pretty much like Sage expected. Small with what looked like second-hand furniture neatly placed around the small living room—a plaid couch, a small TV on top of a scarred vintage coffee table, and two mismatched lamps on opposite sides of the couch. The walls were a neutral white but a dozen or so framed movie posters brightened things up. The look of the apartment along with the smell—tomato sauce mixed with nail polish remover and weed—gave it a distinct college student vibe.

"Thanks for inviting me over," Sage muttered. Why was she here again? "Can you point me to your shower?"

"Yeah, yeah, sure!" Crystal looked happy for something to do besides stare at Sage. "It's through here." She led the way down a short hallway and opened one of the two doors. "I have towels and wash rags on the shelf. Use anything that you want."

The bathroom was clean as the rest of the apartment. Built-in shelves held neatly folded towels and face cloths, slightly faded and mismatched, and a tropical patterned shower curtain surrounded the combination tub and shower. A pair of pink floral panties hung from the shower rod. Crystal snatched up the underwear the moment Sage's eyes landed on them. She ducked her head.

"I...uh...wash them when I shower."

Sage gave in to the faint trickle of amusement. "Are you from Jamaica? That's some shit my country cousins used to do."

Crystal's eyes darted to Sage. "I am, actually."

For real?

"Damn. Me too."

"Yeah, I figured."

Right. Her accent. As much as she'd tried in the early days of being in America, she hadn't been able to completely get rid of it. Crystal though, had no trace of an accent. As far as Sage could tell, she could've been from anywhere in America.

They stared at each other again, awkward in the tiny feeling bathroom. Then Crystal scratched at her nose and slowly backed away and out the door. "Let me know if you needed anything."

Sage was looking for how to turn on the shower when Crystal appeared again behind her. "You can give me your clothes and I'll throw them in the wash. It doesn't cost me any extra."

"Sure." Then because she didn't feel like putting on a show of modesty, Sage quickly got out of her wet clothes, minus the underwear, and passed them to her. "Thanks a lot."

"Okay." Crystal squeezed her eyes shut for a moment, then darted close enough that Sage thought she was trying for a kiss. "Uh...you turn it on like this." She got the shower going with a sharp tug at some mechanism hidden in the mouth of the bath spigot. Crystal yelped and jumped back in time to avoid getting her hair wet. Her cheeks darkened with a blush.

"Thanks."

"Sure." Then she was gone again, this time closing the bathroom door behind her with a click.

Sage stood in her underwear, staring at the rushing stream of water, for far too long. Thoughts rushing through her head, as quickly as the water left the spigot, too fast for her to catch. This was a kind of escape, a path she'd taken many times before.

Was she going to keep going to its inevitable end?

Enough of this thinking crap.

She peeled off her underwear and climbed into the shower. Twenty minutes later, she got out, surprised to see a pair of sweats and a T-shirt waiting for her on top of the closed toilet seat. She hadn't even heard Crystal come back into the bathroom.

"Thanks for the clothes," she said to Crystal as she stepped out of the hallway.

The apartment was small enough that she could see Crystal's front door, her kitchen, and the door to what looked like a small balcony from where she stood. Only a low breakfast bar separated the kitchen from the living room, so Sage had a clear view of Crystal stirring something in a pot. The scent of something creamy and tomato-rich flooded the small apartment.

"You're welcome." Changed into a loose gray dress and with her hair pulled back in a sloppy ponytail, she looked much more comfortable than before. "Do you want something to eat? I'm making grilled cheese with tomato soup.

Sage hadn't had that in years. Not since Claudia, "Mrs. Nichols" to her and her friends back then, used to make them as an after-school snack. Her stomach rumbled then, answering the question for her.

"Sure," she said anyway. "That would be nice." All she'd had was the glass of orange juice at Nuria's and the promise of the Bloody Mary that had spilled all over her morning. "Thank you."

Crystal looked away, her ponytail swinging, then went back to the stove. "It'll be ready in about ten minutes. Just..." Over her shoulder, she gestured toward Sage and the rest of the apartment. "...make yourself comfortable. Or whatever."

Or whatever. That was quite an invitation. Despite the shitty last few hours she'd had, Sage found herself smiling.

This wasn't going how she thought it would at all. Maybe that was a good thing.

Away from the hectic pace of the restaurant where Crystal worked, the girl was sweet, almost shy. Or maybe she was just acting her age.

Sage finished drying her hair with the towel, tossed it over her shoulder and explored the living room, the books on the shelf, gaming console hooked up to the TV, the posters of movies on the wall that she'd never seen. Crystal was apparently into foreign flicks.

"Do you speak any foreign languages or do you just read the subtitles?"

"I speak a little Spanish, that's it," she said.

The sound of something fattening, either butter or cheese, sizzling in a pan came from the kitchen. A buttery scent teased Sage's nose. Moments later, the rich smell of heating bread made her stomach clench with remembered hunger. When was the last time she ate anything?

"Those are mostly my mom's posters though," Crystal continued although Sage was half-ashamed to have tuned her out for those few seconds where her hunger had been more important than her manners. "She was really into the old stuff barely anybody's ever heard of. I keep them because they remind me of her."

A delicate pain throbbed in Crystal's voice despite the careless way she spoke.

"Is she...?"

"She died."

"I'm sorry to hear that."

"It's cool. You didn't kill her."

Sage turned away from the black and white poster with the movie title written in Portuguese. "I don't have to be her murderer to be sorry."

"Yeah..." Her voice tapered off into nothing.

Sounds from the kitchen swallowed up what would've otherwise been an awkward silence. The bookshelf seemed a safer part of the apartment to explore so she made her way over there but, just in case there was some pain there waiting to be triggered, she didn't comment on anything she saw.

Minutes later, Crystal left the kitchen with a round tray in her hand. It was loaded down with bowls of soup, a plate of grilled cheese sandwiches, and cold water in Star Trek glasses. Spock and Uhura. "Do you want to eat over here or on the couch?"

Sage tore her eyes away from the Star Trek glasses, wondering again how old this girl was. She turned her mind to the real question at hand. The breakfast bar would be more comfortable. But then they'd have to carry on an actual conversation and Sage didn't think she had anything to talk to Crystal about.

"The couch is cool. Maybe we can watch some TV or something."

Nibbling on the corner of her mouth, Crystal came into the living room and gently put the tray of food on the coffee table.

"Have a seat," she invited with an awkward little wave of her hand.

She put the food in two places on the wide coffee table—a bowl of soup, a plate piled with four triangles dripping with three types of cheese, two tall glasses of water with lemon wedges perched on their sides. She put the spoons on separate folded napkins, adjusted them at least twice before sitting down. Then she picked up the remote and sat back in the couch. Her knee jumped with obvious nervousness.

Sage said, trying to do the semi-decent thing and ignore how much the girl seemed to alternate between being nervous out of her skin and poised on the edge of seduction. Then and there, she decided not to take advantage of either state of mind. Crystal was young. She didn't have any business inviting a stranger to her place.

"What do you want to watch?" Crystal asked.

"Pretty much anything," Sage said. "I'm easy."

The truth was she didn't watch much TV. Whether she was hanging by herself or with Phil, she'd much rather read or listen to music. The intimacy of silence was something she loved. And something she especially loved to share with her girlfriend. A lump of emotion rose up in her throat, threatening to choke her. Tears pricked her eyes and she coughed, covering her mouth with a fist and looking away.

Fuck. What was she even doing here?

But she knew the answer to that question. Avoiding her life. Turning her back on the things that should have been familiar and now reminded her too much of how much in her life now was unknown. Unfamiliar as Mars or walking on the moon.

At her side, Crystal messed with her spoon again, knocking it against her water glass. "You probably don't watch much TV then huh?"

Sage thought about lying, then discarded the idea. This girl was a stranger. Lies would be meaningless between them.

"No, not really. But when in Rome..." Sage shrugged.

She sat down in front of the food, the warmth of Crystal's thigh only inches from hers, and picked up her Spock water glass. "Thanks for the food, and for everything."

Their glasses clinked together.

"You're welcome." Crystal sipped her water, then cleared her throat. She put the glass on a coaster, not looking at Sage. "I'm actually surprised you came home with me."

"I'm surprised you asked me. Aren't you afraid I'll murder you and steal your..." She looked around the small apartment for something worth taking. "...Star Trek cup collection or something?"

A smile darted across Crystal's face. "Not really. Your watch can probably pay my rent for a year." She eyed the Cartier pointedly before picking up her spoon. "I figured I was safe."

The smile stayed on her face while she sipped from her spoon.

"I could be the kind who kills for fun, not necessity," Sage said at the same time she realized how creepy that sounded. "Forget I said that."

"Yes, please." Crystal rolled her eyes, her smile showing more teeth.

Sage picked up her sandwich and took a big bite, sighed at the distinct bite of gorgonzola cheese, the unexpected scent and crunch of caraway seeds. Sharp cheddar and maybe parmesan was mixed in there too. The combined flavors were damn near a party for her taste buds. Though, truth be told, it was damn near impossible to mess up a grilled cheese sandwich.

"This is good," she said once she'd swallowed the bite and, irresistibly, licked a smear of what tasted like browned butter from her lips.

"Thank you." Another smile, this one full of self-satisfied mischief, curved Crystal's mouth. Her eyes sparkled behind the lush thicket of lashes. "I got the cheese from work."

"And the sandwich recipe?"

"Yeah, that too. As much as I love cheese, it never occurred to me to mix them like this. It's good but I can't afford to buy it so..." She shrugged and didn't look the slightest bit ashamed.

"I'll make sure to order it when I come back to the restaurant."

"Or you could just come here and eat it anytime you want."

The words hovered between them, an invitation of a whole other sort. Even though they hadn't touched, and Sage had no plans on *ever* touching the girl, the air in the apartment suddenly thickened and became ripe with intention. None of it hers. Sage put down her sandwich and rubbed the tips of her butter-slick fingers together.

"Listen, Crystal..."

A damp mouth crashed into hers and Sage's arms were suddenly full of a squirming, young girl half her weight but with twice the determination to get closer.

The soft weight tumbled into her and she grunted, releasing a startled breath immediately swallowed up by a hot mouth that smelled of tomato soup of melted cheese. She gripped Crystal's arms, but her slick hands slid over the bare skin and they tumbled back into the couch, the blanket draped over the plaid couch smelling like fabric softener and lemongrass incense.

"Wait..."

But wait for what?

But her body was already responding to the signals that had compelled it for years—firm breasts pressing into her chest, a willing woman with desire armed directly at Sage, even if the mouth on hers wasn't exactly expert.

She tore her mouth away. "Crystal, this isn't a good idea."

Who exactly was talking? Right, the adult.

Crystal moved her mouth away only to press it into Sage's throat, teeth nibbling, tongue licking that spot under her ear that made Sage weak. "Isn't this what you came over here for?"

The familiar heat curled into her belly, sliding low to plump her pussy lips and make her wet.

"No, not really." But the words came out on a tremor, especially when warm hands slipped under the loose shirt and covered her breasts. Crystal's thumbs swept over her nipples with a knowing touch. Maybe Crystal wasn't as inexperienced as she first thought. And maybe she wasn't as immune to teenagers as she first thought.

"How old are you anyway?" She gasped the question while her mind was still hers, the desire to be naked and to have the girl's mouth on her nipples she touched so firmly and expertly quickly taking over.

"I'm old enough." Like she'd read Sage's mind, Crystal moved her mouth lower. "I was serving you liquor the other night, remember?"

Waitresses who served liquor had to be at least twenty-one, right?

Then Crystal shoved the borrowed shirt all the way up, latched her mouth to Sage's nipple and pushed any other coherent thought not related to cumming straight out of Sage's mind.

God, she felt good. Uncomplicated. The thin fingers tugged and rolled the nipple not in her mouth. Between her legs, Sage was rushing wet, and she was certain the crotch of the sweatpants were already desperately in need of the laundry. Groaning, she gripped Crystal's shoulders just for something to hold onto. The girl hummed with pleasure as she sucked Sage's breasts, one then the other, fingers driving her wild and she hadn't even touched Sage's pussy.

That didn't stop her from grinding up on the girl, searching for something to rub her clit and pierced hood against. God...she was so desperately horny. So desperate to forget the last day had happened.

If she let this run its natural course, then maybe, just maybe she'd leave this stranger's bed—or couch—and go back home to see everything returned to normal. Phil in the walk-in closet, trying on her latest dress, ready to drag Sage out to the latest play or bar or sex party, her melting brown eyes filled with love and the forever they hadn't talked about but were drifting toward together.

"You're so hot!" Crystal groaned into Sage's skin, her fingers plucking, a steady pinch and release that shocked a cry from Sage. Her mind flying back to the here and now, the reality of a too-young girl intent on making her come without touching her pussy.

Crystal moved, adjusting on top of Sage until her thigh fell between Sages.

Finally!

Sage shoved up, grinding up and into the girl's slender thigh, her pussy so damn wet, the arousal nearly painful as it pulled tighter in her belly, her pussy aching for a mouth, a tongue, anything. But this—she shoved up, grinding frantically now—this might be enough. Teeth scraped over her nipple, fingernails pressed into her soft flesh of the other breast. Crystal moaned into her flesh, the sound like she was eating something so damn good she couldn't bear to take it out of her mouth. Hips twisting and frantic, she humped Sage like a teenager in the backseat of a car fighting against curfew. And Sage completely lost her mind.

She screamed until her throat was hoarse. When she came back to herself, all she could hear was the sound of their heavy breathing in the room. Her heart raced and her mouth felt desert-dry. Crystal lay slack on top of her, her mouth still sucking weakly at Sage's breast, but her hips were still. Sage felt a big wet spot on her thigh. Like someone had spilled another drink all over her clothes. But this wetness wasn't cold.

Crystal was a squirter. Nothing like Phil whose subtle orgasms she'd had to learn then tease out over the years they'd been together.

A dull ache settled in Sage's chest, and she squirmed under Crystal's slight weight.

The girl licked her lips, looking down at Sage with the sweated-out edges of her wild ponytail. "Is this where you tell me we shouldn't have done this then walk out of here in your half-dried clothes?"

If Sage were a good person, she would answer yes and climb from under the wet, still shuddering girl and take her ass back home to face her problems. But Crystal moved and the undulating press of her thigh against Sage's clit re-lit an ember that hadn't quite gone out.

"No," she said and felt a strange satisfaction at the girl's look of surprise. "I want to see these pretty titties of yours." The girl's back was warm and damp as she dragged her hands down its length, pulling the top of the dress with her. "Then I want to taste you from top to bottom."

Reality could wait forever as far as Sage was concerned. She leaned in and pulled the dark tip of Crystal's nipple into her mouth.

The girl moaned, a long and clit-buzzing sound.

"I'm so glad I got the right one." Crystal panted through a moan, her fingers flexing into Sage's shoulders with each bite of Sage's teeth into her nipples.

Crystal scrambled up to her hands and knees on the couch, crouching over Sage and sticking her ass up and out. She wasn't wearing any underwear. Sage sighed into the addictive taste of the fat nipple in her mouth, her fingers slipping up a warm thigh and into the welcoming and wet pussy. They sighed together, the couch groaning with their weight, and Sage lost herself to the wet, decadent sound of her fingers fucking a pussy that, in the moment, was dripping for her and only her alone.

CHAPTER NINE

Sage didn't do stress well. When life pressed in on her, she either fucked the pain away or sang about it until all memory of it disappeared. Avoidance her mainstay, fear of being killed by the very people who professed to love her was another reason she'd never come out to her parents. The memory of Clarence's inside-out face flashed briefly behind her eyes.

She swallowed the familiar fireball of terror and pain. They would hate Sage the lesbian. They might even want her dead. Better to have their conditional love than no love from them at all.

Sage clenched her hands around the steering wheel and pressed down on the gas. The truck bucked under her and sped up. On the worst days, she felt like a coward. On other days, she wished she'd been born straight, or could at least fake it.

After making vague promises to call, she left Crystal's apartment and walked back to the restaurant to get her car. From there, she headed to the music studio. With Dennis Brown blasting on the stereo, the windows of the SUV all the way down, she roared down I-95 toward Coconut Grove.

I never thought that you would ever let me down...

She sang along to the old tune, nostalgia for her pre-teen days in her parents' kitchen, their helper Miss Opal cooking up Sage's favorite food while her bare heels knocked back against the edge of the stool she perched on. Miss Opal, who'd never had children of her own, indulged Sage in nearly everything she asked for. Food. Music. Any fruit she passed on her way to work in the mornings. Especially the June plums Sage was addicted to.

The song rolled on and Sage's memory tumbled back in time.

She often thought of Miss Opal when she listened to certain songs. Old songs that had played in the background Miss Opal worked and Sage endlessly pestered her. Guilt grabbed her throat most of the time. She'd happily left Jamaica for high school and her big lesbian life, not thinking of the things and people abandoned in her rear view.

Sage loved Miss Opal, maybe even as much as her parents. And because of that love and fear of being rejected, she allowed the connection they had to grow frailer every year. Sure, she visited Jamaica and made sure to see Miss Opal each time, but as she grew more certain in that lesbian identity, she held her real self back.

The phone chimed, the electronic tone dragging Sage from her heavy thoughts.

The Bluetooth display showed a Jamaican number, but not a familiar one. Sage frowned. She'd been expecting her parents—or at least her mother who spoke for herself and her husband as a unit—to call and confirm their airport pick-up time. With things happening with Phillida, she'd conveniently allowed herself to forget about their visit. But now, that brief respite was apparently over.

No delaying the inevitable, right?

Sage answered the phone with a tap of a button on the steering wheel. The music automatically stopped.

"Hello?"

"Baby love!"

That was *not* her mother's voice. And her mother would never greet her like that.

"Um... Hello."

"It's Miss Opal, darlin'."

Did she just conjure the woman out of the air?

"Hey, Miss Opal... What—?" Even though she hadn't seen the woman in almost three years, they occasionally talked on the phone and managed to exchange at least four letters a year. One for each of their birthday, Christmas, and Jamaican Independence Day. None of those days were coming up soon.

"How are you?" Sage finally had the presence of mind to ask.

"Good, baby. Good." The sound of rattling pans came through the phone, then a voice speaking in the background."

"Hush, man! Can't you see I'm on the phone?" Miss Opal's voice dimmed for a moment before it came back strong on the line. "Your mother is coming up there, and your father too, I suppose, but she and I were talking this morning and she just invited me to come up with her."

The shock of it almost had Sage veering off the road.

"You alright, baby? I just heard a strange noise from over there."

"I'm good." With a quick jerk of her hand, Sage righted the wheel and cursed when the car tires screeched, nearly overcompensating and slamming into the concrete barrier. "Just driving."

"Be careful, baby. I hear they try to kill you out there in Miami."

"No more than in Jamaica," she said, automatically falling back into their natural banter despite her surprise.

"Anyway, babes. I just wanted to tell you the news, so you don't get too shocked when you have to pick up three of us instead of two next week."

Next week?

Sage didn't even bother to ask how her parents managed to get Miss Opal a Visa to visit America. It seemed like they were as hard to get as rim jobs in church.

"Do you know what day and time your plane is supposed to land?" Because she wouldn't put it past her mother to call her from the airport to tell her she was waiting on their Miami-bound flight to board. Or worse yet, send her a quick text when they were already on the other side and heading to customs at Miami International.

"Yes, let me see... Mrs. Bennett already bought the tickets and I have the information right here on the fridge."

She must have been calling from her own little cottage then. It was on the same piece of land as her parents' house. Sage's parents didn't allow anything on the refrigerator. Not even a grocery list.

"Ah, here it is." Miss Opal rattled off the day and time that made Sage's hands clench around the steering wheel. This time, she managed not to cause a multi-car pile-up with her reaction.

"All right, Miss Opal. I'll be there to pick you up."

"Thank you, honey. After all this time, I can't wait to see how you live over there in America."

Oh, you mean my big dyke life?

"I'll make sure to have someplace nice and comfortable for you to stay," she said, grateful she wasn't on FaceTime, so Miss Opal couldn't see her panicked face.

"I know you will, baby love. That's just the kind of sweetheart you are."

Miss Opal's words made Sage smile.

"Anyway, darlin' dear. I have to finish making this soup and get this worthless boy here to help me. Talk with you soon." Muttering in the background made Sage suspect the "worthless boy" had heard her comment.

"Okay, Miss Opal."

The call disconnected.

"Fuck me..."

The adult thing for Sage to do would've been to call her parents and confirm their date of arrival and that Miss Opal was coming too. But there was only so much adulting she could do right now. She switched the music to Drake and allowed the thumping beat to obliterate any useless thoughts for the rest of the drive.

At the studio, she let herself in with the key. About a year ago, a relatively well-known lesbian director asked her to write a couple of songs for an upcoming movie. Sage immediately said "yes." It didn't hurt that an actress she'd had a massive crush on as a kid played the lead and very dykey role.

Sage had already written the songs, and they'd been "approved," but she wanted to record them herself in the privacy of the studio before the producer got involved. And it didn't hurt that the next couple of hours gave her a legit reason to avoid Phil and home a little bit longer.

Tucking her keys in her jacket pocket, she walked into the reserved room. It didn't take long for her to find who she was supposed to meet. A pale, bald-headed figure already sat at the soundboard, headphones over one ear, fingers manipulating the knobs and buttons.

"Hey, Leda."

Leda Swann—and Sage strongly suspected that wasn't her real name—was one of the behind-the-scenes music folks attached to the movie. She was in town for the next couple of nights and wanted to be there when Sage set down the first tracks.

Although they weren't besties, they'd talked enough on the phone and in person over the last year enough to know each other a little bit.

"Hey, doll face." Leda, short and sexy-ugly with her pale skin, red lips, and full sleeve tattoos, gave Sage a worried full-body glance. "Everything good?"

"As good as they'll get for now," Sage said, not bothering with a lie.

"If you wanna talk..." Leda hitched up a shoulder to indicate what was left unsaid.

"Thanks, but I just came to forget all that shit, get some work done, and maybe meet this deadline to get my manager off my ass."

"Good enough." Leda clambered onto the stool in front of the digital console, abandoning whatever she'd been working on when Sage walked in. The soles of her thick boots thumping against the floor as she got herself settled. She picked up an iPad. "I love the song you wrote for the break-up scene, but I want you to consider a slight change..."

"All right. What do you have in mind?"

With Leda by her side, Sage lost herself in the rhythm of the work.

It was work she loved although, until Nuria suggested it, she never thought she'd do anything more with her voice than occasionally sing at Rémi's club. But as soon as she started taking her singing seriously, the work came pouring in. Songs on indie movie soundtracks, local club appearances, a few commercials here and there, even a couple of music festivals in Europe.

Some days, the music was almost as good as sex. For those minutes that she recorded in the studio or sang under the hot stage lights, it transported her to a place inside her mind where nothing hurt, and everything was perfect. It was a place she needed now more than ever. With Leda watching her from outside the soundproof booth, Sage adjusted the headphones around her ears. After a deep breath that better rearranged all the separate parts in her body, she started to sing.

Everything else, she'd deal with later.

CHAPTER TEN

Later came sooner than she wanted.

Sage had just finished up the second track, with a few spontaneously re-written lyrics, and was listening to it with Leda through the headphones. The music was beautiful and felt good in Sage's ear. It was a balm to the riot in her heart. Leda nodding along to the slow and sensuous beat with a smile.

"How about repeating the second verse here? It sounds great as is, but those lyrics are perfect and worth showing off." She hummed the verse and Sage nodded too. It made sense.

MY HEART IS the moon
a place you colonized
then abandoned to explore
an easier world.

"YEAH, YEAH." Sage made a quick note on her phone.

The door banged open making her jump.

"It's occupied! Can't you read the damn sign out front?" She shouted the words over her shoulder and kept typing notes app without looking to see who it was.

"Um...Sage." Leda's voice brought her head up.

"What?"

Leda pointed. And Sage swallowed the sudden and barbed lump in her throat. Phillida stood in the doorway, still wearing her yellow dress from the night of the movie premiere. Phil's bright dress, her bangles, the thick cloud of hair pulled back from her face. Almost everything about her looked just like it did that night. Except for her face.

Smudged red lipstick painted her mouth, chin, and under her nose. Her mascara and eyeliner were smeared, making it look like she'd been punched in both eyes. Phil looked wrecked.

Sage's fist clenched at her side.

"I can read the sign just fine," Phil said, closing the door behind her with a sharp snap.

"I think I'll..." Leda pulled off the headphones, and carefully put them next to the soundboard. "...go take a cigarette break." She grabbed her bag from the back of the chair and walked out in a thunder of heavy boot steps.

Sage appreciated her Leda's tact. The woman didn't smoke, she was just giving them some room. The sound of her leaving left them drowning in silence. Sage shifted, dropped her headphones next to the ones Leda had abandoned. She wasn't ready for this. Her stomach churned with anxiety.

"What's on your mind?" she finally asked when Phillida only stood on the other side of the closed door, watching her.

Her face was naked with pain. "You can't keep avoiding me," Phil croaked.

"That's not what I'm doing." Sage winced even as the words

came out of her mouth. She'd always been a shit liar. "I came over this morning."

"And?"

"And what?" Sage shrugged. "You were asleep, so I left."

"You could have stayed. You could have woken me up."

Yes, she could have. But the coward inside her had raced out the door and directly between the open legs of another woman. But she wasn't the one in the wrong here. She wasn't going to feel ashamed.

"Stay for what?" Sage asked, her lips curled in a snarl. "For you to lie to me some more?"

Phillida recoiled like she'd been slapped. "I never lied to you."

"But you never told me the truth either. You've been hiding this from me for months now." Once Sage started talking, she couldn't stop. "I knew something was wrong. I fucking knew it. I just never in all my nightmares thought you'd want to ride a dick straight out of my life."

"You're not being fair. I never cheated on you. I never lied. I just...I just knew you'd react this way. This is the reason I didn't tell you. Not yet. I never wanted to see *that* look on your face." Phil stabbed a finger at Sage. "—that look you always get when you talk about 'those disgusting bisexuals,' turned on me."

"What? I don't want to eat after some guy, and I sure as fuck don't want my wife or the mother of my children to kiss me with the same mouth that's been sucking dick and—."

The shocked gasp from Phil brought her tirade to an abrupt halt.

"Wife?" Phil clutched at her throat, thin fingers trembling. "Wife? Did I miss you proposing?"

They'd only talked *around* marriage. Sometimes making laughing speculations about the married lives of their friends, how boring they must be even when something beneath their laughter had obviously been strained in a way that neither of them had been bold enough to confront.

"No. And I'm sure as hell not going to now." Sage couldn't take back the words. Not now.

"You're a real bastard, you know that?"

The naked pain on Phil's face tightened the ache in Sage's belly. "I never said I wasn't," she muttered. That was one of the things Phil had said about Sage at the beginning of their love affair. That Sage was an asshole to just about everybody but those she loved. Part of why people were so charmed but also intimidated by her.

She didn't have the heart-stopping good looks of Rémi, Dez, or even Nuria. But her constant snark, her willingness to confront everyone on their shit and give out compliments when she felt they were due, drew everyone under her spell and sometimes even begging for her approval.

"No," Phil said softly. Her arms fell to her sides, limp. "You never did."

She looked defeated, nothing like the fierce woman who always gave Sage back just as much shit as she dished out. Not that Phil could've done that now. This was far from one of their usual arguments. Arguments that had revolved around stupid shit that didn't ever really matter. If this had been one of those old arguments, they would've been on the studio floor by now, furiously kissing, one of them half-way to being naked while they pledged their ever-lasting love for each other.

But that was never going to happen.

A sudden pain lanced through Sage's chest, and she bit back a gasp. "I think you should go," she said, abruptly exhausted. "It wasn't smart of you to come here."

Outraged heat flared in Phil's eyes, and Sage was almost glad to see it. "Are you calling me stupid now?"

"We both know the answer to that question." Phil was by far

the smarter of the two of them, and she had her Ivy league degrees and Mensa membership to prove it.

"Then what are you saying to me exactly?" Phil demanded.

The words were stuck in Sage's throat, but she managed to cough them up. "I'm saying I just can't—can't be with you right now."

"At all?"

"At all."

The air hissed from between Phil's teeth like a balloon deflating. Then her crossed arms formed a barrier over her chest, across her heart. Slowly, her face rearranged itself. Became cooler, then cold. And the tears that had been gushing up from the edges of her eyes stopped like they were being sucked back in.

"We still need to talk," Phil said finally, her voice low and measured. "We have to resolve this."

Sage shook her head and took an uncertain step to the side and away from Phil. Everything she'd built with Phil over the past twelve years was really gone. The thought struck Sage like a blow to the chest. If she hadn't been leaning against the soundboard she probably would have fallen over. Her mind flew through all that had happened in the last day and a half.

And now her parents would be here too.

Her parents. *And* Miss Opal.

It was too much.

The breath churned in Sage's lungs. Her stomach roiled, but she fought for control and swallowed hard. Her tongue dragged heavily across the sandpaper dryness of her lips. "If... Can you leave the house for a few days next week? That's when my parents are coming."

Scorn flashed in Phil's eyes obliterating any trace of hurt. With a sneer, she pulled herself up to her full height, her chin jutting out. Sage braced herself for the full blast of Phil's temper only to watch Phil quietly turn around and walk out of the studio.

In the shocked silence, Sage realized then that Phil's feet had been bare. The slap of her lover's naked soles against the smooth hardwoods echoed, empty and loud, long after the door closed behind her.

CHAPTER ELEVEN

After leaving the studio, Sage got a room at the Four Seasons for the next few days.

She tried to convince herself it was to give Phil time and privacy to pack up her stuff and leave, but the reality was that Sage was too much of a coward. Even though this was what she wanted, the thought of watching Phil separate herself from the home they'd built together made her feel sick.

She'd done this before with Phil, asked her to take off and leave their house for the brief length of her parents' visit. Phil never liked it. And she'd always used those times to reason with Sage about coming out to her family. This time, Sage wouldn't have to deal with that aggravation or worry about whether or not Phil left remnants of herself at their house. She wouldn't have to deal with anything where Phil was concerned. Not anymore.

Barely an hour into her pity party for one at the hotel bar, Sage's mother finally called her about their Miami visit.

"Opal can't wait to live in the same house with you again. Even if it's only for a week." Her mother opened with that when Sage answered the phone.

"Good morning to you too, mother."

"Don't be a smart ass, Sage Danielle."

As if she'd dare at this stage of the game. Sage balanced her phone between her ear and shoulder and nodded her thanks to the bartender when he slid her a second rum and Coke in anticipation of her finishing the one in her hand very soon. Someone bumped into Sage with a laugh, one of a group of suits who looked like they were celebrating an early morning something.

"Sorry," the suit said with a laugh and went back to her companions without waiting for Sage's response.

"Are you at a bar?" Sage could hear the outrage in her mother's voice even from so far away.

"It's way too early to be drinking," Sage said, neatly sidestepping the actual question. She'd had lots of practice with that over the years. The bartender passed her with a vaguely upraised eyebrow. Sage ignored him. "What's going on, mother?"

Puttering sounds in the background and snatches of a nearby conversation reached Sage though the phone. Good, her mother couldn't give her full attention to giving her shit for living her life. "No, Trevor, not that one. Wait...Sage!"

"Yes, mother." She took the last swallow of her first drink and slid it toward the bartender, then reached for the fresh one he'd just dropped off. "I'm still here."

"We're coming in on Saturday afternoon. Do you have time to pick us up or should we get a taxi?" It wasn't a real question. If Sage even hinted that she was too busy to pick her mother up from the airport, she'd be hearing about her failings as a daughter all the way to the grave.

"I'll come pick you up. No problem. Do you have the flight information?"

Her mother gave Sage the same details that Miss Opal had provided. "Got it. I'll be meet you once you get through customs."

"Good."

And that was that.

"We might be too hungry to wait for you to cook so you can just take us out for a nice early dinner."

Good to know she was already planning Sage's day and evening too.

"Of course."

One of the suits was paying far too much attention to Sage's conversation, or maybe just to her, eyeing Sage over the rim of her martini glass while the others in her party chatted on about some business deal or other.

The woman looked uptight, her hair in an up-do that pulled at the edges of her face like an instant face-lift. The navy suit she wore wasn't doing her body any favors, but her face was interesting enough with its fat, red lips and the mole at the corner of one eye.

"I have to go, mother. My friends just got here." Sage kept her eye on the woman who didn't look the slightest bit embarrassed to be caught staring.

"Okay, honey. See you Saturday."

"All right, Love to Daddy and Miss Opal."

Once her mother hung up, she slid the phone in her pocket and leaned her forearms on the bar. The condensation from her drink soaked into the coaster and the drink itself was steadily on its way to becoming half water and ice. Although she'd badly wanted a drink when she came down to the bar, now the thought of getting drunk had lost some of its appeal.

Her parents were coming. Phil was gone. If she kept going, she'd only give herself the sweet gift of a hangover the next day. A pounding head and a trick stomach would only compound the misery of having to pretend not a big, butch dyke once her parents and Miss Opal got into town.

"Fuck..." she muttered.

"That would be nice right about now, wouldn't it?"

The suit was closer to Sage than the last time she looked, having taken the place of the one who'd stumbled into Sage during her phone call. The stranger licked the rim of her martini glass and gave Sage the most thorough eye-fucking she'd had in a long time.

Sage decided to play dumb. "What would be nice?"

The woman didn't allow her to play dumb for long though. "A nice, long fuck." She took a slow sip of her martini, her tongue pressing into the glass, long and flattened enough to show off the silver stud piercing through it. "I have a room upstairs."

The glimpse of silver in the woman's tongue kicked a sharp response in Sage's belly. But probably not the one the woman wanted.

Phillida. Her ring. Her promise.

Sage squeezed her thighs together and the curve bar through her clitoral hood pressed back, sending a bolt of pleasure straight to her core. They'd gotten the piercings together, an unofficially-official sign of their commitment only they knew about. They were both made of titanium and, when Phil went down on her, she loved to flick her tongue to click the metal balls together. She said it was their own special music.

Sage swallowed the burning lump in her throat, then took a long sip of her drink when that didn't help. She cleared her throat, glanced at the woman once before turning back to face the bar and the bartender who hovered nearby, watching the sparse bar crowd and polishing glasses now that there was no one around needing fresh drinks.

"Good luck with finding that morning fuck," Sage said. "This seems like a good place for it." She knocked back as much of the drink as she could in one swallow and walked away from the bar.

CHAPTER TWELVE

Sage saw her parents before they saw her. They came out of customs, her father pushing a luggage cart loaded down with three suitcases that looked over-weight from where Sage was standing. Food from Jamaica, most likely. Even after all these years, they had Jamaican friends who lived in Miami and asked them to bring back what they probably thought of as the best part of Jamaica. Food. Fried sprat. Roast breadfruit. Chippies banana chips. The chocolate candy Sage used to love as a kid but couldn't stand the taste of now.

She pushed away from the column, sent off one last text to Nuria to wrap up the distracted conversation they'd been having about Sage's so-called biphobia and tucked her phone away in her back pocket. She lifted her hand to wave the same moment her father wheeled the cart in her direction.

"Sage!" His big voice boomed out through the busy concourse.

Being away from him, away from them, it was easy for Sage to forget what a forceful man he was away from his wife. His wide chest, powerful body, and carrying voice hinting that he was a man in control of all things in his world. And away from his wife, he took up more space than when he was with her. A case of a powerful man ceding control to someone smaller than himself by choice. It was an interesting dynamic if Sage allowed herself to think about it. But she purposefully did not.

"Daddy."

He deftly maneuvered the cart through the thick weekend crowd, his smile wide and very much pleased. At his side, his wife, pretty and conservative in her "airport clothes" which consisted of a black skirt suit and low-heeled shoes, had her phone in her hand and used it to wave at Sage. Miss Opal, who Sage hadn't seen in years despite talking with her at least once a month since she left Jamaica as a child, looked like she was going to church in her wide yellow hat, white dress, and yellow shoes.

She held a plate wrapped in tin foil in front of her like a shield while her wide-eyed gaze bounced around the airport. But once she saw Sage, her eyes focused like a laser beam and her smile nearly split her face in half.

"Sage! My honey child." She rushed through the crowd, miraculously avoiding getting shoulder-checked, to wrap her arms around Sage. The edge of the plate dug into Sage's back as they hugged. Miss Opal smelled like rose water and cooked ackee. Like home.

"I hope we didn't keep you waiting too long," her father said. "That immigration line was murder."

"No, not at all. It was no problem to wait," Sage said over Miss Opal's head, still squeezing the woman who'd managed to shrink at least two inches since they'd last seen each other but whose affection had only grown. "I keep myself occupied."

"You look good, babes," Miss Opal said. "A little skinnier than last time, but still good." She plucked at the neckline of Sage's shirt.

Despite the heat, Sage wore a long-sleeved button-down shirt and slacks, keeping everything covered except for the V of skin revealed by the two open buttons of her shirt. Her parents had seen her since the last set of tattoos, but Miss Opal hadn't. She didn't want to spring them on her just yet.

"You have a man here treating you right?"

Sage winced. "No man..."

Did she imagine it or did her parents just share a look over Miss Opal's head?

Her mother breathed a gusty sigh that lifted the cloth over her significant bosom. "All right now. Everybody ready?"

After exchanging a quick set of hugs with her parents while keeping her arm firmly around Miss Opal, Sage escorted them to her parked car. Once they were buckled in, she navigated the hectic airport traffic and streamed out onto I-95 with the rest of the cars fleeing the airport. She didn't know which traffic was worse, coming or going.

"You guys want to eat first or freshen up at home before heading out to eat?"

"Let's drop off these bags," her mother said. "I don't want some worthless criminal to break into your car and steal our luggage. It took Miss Opal nearly all day to bake the plantain tarts."

"Plantain tarts?" Sage perked up. From the passenger seat, Miss Opal gave her a wink. Plantain tarts were, hands down, Sage's favorite of all the delicious things Miss Opal made. "We definitely don't want that," she said and turned the car toward home.

Since they weren't going to stay long, Sage didn't bother opening the garage door to park inside. Her insides tripping with near-anxiety, she pulled up to the house and parked the car in the circular driveway. The street was quiet and the tall palm trees around their property gave the front yard a feeling of privacy, despite the actual close proximity of their neighbors.

"Wow! This is nice!" Miss Opal tumbled from the car, still clutching the foil-wrapped plate. She looked around with awe written all over her face.

Sage tried to see the house through Miss Opal's eyes, a home that was smaller than where her parents lived. The two-story, Mediterranean style house with a sleeping porch on the second floor and an explosion of purple flowers trailing up the driveway, flowers the landscaper was paid well enough to take care of. Purple was Phil's favorite color.

"Come on in. The inside is even better." It had the A/C on for one thing.

With her mother's massive Louis Vuitton bag dragging down her shoulder, Sage unlocked and opened the door, moved through the brightly lit foyer with light streaming in through the stained-glass mosaic over the front door. "I'll just put your bags in your rooms and you can freshen up or do whatever you need. We can leave whenever—" both her feet and words stumbled. "—you're ready."

Her brain couldn't process what she was seeing, or what she wasn't.

From her long-legged sprawl on the couch, Phil stretched and yawned, and the top of the pajama pants set she wore—white and silky—rode up to show her flat stomach and the platinum belly chain curved just beneath perched her navel. Her laptop was open next to her and her cell phone sat on the ottoman next to her feet.

"Hi there." She leveled a challenging gaze at Sage before turning a smile to her parents.

"What are you—?"

"Phillida! What a nice surprise to see you."

Sage's father dropped his bag in the middle of the living room floor and crossed to where Phil was gracefully getting to her feet. His grin was wide and happy.

"It's good to see you too, Papa Bennett. I didn't know you were getting in today."

A pulse thudded wildly in Sage's neck and she gripped the strap of the bag over her shoulder like she was trying to strangle it to death. Better the bag then Phil's damn neck. She couldn't help but notice her mother who stood at the entrance to their wide living room looking like she'd just sucked on a lime, her lips puckered and disapproving, while she looked anywhere but at Phil.

"That's fair since we didn't know you'd be here," Sage's mother said.

"That makes two of us," Sage muttered.

Apparently unbothered, Phil practically floated from Sage's father and his warm welcome to stand in front of Miss Opal. "You must be the most amazing woman alive," she said to Miss Opal, her smile genuine and setting her brown eyes to sparkling. "I'm Phillida, Sage's very good friend."

Sage nearly jumped out of her skin, but Miss Opal was preening under Phil's skillful seduction. Her oak skin gleamed with pleasure and the denture-baring smile made her seem almost like a child.

"Mr. Bennett talks about you sometimes dear. You've even prettier than he said," Miss Opal said.

Another sound from Sage's mother. Which Phil ignored as she shared a hug with Miss Opal like she was a fond and long-lost relative. When she pulled away, Miss Opal followed her with her eyes, looking pleased indeed, as she made her way to Sage's mother who still looked like she smelled something long dead and rotten.

"Mrs. Bennett, it's good to see you again." They didn't so much as exchange air kisses.

"You look...comfortable, dear heart."

Phil's smile didn't falter. "I try to be as much as possible."

Then she spun around, the white silk moving gracefully around the lines of her tall and elegant body. She must have been wearing underwear because the tips of her breasts that usually made themselves eagerly known in the silk were noticeably absent.

"Sage, you can show your parents to their room and I'll take Miss Opal's bags to the other guest room."

Her father blinked in confusion, but Sage did the only thing she could do, which was what Phil said. The bag on her shoulder suddenly felt ten times as heavy, especially with the added weight of her mother's suspicious stare. Her parents followed her down the hall.

In the guest room, done in shades of brown and sapphire blue, she put down her mother's bag and the massive rolling bag of her father's that she carried.

"Here you are." She swallowed past her dry throat and fought the age to clear the massive lump that had formed there in the last few minutes. "The bathroom's through there if you want to tidy up before we leave."

And she thought that was going to be that, but she should have known better, at least from her mother.

"What the devil is she doing here? She looks well comfortable in her nightie and with her stuff scattered everywhere."

"Uh..." Sage's brain had shorted out completely.

"No matter. That girl is always a welcome sight," her father boomed, rustling in his carry-on and pulling out his Dopp kit. "She could come to eat with us." Then he disappeared into the bathroom, leaving the door wide open. He took his phone from his jacket pocket, fiddling with it as he squinted at the screen through his bifocals.

"Don't you dare invite her out with us, Sage Bennett."

An indecipherable noise floated from the bathroom. Her

father muttering to himself. The familiar chime of a text being sent came from his phone.

From down the hall, Sage could hear Phil's soft voice, then Miss Opal's loud and open-throated laughter which somehow made her mother frown. Sage felt her stomach cramp all over again.

"I like her." Her father came out of the bathroom wiping his hands on a small towel. The smell of mint mouthwash followed him into the bedroom. "She's really smart. Did you read her article in Science Journal America about the in microbial gut populations in vegans versus vegetarians? Really interesting research that." Passing the full-length mirror, he brushed a hand over his jaw, critically eyeing this still stubble-free jawline before patting his back pocket to make sure his wallet was still there.

Sage blinked. "I did read that article," she said after a moment's surprised silence. "Most of it went right over my head, though."

Her father grunted out a laugh. "Me too."

Sometimes she forgot how well Phil and her father got along, and how much they had in common. Although Phil called herself a science hobbyist, she kept up with the information in the obscure scientific journals she subscribed to and kept a lab across town with some of her Mensa friends. On one of her father's long-ago visits, Sage had even exchanged email addresses with him, another so-called science hobbyist.

Sage's mother made a disapproving noise and moved toward her husband.

And that was that, Sage thought with more than a little relief. What her mother wanted, she usually got.

She walked out of the room, heading toward the bedroom she and Phil shared. Used to share.

Phil was there, naked except for a pair of black thong underwear and a matching bra offering up her breasts for inspection.

She stepped past Sage and walked into the closet, dipping her shoulder to the side to avoid touching Sage.

"What the fuck are you doing here? You should be gone." Skin shivering with the rush of sudden anger and helplessness, Sage stalked after her.

"This is my house too, in case you forgot."

Phil pulled a black dress from its hanger, shook it out, and held it in front of her. Was she getting ready to leave? Something about the way she looked at herself reminded Sage of her father in that moment. After a nod of satisfaction, Phil stepped into the dress, sleek and black that hugged her from knees to shoulders, and Sage stepped forward on automatic pilot, to help her zip into the dress. After the barest pause, Phil turned her back and stood still as Sage smoothly tugged up the zipper, breathing in the faint scent of coconut oil that lingered in Phil's hair.

Sage froze. No, they couldn't have this "normal" between them anymore.

When Phil moved to turn away from her, Sage grabbed her arm. "We can't do this. Not with my parents here."

"Let go of me." Phil's eyes snapped fire, anger all tangled up with hurt.

Sage dropped her hand as if she'd been burned. She struggled to find her footing in this new dynamic, this disaster they'd become. "You're supposed to be gone." She hissed the words, an accusation.

"And you're supposed to act like an asshole to me and try to throw me out of the house that I half own so maybe we're even for now." She spun, slipped her feet into black heels, tipped lipstick into a small black clutch and left Sage to stew by herself in the closet.

By the time she got back to the living room, her parents were there, her father wearing a pleased smile while he showed Phil something on his phone. She matched his height in her high heels. Her mother sat on the couch, stiff and upright, her purse on her lap and clutched between her hands, her eyes glued to the door like she was waiting for a jail sentence to be over. Sage looked from one face to the other, sure that she'd missed something. Before she could ask what it was, Miss Opal's voice rang out from the kitchen.

"This stove is nice and big. And so clean. Do you even cook in here?"

"Yes, but I clean up well." Sage flashed a look around the room, trying not to let her anxiety show, wanting everyone to be happy, or in her mother's case, as happy as they could be and not start any shit. She took a few steps toward her mother who looked like she was chewing on nails, changed her mind and went into the kitchen instead.

Miss Opal was halfway inside the pantry, bending down to look at the lowest shelves.

"I don't recognize most of the things in here," she said, sounding pleased.

Miss Opal loved to cook, for herself as much as for the kids who had moved into and out of her life. Many a day Sage had stopped by her house to find her in the kitchen, the house empty except for her, backing or cooking, reading a paperback romance while a pot bubbled, and the kitchen overflowed with delicious scents.

"You can use whatever you want in here." Sage stood with her back to the counter, fingers clenching and releasing around the edge.

"Of course, baby love," Miss Opal said.

Sage rubbed a finger along the smooth granite edge of the counter. "We're ready to leave whenever you are."

"Of course! I didn't mean to hold you up. I was just being nosy while everybody was putting themselves together."

"You're not holding us up."

A soft snort and a quick smile. "I think Mrs. Bennett might feel a bit differently," Miss Opal said. "She's been holding down that settee for what she probably thinks is a whole hour now." Her voice was soft, secretive, but teasing. She'd worked for Sage's parents long enough to know all their faults.

"It's fine." Sage pushed away from the counter, relieved to find something to smile about. "Ready?" She offered her arm to Miss Opal and they left the kitchen together.

In the living room, things were just as she left it. Phil, now with a chunky star-shaped necklace resting just beneath her collarbones and her phone tucked away, was attempting a conversation with both Phil's parents. It wasn't working out too well.

What was she still doing there?

"All right." Sage forced a cheerful smile. "Everybody ready?"

"Of course, daughter." Despite his wife's grim look, he practically leaped toward the door, holding it open for the women to walk through.

"Thank you, kind sir," Phil said with a laughing smile.

"You're going with us?" Sage felt stupid for asking.

In the spirit of inane questions, Phil gave her a quick once-over. "Aren't you hot in all those clothes, honey?" she asked, voice low and falsely solicitous. She knew damn well Sage was wearing the long-sleeved shirt to keep her tattoos out of sight.

They sneered at each other.

"I invited her to come along," her father said, ignoring their by-play, his hand on the doorknob, smile easy and unconcerned. "There's plenty of room in your big SUV. Plus, I'm paying, in case you're crying broke these days."

He was obviously joking since it would take just about the world ending as they knew it for Sage, and the rest of her family, to be truly broke. But as financially savvy as he was, her father was dim as a box of rocks where emotions and people were concerned. Like why the hell did he think inviting Phil to dinner with them was okay?

A crack of pain in her jaw warned Sage she was clenching her teeth too hard. She let the other women walk out before her, fussing with her keys to avoid giving her father a dirty look.

It was going to be a long ass dinner.

CHAPTER THIRTEEN

"We should go to that place you got us take-out from last time," Sage's father said. "I haven't had Jamaican food that good outside a yaad."

Of course, he was talking about Novlette's, a restaurant where Sage and the rest of her friends, her very gay friends, hung out all the time. Damn near as often as Rémi's club. But she didn't want to take them someplace where they'd be a risk of someone recognizing her, or her and Phil. This wasn't something she would've thought of before, but Phil in the car with her scowling mother and Miss Opal, who found everything about Phil and Miami fascinating, frightened her into being more careful than usual.

Sage cleared her throat. "Why don't we try someplace a little different?" she suggested. "If you don't like it, we can head to Novlette's before you all leave." And when Phil wasn't with them.

The look Phil gave her in the rear-view mirror clearly told Sage she wasn't fooling anyone.

"Okay..." Her mother looked at her with something like suspicion.

"As long it's someplace where we can sit outside," Miss Opal said. "It's real nice here. I want to see as much of it as possible before I leave."

Sage mentally ran through a list of restaurants in her head where no one knew her, where there was outdoor seating and a decent view. "I know just the place," she said.

In the back seat, Phil sat behind her with an arm dangling outside the car while Sage's father perched in the middle seat between the two women. He looked happy as a pig in shit. His wife did not.

"As long as you know where you're going and the food is good," her father said. Then he went back to fiddling with his phone. He sent a text. "By the way, I invited Errol to come eat with us. I hope you all don't mind."

"You've inviting all kinds of people to eat with us, why should one more be any different?"

"Mother..."

Sage threw her mother a look of frustration, not just because of the sheer rudeness of her statement with Phil sitting right there, but because Errol wasn't just anybody. He was the reason they came all this way.

A soft emotion smoothed her mother's face, her version of an apology, but she said nothing. Phil's smile, such as it was, stayed on her face. "It would be nice to meet Errol. We've heard about him but never met."

"We?" Her mother's face tightened up again.

"It's strange with you living in the same state that you never even met Errol. The world can be so small and big at the same time," Sage's father said. As usual, he was ignoring his wife's rudeness, living in a world of his own creation, seeming to comply with everything she wanted but living his own life regardless.

When her mother first told Sage about Errol, how he was an orphan in Jamaica with no resources, that they were sponsoring him because too many people took on kids from China or someplace else besides home, she had been surprised. She still remained surprised but was glad they'd decided to share what they had to help Errol and other kids like him in Jamaica.

As far as she knew, he was the only one they had actively sponsored and taken from Jamaica, sent to a private boarding school, and promised to pay for his college degree as well. They helped kids at an orphanage back home, but none of the individual kids to this extent.

"It is," Phil agreed. "Like I had no idea when you wrote to me about my article in Science Journal America that you were Sage's dad. Such a small world."

Sage felt a start of surprise. She had no idea that was how they met. She thought it had been just him gradually getting to know Phil through careful and repeated exposure over the years.

"Exactly," Sage's father said. "A happy coincidence."

Her mother made a noise, and for a few awkward moments, silence rang loudly in the SUV. Then, thankfully, they arrived at the restaurant. Sag pulled the car into the lot, relieved that it wasn't overflowing with Saturday early evening traffic. Then again, they were at a lull between lunch and dinner. After six, the place would probably have been impossible to get into without a reservation. At least it seemed that way from the couple of times she'd been there before. For a new place, it was damn popular.

"We're here!" Sage announced unnecessarily.

Phil gave her an unamused look and climbed out of the truck. "Yay," she muttered under her breath.

Sage hopped out of the car while her parents wrestled with their seat belts and began getting out of the truck together.

"You didn't have to come, you know," she muttered under her breath, glad that both her parents got out on the other side of the truck.

"I don't want to be rude to your father. He invited me."

"But you don't mind being rude to my mother?"

Phil rolled her eyes. "This is *so* not the time..." She tucked her little purse under her arm and marched past Sage, her ass rocking under the slim fitting black dress that managed to straddle the line between elegant and sexy as sin. Her palms itched to cup that ass, to feel the muscular glutes she loved to clutch and bite when they were fucking.

With a deep breath, she slammed the driver's side door shut and pocketed the truck keys. The paved parking lot was brand new, smooth with freshly painted stripes diving the parking spots, a valet waiting at the front to take their truck if they wanted, a building that looked new and even more impressive, modern without being cold, something she'd missed the last time she'd been there.

Her parents and Miss Opal walked arm in arm, leaving Sage to walk stiffly at Phil's side toward the double doors of the restaurant. The wrap-around terrace on the second floor was no more than half full. Plenty of space for Sage's little family. And their plus one, she thought, thinking of Errol and his impending appearance.

The hostess seated them quickly and without a wait on the wrap-around terrace, finding room for them on the section overlooking the bay.

"This is so nice," Miss Opal said, dragging out the last word.

The place was decent. Not as good as Rémi's club, of course.

"I still prefer Gillespie's, though," Phil said, echoing Sage's thoughts. She smiled over at her woman before she could think better of it. And for a moment, Phil smiled back at her, an intimate look that said they were on the same page, not just about this but about everything else in their lives.

But that wasn't true anymore.

Shifting in her seat, Sage tore her eyes away from Phil and stumbled into Miss Opal's curious gaze. "What's Gillespie's?" Miss Opal asked.

"Uh... um...Rémi's is... it's... um..."

"It's a club our friend owns," Phil said, easily filling the gap between Sage's flustered mumblings.

What the hell was wrong with her? She couldn't share a single real thing about her life? But this was what happened when you were in the closet. Every truth was a minefield of disastrous discovery, every authentic part of your life you took for granted as good and safe became something to be ashamed of, something to second guess. A quiver of unhappiness rippled over her skin.

"Yeah. It's in town on the water. A much better view."

"Why didn't you take us there? The food is good, right?"

"The best," Phil said, her filled with tender poison.

"I just thought we'd try something a little different for once."

"Well the same for you is different for us since we've never been there," her father said.

Sage squirmed under the combined stares of everyone else at the table. A waitress appeared at their table, and Sage wanted to kiss her.

"Hi, I'm Mattie and I'll be taking care of you today. Can I start you with anything to drink?"

When she left with their orders, her father started up a conversation with Phil about Neil deGrasse Tyson and his likely stalkers. Despite their animated discussion, Sage still felt Phil's gaze on her and she deliberately avoided it.

Not now. Please.

The beginnings of a headache throbbed just behind her right

eye and, her body felt heavy and unwieldy, a reminder that she hadn't slept well the night before. Even the bright, late evening sun, which usually powered her like a battery, didn't help. It seared into her skin through her clothes, the long-sleeved shirt hiding her tattoos, into the back of her neck, through the short but thick coils over her scalp.

Letting loose a silent sigh that shook her entire body, Sage roamed her gaze over the other tables on the terrace where they sat. The crowd at Wilde's was as different from Gillespie's as you could get. Eclectic but with a strong mobster vibe. Guys in blazers despite the heat, probably packing a different kind of heat in holsters under their clothes, girls wearing thick makeup more suited to late night, most wearing enough jewelry to blind the eye if you stared too long. A few tourist types here and there took up random space, but they looked a little out of place. But maybe no more than she and her family did.

Her eyes made another sweep of the place, then, she froze. Was that...?

The long hair, this time wrapped in a topknot like the princess in a Disney movie, was definitely the same. Her eyes drifted from the girl's hair and found a pair of pale brown eyes staring back at her. The surprise of it settled hard in her belly.

Crystal. Like an idiot, she didn't count on Crystal hanging out at Wilde's on her day off.

"You okay, honey?"

Of course, it was Miss Opal who noticed her flinch.

"Yeah, I'm good. Just thought I saw someone I know." No point in lying when her reaction clearly said as much.

Sitting on the side of the table opposite to Sage, Phil twisted around to look. "Who?"

It didn't take her long to find who Sage was talking about. Which was basically because Crystal hadn't stopped staring. "You know her?"

Caught off guard with her unexpected bluntness when she was usually more circumspect around her parents, Sage made a vague motion. "Yeah. I met her a couple of times." Literally twice. Phil's gaze narrowed, and it was obvious she knew exactly what Phil meeting up once or twice with this obviously young girl consisted of.

Her lips twisted. "You going to go say hi to your little friend?"

"Here you are!" The waitress appeared with their drinks and Sage again had the urge to give her the biggest kiss, or at least a tip that equaled to the same thing. With a smile firmly in place, perky Mattie efficiently served the drinks around the table. "Are you ready to order your meals?"

"Yes!" Sage jumped in like the idea of food at this place was the best one she'd ever had in her life. But she didn't remember anything the girl said about their specials and she sure as hell hadn't even glanced at the menu.

"I'll have the special," she said.

Mattie frowned. "Which one?"

Every restaurant had fish on their menu, right? "I'll have the fish."

The girl's smile looked pained. "I'm sorry, miss...but which one?"

With a sound of impatience, Phil sat up in her chair. "She'll have the lamb."

"She said she wanted fish," Sage's mother said.

Phil tried her most sincere-looking fake smile at Sage's mother. "She wasn't paying attention to what Mattie said earlier. She loves lamb. She'll rather have that than the fish."

Without waiting for a reply, she nodded once at the waitress then rattled off her own order. By the time the waitress had gotten all their orders and run off to tell the kitchen, Sage was squirming in her chair. Not just from the looks her parents tossed between her and Phil but the poisonous glare Phil threw her way.

"Oh, God! Sorry I'm late! I got so lost on the way here." The high-pitched voice dragged Sage's guilty gaze away from Phil and her parents. A slender boy, feminine in a thin, asymmetrical shirt that skimmed down to knees in the front and brushed against his calves in the back, skinny jeans that might as well be yoga pants, and clunky boots he wore unlaced, dashed up to their table. "Does that mean I don't get any food?" His teasing words were obviously aimed at their table, but Sage was damned if she knew this obviously flaming gay kid.

But her mother got to her feet just a beat behind her husband. "You're right on time, honey!"

Sage's mouth dropped open as her parents swarmed the boy with hugs.

CHAPTER FOURTEEN

"Errol?" Sage couldn't have hidden her shock even if she tried. The boy was as visibly gay as she was, his hips swishing under the thin shirt and tight pants, his hair straightened and hanging down past his shoulders in sleek and thick waves.

From the shelter of her parents' arms, the kid looked over at Sage. "Yes, that's me." His smile was blinding, and sweet. He gently extricated himself from her parents' arms after giving them each one last kiss then slipped close to Sage even though she was still sitting. "It's good to finally meet you, almost-sister."

Almost-sister.

Sage was too surprised to do more than tolerate his hug when he leaned down to hug her in the chair. But Phil had better manners—or maybe she was less stunned—so she stood up to hug the boy.

"I'm Phillida," she said, looking like both a proud parent and some sort of fan. "You're *so* very pretty."

He actually blushed, his pale pecan skin coloring like a princess in a storybook. "Thank you!" He gripped her in a full-body hug and they stared at each other, an instant mutual admiration society, because it was very obvious how beautiful Phil was. To Sage, it felt like a long ass time before Errol let Phil go so he could sink gracefully into the empty seat Sage's parents saved for him. "Sorry again to be so late. This restaurant is a little hard to find."

"Yeah, it's so new that even the GPS was confused." Phil fluttered long fingers to dismiss his apology. "Don't worry about it. We're just glad you made it."

Sage cleared her throat. "Um...yeah. And...uh...congratulations on finishing school with a 4.0." Her parents had gushed about his excellent grades during more than one phone call. "Mama and daddy are very proud."

Errol reached out both hands to touch the couple on either side of him. "Viv and Trevor are the only reason I come this far. They saved my life. The least I can do is study hard and show them they didn't waste their time on me." His soft voice vibrated with sincerity and passion.

"Even if you'd been dead last in your class, to see you happy and thriving is enough for us," Sage's mother said. The lemon-face she'd been wearing disappeared when Errol showed up. She looked so genuinely happy to see the boy that Sage was having a complete mind-fuck around the whole thing.

"He has too much discipline to be last in his class," her father said. A muscle clenched in his jaw from his intense emotion. "We are very proud of you, Errol."

The boy blushed again.

The waitress returned to take Errol's order, and the boy, so sure and confident of himself, scanned the menu and made a choice quick and decisively. Sage's parents looked at him with adoration as Mattie left the table to put in his food order.

"So tell us, honey, what are you doing now that you're about to have the whole summer off?" Her mother leaned in, her chin propped up on her upraised palm, apparently eager to hear all about her nearly-adopted gay son's summer plans.

It was all fucking unreal.

Sage pushed away from the table, muttering something about the bathroom, then practically ran across the restaurant toward the restroom signs. Barely a minute passed before the bathroom door opened behind her and Phil stalked in on her high heels.

"Do you think they know?" Phil asked, keeping her voice low.

"You mean about Errol being a giant queer?" Sage's entire body felt too warm, her cheeks burning like she had a fever. She splashed water on her face, making sure not to get any water on her shirt. "Well, if they managed not to see my big gay ass for this long I can see how they might easily not see his."

"But what if they already know about you?"

Sage jerked around to look at Phil. "What?"

"You heard me." Phil stood with her feet braced apart, hands in the pockets of her dress. Her gaze pinned Sage where she stood. "What if they already know you're a big dyke who likes nothing better to eat pussy and strap up to fuck me when I let you?" She lifted her head in challenge.

Sage couldn't even begin to imagine a world where that was true. "They can't know," she said, her voice coming out so rough that it hurt. "They can't." Then that would mean she'd been shielding herself for nothing, hiding Phil and the miraculous thing they shared—*used* to share—because she was the one who was afraid. "No," Sage said again.

Phil snorted, but it was a gentle, almost kind sound. "Okay, honey."

Sage couldn't think of anything else to say.

Moments later, they left the bathroom together without saying another word and headed back to the table where her mother treated them to a suspicious and narrow-eyed stare. Her father and Miss Opal barely looked at them.

Did they know? Sage's heart beat double-time at the thought.

But as the time passed and no one said anything, she gradually relaxed. The rest of the meal went by in a surreal rush. Sage's parents freaking *fawned* over Errol and encouraged him to eat, asking him what his plans were now that he was graduating high school—enrolling in an art school in Boca Raton apparently—and asking what help he needed while they were there.

Sage couldn't help it. She kept glancing at Phil to see if she was reeling as much from this big Errol revelation as much as Sage was. But she seemed as swept up in the Errol love fest as Sage's parents, asking him questions, inviting him to brunch whenever he had a free day next, even asking if he was seeing anyone.

"I am hanging out with this one guy," he answered. "He's cool but I'm mostly focused on my school plans, you know."

"That's smart," Sage's father said and just about gave Sage a heart attack.

Phil just beamed at the boy. A child of genius parents, she'd finished at least three advanced degrees by the time she was eighteen and only came back to Miami to attend school with kids her age because she wanted to be "normal." School had been her everything until that last degree and by that time she'd been focused on reclaiming all the fun she'd missed out on. It was obvious that she loved how much Errol enjoyed school.

But because Phil was caught up in Errol didn't mean she didn't notice Sage. A few times, Sage caught her pitying looks, but they didn't linger.

They wrapped up the meal with Errol inviting Sage's parents to a gallery in Wynwood that had a few of his art pieces—he did surrealistic oil paintings that were a mashup of Dali and Kehinde Wiley—that he was excited to show them. He very obviously, Sage thought, didn't invite her and Phil. Maybe because he wanted to have his nearly-parents all to himself.

"That's great, sweetie," her mother said. "I'm excited to see them in person. I bet the cell phone pictures don't do them justice."

Errol's expression of bashful pleasure amped up Sage's guilt, and shame. In the four years since her parents had been sponsoring him, she never once thought about going to see him much less to ask about his work. Other than to check with her parents to make sure he wasn't scamming them, she'd ignored his presence in their lives. The assumption of him being another Jamaican who'd talk shit about gay people had made her erase him from her mind. Things were obviously different now.

She'd have to remember to make a trip to see his work.

"Drive safe, Errol," she said. "You know Miami drivers are nuts." He was taking her parents and Miss Opal to the gallery in his own car.

After a brief hesitation, Sage plucked the house key from her key ring and passed it to her father. "Take this and let yourselves in whenever you get back."

Everyone was standing around the wreckage of empty plates, cups, and crumpled napkins on the table. Her father tucked his wallet back in his pocket after paying the bill and hiked up the waist of his slacks from what looked mostly like habit instead of necessity.

"No, darling. We'll just call you when we're on the way back," her mother said. "You'll need a key to get into your own house."

What she should have done was make a copy for her parents, but her mind hadn't been functioning properly the last few days. "It's no problem. Phil has a key too."

Her mother frowned, the first negative look on her face since Errol showed up.

"Don't worry about it, Viv." Sage's father tucked the key in this pocket and brushed a hand against the small of his wife's back. "Let's get on the road before the gallery gets too crowded."

They trooped out of the restaurant, Errol chattering about how happy he was the Bennetts were in town again, his voice a rising and falling rhythm that sounded a lot like singing.

While they'd eaten, the restaurant had grown more crowded, at least more people were sitting at tables than when they first got there, and as they walked out, taking a winding path through the packed tables, Sage became aware again of Crystal watching her, the girl's face a mess of lust and hope.

Crystal sat at a big table with at least three other people who had joined in on the staring. Phil glanced back at Sage but didn't say anything, even when they were in the parking lot and waving goodbye to her parents and Miss Opal who took off in Errol's old but clean 4-door Honda Civic.

An unpleasant something sparked in Sage's chest. Despite the nerves she had about being around her parents and Miss Opal, she couldn't help but feel a little abandoned by them. Yes, they'd come to Miami for Errol's graduation, but she was their daughter, dammit. And Miss Opal was...her Miss Opal. That *something* was probably jealousy.

Hands in her pockets, Sage watched as they drove away, tracking their progress through the large parking lot then out into the street when Errol carefully joined with the flow of traffic. Once she was sure they were out of sight, she rolled up the sleeves of her shirt, unbuttoned the one more button at her collar.

Beside her, she could feel Phil vibrating with the need to unload exactly what was on her mind. She squeezed her eyes briefly shut then started toward their SUV. At the driver's side door, she turned to Phil who had kept silent pace with her.

With a sigh on her lips, Sage turned, arms crossed over her chest. "Just spit it out."

"Spit what out, exactly?"

"Jesus fuck! Is this what you're going to do when it's damn obvious what's on your mind?"

"If it's so obvious, then you tell me." Purse tucked under her arm, Phil put her hands on her hips, an eyebrow at a disdainful arch. It was a pose Sage was well-familiar with. Phil was pissed and ready to get into her face about something. But this time instead of shoving into her space, Phil kept her distance. About four feet yawned between them, and that space felt as wide as an ocean.

"You're pissed I slept with that girl." Although Phil had no moral leg to stand on in this particular disagreement, Sage couldn't keep the defensiveness from her voice.

"O-kaay..." Phil said in a slow and mocking drawl.

"Okay, what?"

"That's all you got from your amazing mind-reading abilities?"

Sage growled. She wanted to strangle Phil, but she didn't move. Although even in the midst of their most intense arguments, they'd never laid hands on each other. Not like that.

"I fucked her a few of days ago when I was pissed at you, okay?" she snapped. "Is that what you want to hear?"

Before Phil's big bisexual revelation, they had a rule against revenge fucks. If they were pissed at each other, they didn't take out their feelings on the bodies of strangers. They talked things out. They fucked the anger out of each other.

"You were the one who broke our rules."

Sage frowned hard enough to give herself a Klingon forehead. "Which rule? The one that said we should be honest with each other? Nope, I kept that one. Unlike you."

"You're missing the fu—" Something she saw over Sage's shoulder cut off the rest of whatever she was going to say. Her teeth snapped together, and her breath came out in a hiss.

Sage turned to see Crystal walking into the parking lot with three guys and another woman who Sage realized then had been sitting with her at her table. The group of five moved purposefully in Sage and Phil's direction.

"What the fuck is this shit?" Phil asked, the picture of feminine aggression.

"Chill," Sage said. "Don't blow things out of proportion. None of this is the girl's fault."

"Do you even know her name?" Phil muttered the question from the corner of her mouth. "Anyway, upsetting your little piece on the side is the last thing I'm worried about," she said the last under her breath as Crystal and her friends came closer. As they approached, Sage couldn't help but notice how hostile Crystal's friends looked. And then, with each step that drew the group even closer, she noticed the similarity between them. Dark skin, long hair, pointy chins.

Phil got one last dig in before they got right up on them. "You may have fucked her, but I think you might be the one who's fucked now."

The group of Crystal-lookalikes spread out in a semi-circle in front of Sage and Phil. Her girlfriend tucked her tiny purse under her arm and faced them with hands loose by her sides. They didn't have to wait long to find out what was going on.

"Are you the perv that fucked our underage sister?"

Underage?

But Sage didn't hide her shock. At Phil's quickly indrawn breath, she half-turned, a denial on her lips. But Phil shook her head once, a sharp motion that reminded Sage to keep her head in the game and focus on the important part of what was happening now. Namely that this group of protective siblings seemed intent on kicking her ass.

"You're underage?" She asked Crystal the question, trying to keep calm.

Dammit, she knew fucking her had been a bad idea the

moment it stirred in her pants. When the hell would she learn to listen to her gut instead of second-guessing herself? "But I asked you how old you were."

Panic flashed across the girl's features and she bit her lip, saying nothing.

"How could you *not* think she's jailbait?" One of the men jabbed a finger toward Crystal. "She looks like she's still in fucking high school."

Although Sage disagreed, she didn't think now was the right time to voice that. "I didn't know she wasn't legal."

"Exactly how underage is this girl?" Phil aimed her question at the man who seemed in charge of this whole confrontation.

"Her high school graduation is this coming weekend," the woman chimed in, obviously spoiling for a fight. Her chest puffed up under the studded leather jacket and her fists clenched and unclenched at her sides.

High school?

Crystal had a college ID. She lived by herself in a dorm-style apartment. Were these idiots for real?

"I was twelve when I graduated from high school." Phil stood tall and straight, her chin slightly lifted to look down on them all, Sage included. "You have to be more specific."

"She just turned eighteen," one of the guys shouted.

Another indrawn breath from Phil, and a look that clearly said what an idiot she thought Sage was. And Sage *did* feel like an idiot, a hypocrite even. She'd been the main one talking about how she didn't fuck or date young chicks. She cringed remembering all the shit she talked the night she met Crystal. Rémi and Dez were going to give her hell for it for sure. Nuria would just laugh her ass off, then throw jailbait Sage's way for the rest of her life. Which would probably be about ten minutes if these pricks had anything to say about it.

"What exactly do you want to do here?" Phil demanded.

"Sage didn't know this chick wasn't old enough to fuck, at least not according to your standards. She's not R. Kelly, on purpose out to trap underage tail for shits and grins."

A comparison to pedo Kelly. Shit. Could this day actually get any worse?

That, amazingly enough, didn't lower the aggression coming from the big group.

"She fucked Crystal and took off," one of the guys said.

"Yeah, she's not exactly a kid but this chick just bailed just bailed on her." This came from one of the more reasonable siblings.

"Did you want something else than what happened that day on the couch?" Sage asked. Okay, maybe that was too much detail. One of the men growled for real, or it might have been the sister.

Crystal still didn't say anything, just looked more embarrassed than anything.

"Look, if there's no point to this little tête-à-tête, we're going to leave. I haven't hung out in parking lots since high school." Phil's mouth twisted and aimed a pitying look at Crystal. "Although apparently that was last week for you."

She held out her hand, palm up.

Sage dropped the car keys in Phil's hand and Phil coolly unlocked the SUV and pushed Sage in and completely over the center console into the passenger seat. She climbed in beside Sage, settling behind the steering wheel before locking the door. Crystal's minions stood frozen for a moment, probably as shocked as Sage was, before rushing toward the truck as one. Phil started the car, didn't give any warning whatsoever before tearing out of the parking lot. They weren't stupid enough to stand in the way.

They drove in silence for a too-long while, the sound of the road moving swiftly beneath the truck's tires the only sound between them. Sage's belly twisted with guilt. Barely a mile from the house, Phil finally spoke.

"This is the shit you do when you're pissed at me for real, huh?"

"Pissed at you?" Sage twisted around in the seat to stare at her. "This is a little more than me being pissed at you."

Phil adjusted the air in her throat. "You're being such a dumb ass right now."

"Look, I know I don't win any points for smart thinking when I jumped into the sack with Crystal, but you...you..." Sage sputtered to a halt, the feelings that had washed over her during the last few days coming back to drag her under a fierce tide. "I don't want this kind of life, Phillida. I told you that years ago when we first got together."

"So, you expected me to stay the same naive twenty-year-old you met back in college? That's stupid." The leather of the steering wheel creaked under the tight clench of her hands. "I never lied to you about what I wanted. I wanted you back then. I still want you."

"But now you want dick too."

Phil winced, her lips thinning until they were nearly a straight line. "It's not that simple."

"Then simplify for me in your words, because from where I sit, shit is pretty cut and dry." A familiar street sign whipped past the window. The turnoff to their neighborhood. "Where are you...?"

"Just shut up and let me drive."

Sage shut up. And they drove. Miles and miles. A twist of Phil's fingers near mile fifteen turned on the radio and killed some of the uncomfortable silence between them. She changed the channels on the satellite radio until Halsey started playing, then leaned back with a grunt, their previous silence now filled with empty sound.

It wasn't long before Sage realized where they were heading.

Sage and Phil had always been wild together. Two elements gravitating toward each other, instantly combustible. An immediate explosion when they first met that had only grown more intense over the years. But sometimes even they needed a place where they could be inert together, away from everything, to settle and allow peace to float over them, if only for the time being.

The place they'd found, they didn't go very often. But when they needed it, it was there.

After less than another hour of driving, Phil parked the car, tucked her shoes and purse under the driver seat then threw the car keys to Sage.

A staticky buzz started at the base of Sage's neck and soon enough spread through her whole body. If she was being honest with herself, she would admit to being scared. But today wasn't a day for honesty.

"Remember when we first came here?" Phil asked.

It was hard to forget. In college, their attraction was so painfully explosive that they had burned too hot in public. Phil at twenty, an odd combination of nerdy girl and exhibitionist freak, shocked her peers at the university. A genius and child prodigy, she did everything well. By the time she got to Sage, she already had a Ph.D., two Masters degrees, and a black belt in some martial art or other. She studied nano-technology for fun and had about a gazillion articles published in world-renowned science journals. It was obvious she was holding herself back academically, so she could fit in. Obvious too that she might have been just a little too uninhibited for relatively tame Miami.

Being with older students most of her life had affected her, jaded her a bit, given her experience that she shouldn't have had, and she was more than happy to share that experience with Sage, teach her, corrupt her. But Sage had loved every moment of it.

One night, they stumbled away from a school party in the middle of nowhere safe. The grounds of an abandoned hotel, private property that was empty and a paradise to them and their college friends.

They'd started making out, kissing in desperation and Sage remembered how her skin felt like it was on fire, the heat coming from inside her body, impossible to extinguish no matter how much she kissed Phil, squeezed her breasts, bit into her soft skin. She felt delirious, out of her mind. It was more than lust, more than infatuation.

They snuck away to one of the empty patches of grass behind the abandoned hotel and fucked until she was rubbed raw, inside and out, her voice hoarse from shouting.

"God damn, you two! Get a room!" Somebody shouted. "This place has about fifty thousand of them."

But Sage needed more than a room. For her, and for Phil too, being around everyone else was too much. The emotions writhing between them disturbed everyone around them, disturbed even Sage. But she didn't want to let them go. Even the thought of that loss paralyzed her on the grass where she lay with Phil's fingers still inside her, her heart beginning to race again but for an entirely different reason than before.

There would be no one else for either of them now, no one who meant this much, Sage thought then. She remembered being elated and frightened at the same time. In the bright moonlight on that still, long-ago evening, Phil's eyes had glowed with the same feeling. Her mouth turned down and serious, her expression a little sad.

With a sound like a wet kiss, Sage tugged Phil's fingers from between her legs, body still electric and too much and just right at the same time. She pulled her clothes on, grabbed Phil, and ran.

She didn't remember exactly how they found the place. Only

that after stumbling over rocks and up sand dunes, they staggered, breathless, onto a barren beach.

White sand lustrous in the darkness, a tumble of high and sharp rocks on both sides of a small stretch of beach. A perfectly secluded grotto. It was absolutely pristine with none of the signs that other college kids or careless partiers had found it—no used condoms, empty beer cans, or liquor bottles.

They collapsed on the sand together, their bodies starfished, only their hands touching. That connection, though small, felt unbreakable. They didn't have sex again that night, only lay together, breathing and overwhelmed.

Now, that night felt eons away.

With Phil, Sage followed the long familiar path, gasping and trudging through the sand, their hands linked, more so from habit than any desire to cling to each other. But when Sage found her fingers gripping Phil's she reevaluated that thought. Maybe she *did* want to hold onto her, at least this last time before everything that was "Sage and Phil" finally shattered and the pieces blew away on the wind.

The powdery sand pulled at her feet, bare from Phil's example and the experience of trying to climb up and down unstable sand dunes in dress shoes. They were both panting by the time they got to the top of the dune and began the blessed descent to the grotto, gravity pulling them inexorably down to that place where they were most raw with each other. Most real.

At the bottom of the dune, breathing heavily despite the fact they both worked out semi-regularly, they stared at each other under the half-moon. Phil dropped Sage's hand and stepped away, but their eyes stayed connected.

The tide rushed up to their feet, higher than Sage remembered from before. Otherwise, their sanctuary was the same. The sense memories rooted in each grain of sand, every transient rush of water, and every lungful of air nearly overwhelmed Sage. She clenched her teeth hard, but that didn't stop the pain.

More than twelve years they'd known each other, and nearly all of those years spent in each others' beds, wrapped up in each other even while other lovers had come and gone.

All that was over. Gone.

"Why did you bring me back here?" Sage asked, the pain turning her voice vicious. She crossed her arms over her chest hopefully tight enough to keep herself from flying apart.

Phil pressed her lips together and turned away. She was quiet for way too long, the long line of her back to Sage, dark dress fluttering around her body from the insistent wind. And then. "I love you."

"Don't you think I know that?" Sage wanted to scream and barely just held herself back. "That's what makes this worse."

Phil finally turned around, and Sage could see the tears glittering like captive diamonds at the corners of her eyes. "I'm not doing this to hurt you, Sage."

"You could've fooled me."

"Do you think I want to be dealing with this shit?" Phil looked stunned, hurt. Miles away from the confident and mocking woman who'd driven Sage crazy at dinner with her parents. She shoved the thick cloud of hair away from her face, hands visibly trembling in the moonlight. "Everything I thought I was, everything I built my identity around is...is different now. I feel completely lost." Vulnerability hung from her like torn and bloody bandages, and it took everything for Sage not to cross the space between them and pull Phil into her arms.

"How do you think I feel?" Sage demanded.

Phil stopped dead. "This isn't about you."

"You're right," Sage said. "This is about *us*, and why you want to blow what we have out of the water."

For years, she thought her parents would turn her away once

they knew who she loved. Because of that, Phil and the friends were all Sage had. Now, with a single confession from Phil, she lost half of her life's foundation.

"You're so damn selfish..." Phil pressed fingers to her temples, her frustration obvious. "But fine. We can do this the way you want. You don't want to marry me now. You don't want me to hang out with your parents. Shit, you don't even want me living in *our* house anymore." Phil spat out a curse and stalked toward the water's edge, ignoring the waves sliding over her feet. "You're fucking afraid!"

"You mean my fear that you'll leave me for the first hard dick that pops up?"

Saying the words actually made her a little sick. She twisted away from the agony on Phil's face, feeling like it was a reflection of her own.

When she turned back to Phil, the woman she once loved was staring at her with an odd, unreadable expression. Sage squirmed. Usually, she didn't have to guess what Phil was thinking.

"Okay," Phil said after a tense moment, her mouth thinned and most of her lipstick gone. "Let's just stop for a second and regroup."

Phil backed away and the wind plucked at her hair and the dress, fluttering it around her slender and graceful body. A sigh blew past her lips and she stalked away from Sage to root around in the gap in the rocks where they kept a blanket and other essentials.

"Okay..." With her arms still crossed tight, Sage stood back and watched Phil spread the oversized blanket on the sand and sit down cross-legged. All in silence. Sage sat down on a corner of the blanket. It wasn't like she would spite anybody but herself by standing up and watching Phil roll around on the blanket that had been her idea to stash out here.

Phil took a deep breath. "Sage, you and I have just been reacting since that night at the premiere. You've had a shock, I get it. But we've been together for twelve years. We can't throw that away." Phil drew another breath like she was getting ready to dive off a cliff. "I want us to work this out."

Sage's breath hitched. She wished it was that simple, but it wasn't. She couldn't be with Phil if Phil wanted to fuck men. No way. "No," she said. "There's nothing to work out."

Among the sound of the waves, the breeze battering the rocks, she heard Phil's quickly indrawn breath. She squeezed her eyes shut, unable to look at her ex-lover. She wasn't bi-phobic or whatever Nuria wanted to call it. She just knew what she wanted.

"Tell me," Phil said. "Tell me exactly what you mean so there's no misunderstanding."

Even from so far away, Sage felt the quivering in Phil's body, but with the dip of her head, the whip of the wind that drew the dark clouds of her hair across her face, she couldn't see her expression.

"Tell me," she said again.

"I want to be with you," Sage said, the rest of what she had to say resting bitter and wrong on her tongue like a dirty confession. "But I don't want to be with the *bisexual* you."

Although Phil's expression didn't change, her legs jerked suddenly on top of the blanket, bare feet digging into the sand. Flecks of white sand dirtied the smooth dark of her skin. She looked like a puppet with cut strings. Her eyelashes fluttered wildly.

"And that's it?" Her voice was barely a whisper. "There's nothing else I can say to make you change your mind?"

Sage's heart jolted in her chest. "No."

"God, Sage!" Phil gasped, and the sound was like pain. "After everything we've been through together? After all the years we've loved each other and lasted through...through everything?"

"This is different, and you know it." They were lesbians together; their world was a world of women. When they played together, they only played with women. Changing that was like changing her blood to vinegar. It hurt. It destroyed everything.

"But what about this?" Cool fingers curled around the back of Sage's neck, a balance of possessiveness and tenderness Phil had always held her with. And God, it hurt. "What about the way I make you feel?" The fingers slid higher into her hair, up to rake through her scalp. Sage shivered. Skin goose-dimpling, nipples hardening under her thin shirt.

"That doesn't mean a fucking thing," Sage said, fighting the arousal that flicked like a warm tongue between her legs.

"Liar." Phil kissed her.

The press of her mouth was familiar and immediately tender. If she had tried to take, to be rough, Sage would have pulled away with some insult on her tongue. But it was too much like they were always with each other. A light press of soft lips, warm breath huffing over her face, fingers cupping her cheeks and their bodies moving inevitably closer.

No... This wasn't right. This wasn't what she wanted.

But the kisses continued. A delicate touch on one corner of her mouth, then other, tingles of warm moving from that soft point of contact and radiating through all of her.

This was Phillida. Her love. Her lover.

The first one to touch her heart. The last.

Phil pulled away and her eyes were a universe of pain, dark with dots of light too vast to be mere stars. "No one else can make you feel the way I do," Phil murmured. "Nobody." Her warm and firm breasts pressed into Sage. The blanket shifted under them and it was like their world was moving, falling away and falling apart. Sage clutched at it.

"No!" She opened her mouth and devoured what she didn't want to lose. Their teeth clicked, lips bruised while Sage deepened and roughened the kiss.

Hot breath misted over her chin as she pulled back this time, fumbled at the neck of Phil's dress for the clasp the same time Phil dragged her shirt up and off. Her pants unbuttoned, unzipped, a hand dove into her underwear. A knowing thumb flicked her clit, fingers dove into her soaked pussy.

Sage's fingers fumbled for the zipper and still found nothing. Frustrated, she finally ripped the dress away, the expensive fabric tore, giving her the sight of Phil's heaving breasts in the black bra. She tore that away too and latched her tongue to a hot and heaving breast.

Oh, God...

Sage bit her neck, gripped her arms tighter, overcome with desperation. Unnamed and uncomfortable feelings thundered through her, fueling that desperation. If this strange poison was all they had between them now after twelve years of untamed and unconditional love, she would drink up every drop.

The taste of her was familiar, the faintly bitter lotion on her skin that also smelled sweet. This bitter-sweetness combined to confuse the fuck out of Sage's senses, but another tang, of fear and hopeless, struck Sage through the heart. But she drank that up too, opened up her legs to the liquid fuck of Phil's fingers inside her at the same time Phil's nipples pressed hard against her tongue, getting firmer with each decadent suck and hot and panting breath.

"Please..."

One of them was crying now, and Sage realized with a sickening lurch in her stomach that it was her. "Phil, don't do this!" She sucked Phil's nipple into her mouth along with the salt of her own tears. She sucked and begged, licked and begged, scraped her teeth across the fat pebbled tip of a nipple and begged some more even though she didn't know what she was pleading for.

Sensation wriggled through her body. Pleasure and pain and regret and the rolling tide of a shattering orgasm from the relentless thrust and twist of Phil's fingers, the hummingbird flick of her thumb on Sage's clit.

She threw her head back and screamed her pleasure.

This was the last time. The knowledge thundered through her. Battered her. If this was it, and it had to be, then Sage needed more.

She dragged herself across the blanket, the fabric of Phil's dress rucking up on the sand, the sound of her harsh sobs rocking between them. Grains of sand from Phil's legs under her tongue, the loamy smell of Phil's pussy, wet and more intoxicating than the sea, calling her mouth. Her tongue dripped with the desire to taste one last time, her fingers curled tight into the soft skin.

"Sage!" Her love cried out when Sage's mouth latched onto her hard and slippery clit. The musky scent and taste, the salt of her lust. "I love you!" Gasping, Phil pressed her dripping pussy unto Sage's mouth, her voice a desperate plea. "Baby, don't...don't leave us behind."

The wind tore at their clothes. Water splashed up over their legs, drenching the blanket.

Familiar juices dripped down Sage's chin. For the last time.

She sobbed and slipped two fingers in to stroke that spot that made Phil scream, pinching her nipples in rhythm to the motion of her tongue on Phil's clit, Phil cried out, cried, begged. It nearly broke Sage, but she couldn't stop the course of what Phil had started at that movie premiere. She couldn't. Groaning, she trapped her hand over Phil's mouth, muffling her words. She didn't stop her fingers or her tongue.

This felt raw and desperate in a way it hadn't been between them in months.

Phil moved under her, surging and frantic in her search for orgasm. For freedom to shout what she wanted. Even with her mouth locked to Phil's pussy and her eyes closed to shut out the pain on her lover's face, she felt the frantic motion of Phil's head, her head whipping back and forth across the blanket trying to shake Sage's hand from over her mouth.

"Oh, God..."

And Sage tasted salt and wet, realizing it was her tears, not just Phil's desire and desperation. Her hand over Phil's mouth slipped and the sounds came loud again. Fingers plunged into her wet and panting mouth. Hot breath puffing against her fingers, the cries that were part pain, part pleasure, all desperation.

Phil bit her fingers, and they both howled.

Seconds passed. Minutes.

Sage blinked the sweat from her eyes and stared up at the stars. Her pants sagged halfway down her thighs along with her underwear. The waning pulse beats of her orgasm throbbed faintly between her legs.

Beside her, Phil lay on her side, facing away from her, her thighs still spread wide, her dress shoved up to her waist. Her platinum belly chain glimmered in the moonlight. The sound of her panting was loud, even over the rush of the wind. Water slid over Sage's bare feet, soaking into the hem of her slacks but that fact seemed too far away to matter.

"I want to go home." Phil didn't turn over.

Her voice was blank, emotionless, but it couldn't have been more filled with pain if she'd screamed. Yet, the biggest sadness of it all was that they both knew the home she wanted, the home they'd shared for so long and so well, didn't exist anymore.

Sage clenched her teeth hard, but the whimper of pain leaked from her just the same. Starlight and moonlight burned down from the sky. Bright so far away from the city. They'd shared this view a thousand times over the years, a view she never grew tired of. But Sage wanted no part of it now. Breathing through another arrow of pain, she licked her lips, still wet from Phil's pleasure.

She buried her face in her arms, the sadness rushing over her like the tide. "We can go now?"

"Okay."

But neither of them got up.

It could have been an hour or ten minutes or a lifetime later before Phil moved. Keeping her face tucked down, she got to her feet and dragged her dress down, teased her hair into some semblance of order with her fingers. Her back was straight as she stared out to the ocean, all the while avoiding looking at Sage.

Sage wanted to touch her, to stroke that long back and give them both some kind of comfort. But they were past that now. She stumbled to her feet and re-settled her own clothes before grabbing the blanket and stuffing it back into the waterproof chest.

They wouldn't need it anymore.

They wouldn't need their grotto anymore.

Another wave of sadness nearly knocked her over where she stood.

Phil swallowed thickly. "I'm ready."

With Sage driving, they left the grotto together, but as soon as they hit civilization, a stretch of road with small shops and mid-rise buildings along its edges, Phil asked to be let out.

Her demand dragged Sage from her circular thoughts. "Why? What are you doing?"

"That's not something you have to worry about anymore, is it?" She gently closed the door, her shoes on her feet, purse under her arm.

Sage rolled the window down to glare at Phil. Why was she making this harder than it needed to be? "It's dark out here. It's not safe."

"Safety is relative." She was already tapping on her phone.

"I'm calling for an Uber. You can go on to the house with a clear conscience." Then she flashed the phone's screen that showed a car only a few minutes away.

But Sage had never been one to abandon anyone, no matter what the circumstances. The irony of that thought wasn't lost on her even as she tried to convince herself she wasn't doing anything wrong. She clenched her hand on the gear shift, watching Phil step back from the car and move further up on the sidewalk, her heels clicking firmly against the cement.

The Uber came quickly. Only after the tail lights of the dark green Nissan had disappeared down the street and around the corner did Sage pull her truck back into traffic and head for the house that no longer felt like a home.

It was the longest drive of her life.

CHAPTER FIFTEEN

Sage was exhausted. She pushed open the door to the house and flinched at the familiar smells of the place—the vanilla scented oil Phil burned in every room, faint traces of her peony-scented perfume, hints of the lemon tea Phil drank every morning.

Her keys rattled against ceramic when she dropped them in the bowl by the door. Heavy footsteps drew her deeper into the house, through the wide hallway and the living room. She stopped.

Her mother and Miss Opal sat close together on the couch while the TV played some sort of game show, but there weren't paying attention to the gap-toothed host on the screen. Instead, they sat close together, nearly pressed knee to knee, talking.

They fell quiet when Sage walked into the room.

"Are you sure you're okay?" her father's voice came from the kitchen.

Sage's stomach dipped as Phil answered softly. "No, but I will be eventually."

Sage couldn't see them, but she noticed that her mother and Miss Opal glance briefly in that direction.

"Baby love." Miss Opal appraised Sage with a knowing eye. "What happened?"

Shit. Was her mouth still bleeding? She tongued the sore spot where Phil had bitten her, then blushed when two pairs of eyes followed the movement. The look of disapproval that had never quite disappeared from her mother's face became more intense. With the weight of Miss Opal and her mother's stares, she felt every bit of sand clinging to her skin from her time in the grotto with Phil. The hem of her pants dragged from the seawater and she was sure flecks of pale sand stood out against the black of her wrinkled and untucked shirt. Basically, she looked exactly like what she'd been doing—fucking on the beach.

"Nothing much happened, Miss Opal," she said in automatic denial.

"I can tell you're lying." Her father appeared from the kitchen with a cup of tea in his hand. He walked past Sage and squeezed her shoulder, his eyes full of pity.

Why?

High heels on tile interrupted the beginnings of another lie. Phil came from the kitchen with a big mug she usually drank her bedtime chamomile from. She looked just as rough as Sage felt. Her dark dress with bits of sand clinging to it. Her hair wilder than when they'd left Sage's parents earlier in the day. Grains of powdery sand glowing against her skin.

It didn't take Sherlock Holmes to figure out that they'd been together. And that whatever happened between them had not been good. Her eyes cut through Sage and she wove through the living room, making an obvious path to avoid her.

"You can lie to them some more if you want to, but I'm going to bed." Phil threw the words over her shoulder and disappeared down the hallway toward the bedroom. The door slammed.

"What's going on?"

Sage shook her head, a quick and sharp motion that made her dizzy. She didn't know what to tell them since the truth was obviously out of the question. "I'm tired," she said rubbing a hand over her face. "I'm heading to bed, too."

"Sage—"

"Let her go, Viv. I think our girl has some things to work out."

Her father's words followed her down the hallway to the only empty guest bedroom. There, she stripped and climbed into the unfamiliar bed, dirty teeth and all. Sage lay spread out under the AC, her thoughts spinning in every direction.

Years ago, it was simple enough. No bisexuals allowed. At least not in her bed.

That policy never bothered any of her friends as far as she knew, and she never had to check her attitude about bisexuals. But then, Dez hooked up with her little college boyfriend. Rémi fell in love with, and managed to seduce, hetero Claudia. And Nuria kept fucking anyone she wanted to fuck—men, women, and everyone in between.

Through it all, Phil had been a constant. And now she was gone.

Sighing, Sage rolled over and winced. Phil's bite marks. They burned on the skin over her ribs. Tender and throbbing.

The recent memory flooded over her. She and Phil on the sand, panting and desperate. Their blanket dragged halfway from underneath them and barely any protection from the rough sand and the bits of shells digging into their flesh. The hot scent of their sex rising like smoke around them. The desperate and sobbing cries they both made.

Was that how things would end between them? In a memory of pain and sex. Teeth marks and a shattered sense of home.

This is your choice.

A voice that sounded suspiciously like Rémi mocked her.

No, this was Phillida's choice. She broke their agreement. She changed the terms of their relationship.

Another pained breath hissed through Sage's teeth when she rolled over to the opposite side of the bed. Sleep felt even further away than ever. The phone's battery was nearly dead, but it had juice enough to tell her it was just past five in the morning.

Fuck it.

She got up, dragged on a robe, and quietly crept toward the kitchen. A cup of mint tea later, she sat at the breakfast bar staring out the wide windows. Darkness covered just about everything. But she could just make out the outlines of the tall shrubbery protecting their yard from the neighbors' prying eyes.

Years ago, they'd moved from what they'd lovingly called their "fuck house" to this quieter part of Miami. Although she and Phil hadn't talked explicitly about it, they were getting ready for another phase of their lives. Rémi had Claudia. Dez and Victoria were quietly married and considering a kid of their own. And through the conversations they'd found themselves having, she and Phil realized they wanted a piece of that quiet domesticity for themselves too.

But not too quiet, and not so soon.

So, they'd bought the house, slowed down the pace of their partying, given up the drugs that had seemed so necessary before and now just seemed like too much. Now, Sage was about to be stuck alone in a house with no future in it.

"That's a lot of heavy breathing you got going on."

She nearly jumped out of her skin. "Shit!"

With an amused chuckle, Miss Opal shuffled toward her in the dark, her slippers shush-shushing against the floor. A click of the light switch illuminated the chrome and marble kitchen and Sage winced from the sudden brightness.

"Just the regular amount of heavy breathing," Sage said once she got her breathing back under control.

"Uh huh."

Miss Opal made her slow way around the long end of the breakfast bar and to the stove where she sparked a blue flame back under the teapot. She wore a thick robe pulled high up to her neck, the too-long cuffs folded over her wrists. A/C always made her cold.

The pantry door clicked open with a flick of her wrist and she rummaged inside, soon emerging with a fistful of green bananas and the container of flour. She settled in at the sink with the bananas and a grater.

"So, you going to tell me what's wrong?" she asked. When Sage opened her mouth Miss Opal quickly cut her off. "Don't tell me it's nothing. "A blind man can see that you and Phillida had some sort of big argument." She turned on the spigot over the bowl of bananas and started to peel the bananas with a knife. "What did you do?"

Sage shifted uncomfortably on the high stool. "Why do you think I did something?"

"Because you look guilty."

But Sage didn't feel guilty. None of this was her fault.

"It's no big deal." Sage forced the words past her dry throat. "It's not like...like..."

"It's not like you love her? Is that the lie you were going to tell me?"

Sage coughed tea all over the marble speckled breakfast bar. "No!" She coughed again, her throat burning.

Miss Opal had her back to Sage, but it felt like the woman pinned her with her all-seeing gaze, just like when she was a kid.

"I—I... Oh, fuck." Sage stumbled over every possible lie to deny what Miss Opal was saying. But suddenly she was so tired. Her elbows thumped into the hard surface of the bar. She dropped her face in her hands as the world as she knew it shifted under her feet.

"It's okay, darlin' dear. I love you. Your mummy and daddy and I only want the best for you, for you to be happy."

Sage's stomach shot up into her throat like she was at the top of a roller coaster about to fall. Her head swam and pressed her fingers hard into her face.

Finally, she lifted her head. "When did you guys know?"

Only the sounds of Miss Opal rattling around the kitchen broke the silence. A knife clattering into the sink. A metal bowl against the countertop.

"Years. Since the beginning, maybe. We were waiting for you to tell us, but you never did."

Sage's cheeks prickled with shame. She wanted to bury her face in her hands again, but she'd already done enough hiding in the sand. She kept her eyes on Miss Opal's back, the movement of her slight frame as she grated the bananas by hand instead of using the food processor Sage had shown her how to use a few days before. The steady scrubbing sound of a piece of green banana sliding against the metal grater filled the kitchen.

They knew about her.

They *knew.*

"But instead of telling us, you just pulled away," Miss Opal went on. "It... we didn't expect that. Before we knew it, you were grown up and so far away. You were lost to us."

If Miss Opal was telling the truth, Sage had gotten herself lost. She'd assumed her parents were like the Jamaicans she heard about on the news, in patty shops and Fort Lauderdale barber chairs. Instead of waiting for them to disown her, she'd treated them like strangers.

Idiot. Because she'd been the stupidest one in the yard, she'd lost something that could have been hers and now belonged to Errol.

"But you never said anything," she protested, despite knowing very much how hard it was for them to talk about things that mattered. Like feelings, and coming out, and anything else that had the possibility of someone breaking down into an ugly cry.

"I know," Miss Opal said. "And I regret it. I was telling your mother that maybe now we could fix things. But..." She turned around, sadness soaked into the wrinkles surrounding her deep oak eyes. "...you look so miserable now. And I don't think it's because of us."

Sticky, dirty feelings rolled around in Sage's chest. Lips pressed together, heart clenched tight, she wished she could just disappear for a few minutes. Hours. Days. The whisper of approaching footsteps brought her head up.

Her father stood in the doorway, his robe hanging open over his pajamas. "I want to get in on this conversation, too."

He shambled into the kitchen and pulled a mug from the cupboard and made himself a cup of fever grass tea. Once he was done, he took the stool next to Sage at the breakfast bar and sat with the mug of tea between his palms. He gave Sage his "waiting" look.

Discomfort and fear nudged the little bit of tea Sage already had in her stomach, threatening to bring it back up. She swallowed and forced herself to take another sip. It was cold and tasteless. Her tongue, dry and unwieldy in her mouth, was still grateful for the moisture. "I..." And that was as far as she got. What could she say that would make sense to them?

"Just tell us what happened." For the first time in a long while, her father seemed to read her easily enough. Was she just that transparent lately?

More silence. Her father and Miss Opal waiting patiently before she finally just opened her mouth and let whatever was waiting there spill out.

"Phil... she..." Maybe there wasn't much waiting there after all. "When she and I got together, we were both into the same things. Only women." She swallowed. It sounded so trivial once she was actually saying it. "And now, she's...*expanded* her interests. She changed. She's not the person I fell—" she stumbled into the words. "—fell in love with."

She darted a gaze at her father to see how he was taking the revelation. Yeah, Miss Opal said he knew, but it was a big thing for her to just blurt out like that. Her stomach clenched. But he didn't react other than to keep watching, seeming to wait for the rest of whatever she had to say. "Things are just too different now," she finished.

Her father moved the mug from one hand to the next but didn't drink. "You broke up with Phillida?"

Miss Opal turned to stare at her. And Sage could only look from Miss Opal to her father, tongue-tied again. Not only did they except, no *expect*, her to be a big dyke, but they knew she and Phil were—or had been—together?"

"I... we're not together anymore."

"Because she likes men and women and you didn't expect that?" This came from Miss Opal.

"It's not that simple," Sage said, hating that she sounded so defensive.

"Then tell me in a way that I can understand, because I'm feeling a dim here." Her father spoke soft and low. He actually sounded confused.

Sage tried again. "We have a kind of non-traditional relationship. We don't only...hang out with each other."

Her father made a noise. "I swear, you young people think you invented everything. Married people have been swinging since the beginning of marriage," he said. "Not too long ago, your mother and I—"

"No no no!" Sage pressed her hand to her ears. "I definitely don't want to hear this." Not about her parents fucking other people when she could barely face the reality of them fucking each other.

"You're not very tolerant, are you?" Disappointment laced Miss Opal's tone.

Beside her, her father nodded. "So much so that you're doing the same thing to Phillida you expected us to do to you."

Sage gasped. It felt like a thousand-pound weight dropped on her chest. "What? No!"

"Then what is this, Sage?" Miss Opal called her by her real name and she blinked in stunned reaction.

She was *not* being intolerant. "You don't understand," she said, but the fight knocked out of her with Miss Opal's words.

"Maybe it's *you* who doesn't understand, daughter." Her father finally took a sip of his tea, then screwed up his face, the taste apparently not what he expected. He probably forgot to put honey in it. "When you love someone, you just love them. You don't take that love away because they stop being what you expect. Being in a relationship is about sticking with your wife through good and bad, famine and feast. You can't pick and choose what you stay around for."

He didn't understand. How could he when he'd been his wife's bitch for as long as Sage was paying attention to how they were with each other? If he suddenly grew a spine, his wife probably wouldn't recognize him.

"Daddy, I don't—"

"What are you doing up so early?" Sage's mother shuffled into the kitchen with a brush of her slippered feet on the tiles.

Sage groaned. Not her too.

"We're talking about Sage being afraid," her father chimed in.

Her mother looked bleary-eyed but was awake enough not to bump into things. "Is she ready to tell us the thing yet?"

She repeated the actions of her husband from minutes before but took the container of brown sugar with her when she sat at the kitchen island, leaving only the stool in front of Sage empty. That was the only reason Sage saw the smile on Miss Opal's face, a kind of 'I told you so,' while she stirred the pot bubbling on the stove.

Slowly, the kitchen filled with the warming smell of the banana porridge. Sage's mouth fell open and it wasn't because she was hungry for what Miss Opal was cooking.

"She told me," Miss Opal said. Why did she have to sound so self-satisfied?

"Sage slipped and told me too, then we went on to talk about other things," her father said.

"Like...?"

"Like Phillida," Miss Opal said.

Her mother's face screwed up and she looked down into her mug of tea.

Sage blamed her exhaustion on why she suddenly couldn't hold her tongue anymore. "Why don't you like Phil?" she asked.

"I don't dislike her—"

"Pardon my language, mama, but that's bullshit." Damn, she must be really tired to say that out loud.

"Watch it. She's still your mother and deserves respect." Her father didn't thump her but the look on his face said he wanted to.

Sage flinched. "Sorry."

"Like I was saying, it's not that I don't like her," her mother continued like she hadn't been interrupted. "She's just not good enough for you."

Not good enough?

"What? She's the best woman in the world. Nobody could ask for a better friend or lover." What kind of woman did her mother think Phil was anyway? Sage didn't miss the glances Miss Opal and her father exchanged but she was too irritated to call them on it.

"What kind of woman allows her wife or whatever to kick her out every time the in-laws come around?" Her mother frowned at Sage over her steaming mug of tea. "Phillida is *weak*." She snapped the last word like it was the worst possible sin. "You need someone strong who can stand up to you, and who you can stand up for." The tea mug never left her mother's hands. She paused between each sentence, just long enough to take a giant sip of her tea. "There's no way I would let the disapproval of my husband's parents turn my household upside down. Never."

For the second time that morning, Sage's mouth dropped open. Her father nodded along as his wife spoke, his eyes moving between her and Sage while Miss Opal puttered around in the kitchen, busy but obviously paying attention.

"But you never— You –" Sage sputtered, trying to say at least one of the dozens of things crowding up at the back of her throat, anxious to spill out. "You acted like you hated that I was a lesbian and blamed Phil for turning me gay."

"You assumed this all on your own, Sage. You were gay or whatever long before you met Phil. Your father and I know that. Miss Opal too." Her mother paused and looked toward the kitchen to meet Miss Opal's gaze. She seemed to get some sort of strength from the other woman because she turned back to Sage with slightly less strain on her face. "Did you ever think about talking to us about any of this before shutting us out of your life?

With the last word, her mother sounded close to tears, and that tore Sage apart.

This was all her fault. The life she lived separate from her parents. Phil's sadness. The strain in her house right now. She pressed a hand over her suddenly aching chest and wished it was all different.

But she couldn't change the past. "I'm sorry," Sage whispered.

All at once, she was as close to hyperventilating as she'd ever been in her life.

"What's wrong?" Miss Opal's hand gently touched her back.

"Everything." Sage gasped out the single word.

Her chest burned. She couldn't catch her breath. The bullshit Phil had had to put up with over the years, all for nothing. The times Phil had to slink back into the closet every time Sage's parents came to visit. The constant compromising of her strength just to make Sage feel safe in the narrow world she'd made for herself. Sage could count on both hands the times Phil asked her to consider coming out to her family and trust that her parents wouldn't toss her aside.

But she'd said no. Over and over again.

Miss Opal appeared at her side, her hand warm on Sage's shoulder, acceptance and the comforting scent of banana porridge radiating from her. "It's not too late to change the kind of life you have, my heart." Her handmade soothing circles on Sage's back. "If you see you're living your life the wrong way and make no move to do better, that's when you're really—as the kids say these days—fucking up."

Miss Opal's unexpected curse surprised a hiccup of laughter from Sage. When her mouth opened to allow the laugh-free, she tasted tears. And, for the first time, the possibility of change.

"She's right, you know." Her father's voice was soft with sympathy. "It's not too late. We love you, and we're here."

Sage didn't know what to say. Feeling like a child called into her father's office for a talking to, she bit her lip. The pain grounded her, and she was more than a little grateful for it.

"I'm sorry, Daddy," she said and just talking felt like she was gargling gravel. She turned to her mother then, unable to keep looking at the sadness on her face, turned back away. "Mama, I'm sorry." Sage squeezed her eyes shut and almost started crying again. Her shoulders sagged, and her head felt almost too heavy to lift.

"I know you are, baby," her mother said. "We are too for letting it go on so long." She paused. "That is why I think your father, Miss Opal, and I will be going to a hotel today."

Sage's tears stopped.

Sage's father immediately agreed. "True. You girls need to work things out. Us being here in your home—"

"The one you have together," Miss Opal added.

"—is just getting in the way of you being together." Her father continued while nodding in agreement to what Miss Opal said.

"You guys don't have to leave."

"We do, darlin' dear." Miss Opal gave her shoulder one last pat before going back to her porridge.

"The graduation is just in a couple of days, but you need all the time possible to fix your home."

"Take this chance, Sage. You don't want to end up living with regret in this big old empty house."

They all spoke, one after another, but the words sounded like they came from one voice. They were united. They were sure. And there was nothing she could do about it.

CHAPTER SIXTEEN

After everything that went down, there was no way Sage could *not* go to Errol's graduation. Even she wasn't that much of a dick. She didn't know the guy, but now she wanted to. Maybe even needed to. There was a strong chance that if she'd gotten to know him in the first place, she'd also know her parents better, and they wouldn't have become so scary and monstrous in her mind.

After her parents abandoned her for a fancy hotel on the beach and Phil disappeared to wherever it was she'd gone to escape the tension in the house, Sage called Nuria for advice on what kind of gift to get Errol.

"What's going on now?" was how Nuria answered the phone.

Last minute as ever, Sage searched through her closet for suitable graduation attending clothes, the phone tucked between her ear and shoulder. "What are you talking about?" She frowned at an electric blue shirt Phil had always loved kissing her in. "Why does something have to be going on?" Sage bypassed the shirt on kept looking.

"These days you're full of drama, baby. I hope you're self-aware enough to realize that."

Sage didn't bite back her sigh, and even she had to admit it sounded dramatic. "I'm going to a graduation. The guy from Jamaica my parents have been sponsoring over the last few years."

"Yeah, I remember him. You never wanted to meet him because you thought he was going to want to stone you for being gay, or something like that. Right?"

Although Nuria obviously couldn't see her, Sage squirmed. "Yeah, something like that." She stopped with her hand resting on a pair of black slacks, debating whether or not to confess to the full level of her stupidity. "That's not an issue now, though."

"Why?"

She rolled her eyes and pulled the slacks off its thick pine hanger. "Because he's about as gay as I am."

Surprised laughter crackled through the phone. "really?"

"Yeah, really." She could barely get the word out over the sound of Nuria's laughter. "Yeah. Laugh it up."

"Oh my God! Does that mean you were wrong about them? Is he super gay, like rainbows flying out of his ass gay so hard to miss, kind of like you?" Nuria cackled again, enjoying this way too much. "Or is he discreetly queer and you happened to have found out when you walked in on him sucking some guy's dick?"

"What's up with you and your obsession with dick sucking?"

"Answer the fucking question." The laughter still threaded through her voice.

"Rainbow ass," Sage muttered. She backtracked and grabbed the blue shirt.

This time, Sage really couldn't get a word in, the laughter was so loud and long. "You are such an idiot," Nuria finally said.

"Believe me, I know."

Her friend was silent for a moment. "But you know I understand. It's hard to predict how parents will react when you reveal something about yourself they don't expect." Her voice was low, thoughtful. "You know I understand that more than anyone."

Nuria's parents, hell her whole family knew she was bisexual. But they were mostly indifferent to her and her life in general, not really aware of who she was dating, whether male or female, for long stretches of time. Not that Nuria ever dated anyone for long, or even exclusively.

"I know," Sage said, equally quietly. She stopped in front of the shoe rack, her hand braced against the closet wall, head hanging down to stare between her bare feet. Her fingers tightened around the phone.

"So, what do you need from me, honey?"

"Come with me to pick out a graduation gift for a queer as fuck high school graduate."

Nuria laughed again, a low-sound filled with warmth. "I can do that."

She ended up helping Sage pick a nice enough gift, had it wrapped up and, since Phil wasn't at home when it was time for her to leave, showed up as her date to Errol's graduation.

When she got to the graduation, Phil was already there.

"Good," Phil said after a long and thoughtful look at Sage's electric blue shirt. "You guys are right on time. I had to damn near body slam a whole family of rugby players to keep these seats." She moved her purse and a long scarf draped over two seats for Nuria and Sage to sit down.

Skin prickling in the wake of Phil's stare, Sage settled into the seat near her parents and Miss Opal.

"Hey, honey bunny!" Nuria practically sat in Phil's lap after they exchanged brief lip kisses. They'd always kissed each other on the mouth, brief pecks that never bothered Sage before but made her dart a look at her parents and Miss Opal to see what their reactions were. They didn't seem to care. Or even notice.

"What's the plan?" Nuria asked. "Are we going to sing out a cheer or just clap and jump up and down like any other graduation?"

Sage's parents looked at her like they thought she was crazy. But when Nuria winked at Sage's mother—her mother!—her father laughed and her mother smiled back. Maybe there wasn't anything for her to worry about after all.

The graduation went by quickly, with Errol walking across the stage in his summa cum laude gold cords. Nuria and Phil jumped up and down, screaming his name while Sage's father whistled the whole house down. Sage's mother clapped and waved a Jamaican flag she whipped out of her purse at the last minute.

"We're proud of you, Errol!" she shouted.

Errol froze on the stage for a moment, eyes big as he searched the crowd for the source of the cheers. When he found Sage and the rest of the family, his smile was pure happiness.

Sage was left feeling both relieved and unsettled. Was this the kind of unwavering support she could've had if she'd been out to her parents all this time? Her eyes stung, but she refused to let any tears fall. This wasn't a time for regret.

She and the group went to dinner at Errol's favorite restaurant, which turned out to be Novlette's of all places, where their table was only one of several with new graduates wearing a part or whole of their cap and gown outfits. Novlette came out from behind the counter and brought him a small cake with his name on it. Sage didn't even realize they knew each other.

After a while, it got to be too much, and she left the table with the pretense of going to the bathroom. But she went out to the back patio instead. The area was closed off, sloping as it was down to the dock where people could get to the restaurant by boat and dock while they ate either in the restaurant or on their boats.

"You okay, darlin' dear?"

She wasn't surprised that it was Miss Opal, sneaking up on her as always. Sage didn't answer her question right away.

"Why him?" she finally asked by way of answering and not answering.

Miss Opal draped her skinny arms over the railing next to Sage's. The smell of her old-school perfume, rose water with a hint of citrus, washed over her, soothed her.

"Maybe because you never allowed them to love you as the real you."

Sage squeezed her eyes shut, and the tears that had threatened during the graduation surged up against her again. This time, she let them fall. Miss Opal draped her arm over Sage's back. The warmth from her thin and frail-seeming body with all its strength, seeping into Sage.

"I've been so stupid," she gasped through her tears.

"Not stupid, just afraid." Calloused hands made soothing circles on her back. "We all get afraid sometimes. It's what makes us protect ourselves."

"Even when there's nothing to protect ourselves from?"

"Maybe especially then."

Regret pooled in Sage's stomach, churned, then surged up in her throat. It tasted too much like bile. "Yeah..." She tilted her head to lean on Miss Opal's shoulder although it was a longer way than she was used to and threatened to cramp her neck up later, but for now, it was exactly what she needed.

CHAPTER SEVENTEEN

Her parents didn't stay much longer after graduation. At the airport, Sage parked her car and walked them as far as the security line.

"Next time we come, we can stay longer," her father said.

Her mother gave her a tight hug. "Yes, once your family is back together and you're in your right mind again, we'll do more."

"And maybe we can even have a nice dinner with your friends," Miss Opal said.

They'd known about Rémi and Dez for years but had never met their lovers before the graduation dinner. Her mother had been instantly charmed by Claudia and couldn't stop talking about how elegant and pretty she was. If her mother didn't seem so settled down with her husband, Sage would've worried about that spontaneous woman crush.

"Yeah, that would be great." Then she'd spoken out of her raw heart. "Maybe this Christmas? Just tell me when you three can come and I'll get the tickets."

They all exchanged a look.

"Yes, I think we can manage that." It was her father who spoke.

"Yes, definitely." Her mother reached out and hugged Sage one more time. "And make sure your woman knows she's welcome. Be fair to her and to yourself."

A thick lump landed in Sage's throat and she swallowed it hard. "Thanks, Mama. I'll let her know."

"Good."

"Now, go and put your life in order. That woman won't wait her whole life for you."

Sage didn't have the heart, or the balls, to tell her that it was over. "I'm glad you guys came," she said, giving each of them one last hug. "Email or call with your dates so we can get something solid arranged for Christmas."

Miss Opal didn't miss a thing. "At least try, honey." She held on to Sage the longest.

Sage stood watching the slow movement of the security line long after all three disappeared past the creepy body scan thing. She didn't want to go home. Not yet. She'd left Phil there, floating through the house in her silk robe, beautiful and silent, probably waiting for some man to come sweep her away.

She was still staring at the line of strangers and thinking about her shitty home life when her phone rang.

It was Errol.

"Hey." She turned away to head back outside and to her car. No point in standing there like an idiot and thinking about things she couldn't change. "Thanks for calling me back."

CHAPTER EIGHTEEN

"You know I can't legally drink, right?" Errol sat perched on a stool next to the bar where Sage had invited him to sit, still glowing from his graduation, his thin and graceful body covered in what Sage was sure was a graduation gift outfit. A thin, peach-colored linen shirt with three-quarter sleeves, worn untucked over white linen pants. Pink-painted toenails peeked from elegant leather sandals.

When Sage only stared at him, he snorted through a smile. "I graduated from high school, not college," he said. "Which means I'm not twenty-one yet."

She didn't see what the big deal was. At eighteen, she'd never cared much about what was legal, just fun. She'd drank, snorted, smoked, swallowed anything she wanted to get her to the desired altitude of the evening.

"So, you don't want a drink?"

Errol smirked. "I didn't say that."

Sage signaled the bartender over. After she ordered her usual rum and coke, Errol got himself a piña colada. Once she slid over some money, she took him to a table near the railing.

"So, what's on your mind?" Errol asked her as soon as they sat down.

There was no animosity in his voice, just a curiosity to know what was going on.

"Not too much." Sage savored the sweetness of the drink on her tongue, the burst of effervescence that made her nose twitch even after all these years and countless versions of the drink. "Just felt like chatting with you for a bit."

Errol mostly played with his drink, turning the curvy glass around and around between his hands. "Why now, after all the years I've been here?" he asked. "I asked you to come have lunch or whatever with me a few times but you always said you were too busy."

A flush of embarrassment climbed in Sage's cheeks. Yeah, she had been that asshole. In the name of full disclosure, and in an effort to be better than she had been before, she inched toward honesty.

"I wasn't ready to meet the guy who took my place with my parents." The drink bubbled in her mouth again. And she almost didn't notice Errol's breath of surprise.

"For real?"

"Yeah." Sage shrugged. She knew it then but was painfully aware of it now, of how wrong she was.

"Weren't you the one who didn't want to go home much, and didn't have much to say to them when they called?"

How the hell did he know that?

"They talk about you a lot," Errol said, answering the unasked question. "They're proud of you too, I guess. Although..." His voice trailed off and she didn't have to be a mind reader to figure out the rest of his aborted sentence: *Although you're a bit of an asshole.* Which was true enough.

"I was a dick and an idiot. I'm trying not to be so much of one now."

Another smirk. A sly slide of laughing eyes. "How's that going for you?"

"It's been hard as fuck..." Which was a kind of an understatement. She'd pushed everyone away, and it was taking time and humility she didn't possess much of to make things right.

"You don't seem like the type to make this easy," he said, finally taking a sip of his melting drink.

She didn't bother denying it. Anybody who'd been in her company for more than ten minutes could see through to her paper soul. She liked fun. Loved Phil. Was a hypocrite. Clear as glass.

"Well, I'm trying to change it up now, at least a little bit." She chewed on a piece of ice and Miss Opal's voice came at her from the past. *You shouldn't chew ice. You'll mess up you pretty teeth dem.*

"So, shoot," Errol said. "How can I help this poor little rich girl soothe her conscience?"

She rolled her eyes. This boy was a real smart ass. "Tell me..." Sage paused, thinking of all the things she wanted to know. "Tell me how my parents found you."

He squirmed, looking uncomfortable for the first time since they sat down together. "It's not pretty."

"I'm not asking for a fairy tale."

"Are you sure about that?" He looked at her with a faint smile, but there was no humor in it. "Well, I'll give you one anyway. It's called Cinderella, Jamaican style."

Errol played with his soda, hands turning the tall glass around and around, occasionally looking up at Sage, a considering look on his face. Finally, he spoke. "They found me in the gully."

Shock thudded into Sage's chest.

The gully was a shitty place. A series of drainage ditches in Kingston, hellish and filthy, but also just about the only "safe" space for gay boys in Jamaica to escape to. These were kids who'd been chased out of their homes or who just left because they were tired of being treated like crap by their families.

"I'd been there for a few months. It was hard, getting used to sleeping in drainage pipes and being...selling my mouth or my ass to eat. Some of them refused to do that shit." He shrugged as if their choices were ones he understood, were nothing compared to the other thing. The thing that had landed them on the streets in the first place. "They stole or did scams, the prettier, smaller ones pretended to be girls and then blackmailed the straight guys they fucked into paying them hush money."

Dangerous shit. Nothing Sage knew from personal experience. Errol was right, she was a poor little rich girl. She had complaints, but she always had a place to sleep. Always had people to show her they cared.

Shoulders gradually stooping down, getting narrower as he immersed himself in memories of the past he'd escaped from, Errol plucked at the label on the brown bottle while he talked. "When my father threw me out, I couldn't believe it. We had our differences, but everything seemed okay. I was doing in school and working some online jobs to bring in money to the family. But then..." He stopped.

His father got a new girlfriend, pretty and sexually adventurous enough to try anything, even the crazy stuff Errol senior had seen on TV. He'd walked on his father and her often enough to know. And the walls of their small house were thin.

"She didn't want to share him, maybe." He shrugged again. "I don't know."

One day after school, she hemmed Errol up in the front yard. He had his backpack and was excited because he got a new client willing to pay him a decent rate for updates to their website. As usual, he planned to save half, contribute the rest to the household.

"I see what you're doing," she shouted, sticking a boney finger in Errol's face. "You're trying to be a wife to him. Bringing in your little pin money, waving your ass in his face!"

It was crazy. All the times she'd looked at him with poison in her gaze, he never thought something like that was going through her mind.

"It was so stupid. I don't even think *she* believed it. But my father did."

Errol landed on his ass in the street with only the backpack he'd quickly stuffed with clothes and the bank card linked to his savings account.

Between his savings and the work he was able to get, he avoided starving, but he didn't have any place to live. So, he ended up in the gully with a lot of the gay boys and trans girls in Kingston.

"Sometimes a boy or two would go missing. But people didn't care, you know. To our own families we were disposable, how else were strangers supposed to feel about us?"

The strangers who came into the gully were furtive men with money in their wallets and a hunger to fuck something different, unable to be open about what they preferred at home. Sometimes these strangers were cruel. Murderous. Fucking then killing the same boys they had turned to for pleasure. For escape.

The gully almost killed Errol.

"People think life is cheap in Jamaica overall, it's worth even less than a ten-minute blowjob in the gully."

The boys slashed each other up, shot each other, scratched, and tore themselves in two. They had been hurt, they were in pain, and didn't know anything else to do but pass along that pain. To each other, to anybody stupid enough to get close.

"You could've knocked over with a piece of bread the day the Bennetts stopped to help me." He rolled his eyes and smiled, fond and pained at the same time. "I was leaving the library when somebody pushed me off my bicycle. I was cussing and carrying on, trying to get back on the bicycle, get away from the two guys who looked like they were ready to kick me to death. But they stopped their car and helped me up, waited for me to clean the scrapes off my knees. Then they took me to dinner, told me about their daughter—"

Sage winced at that.

Errol continued "Then asked if they could help me." His smile leaked away. "I wasn't proud enough to say no."

"So, they helped you get back in school, helped you get an American visa, and that's it. All because you got shoved off your bicycle in front of them?"

"Pretty much. I think I was just a gay kid they needed to rescue. Because they couldn't rescue you, you know?"

"Rescue me?"

"Yeah. I guess from yourself."

Sage's teeth clenched hard enough to creak in her jaw, trapping the automatic reaction she wanted to spit at Errol. She held herself still. Her hand tightened around the cool glass, and her feelings rushed through her too fast to name. Another sip of the drink fizzed over tongue.

"Do you think I need rescuing?" she asked once she got herself under control.

"I don't know you," Errol said with a shrug. "So, I can't really say."

Although it didn't seem like he was making a dig at Sage, she felt the jolt of it anyway. She'd had the chance to get to know him in the four years since he'd been in America. Her parents told her to reach out to him, saying she might be surprised at what they had in common. But she'd always had excuses. Or more to the point, she hadn't wanted to meet him.

Damn. She could've saved herself so much shit if she'd just—

She cut off that useless train of thought. It didn't matter now. They could only move forward.

She swallowed the last of her drink. "You're right."

"Of course I am." He grinned, showing some of what she realized was his natural vivaciousness. It was kind of cute.

She grunted a short laugh, unable to get where he was yet. "Hey, you want to get out of here and grab a real meal? This place is a little seedy."

"Sure. I thought you were trying to tell me something when you suggested this place."

"No. I was just..." She hitched up a shoulder to indicate her general obliviousness and he laughed like she meant him to. "So, you want to go head over to Novlette's or someplace else?"

"You pick," he said.

Naturally, they ended up at Gillespie's, easily getting into the usually fully booked spot despite not having a reservation. It paid to have friends in useful places.

Sage and Errol settled at a quiet table on the upper floor of the restaurant and bar with a table full of food since she remembered just how much he could eat. Rémi was nowhere in sight but that didn't mean her friend wasn't working. Sage sent Rémi a quick text to let her know she was in the building then went back to paying attention to her lunch companion.

"So now that we got how much of I'm an asshole out of the way, tell me about yourself."

"Damn, you really jump in, don't you?"

"I'm trying to make up for lost time." As if that was even possible.

Over a long lunch, he told her about the new life he'd built for himself in Miami, the guy he was seeing but hadn't had sex with yet.

"Why not?"

"When I have sex next, I want it to be important now that I don't just have to do it to survive, you know."

The boy was too sweet for his own damn good.

In exchange for his confidence, she spilled her guts about Phil and how much of a dick she'd been.

"I would've dumped your ass in a minute," he said, giving her some serious side-eye.

"Good thing you're not my girlfriend then," she said with an unrepentant grin, only to joke about it now that things were...better.

After their meal was over, she invited him over to the house later in the week for a family dinner and told him to bring his boyfriend if he wanted to. No sex didn't mean no companionship.

He said he'd think about it, then he drove off, waving at her through the window of his clean Honda Civic with a wide smile. Sage didn't feel like the idiot she thought she would when she grinned and waved right back.

CHAPTER NINETEEN

"This is the sweetest Cuban spot I know of right now." Nuria tossed the comment over her shoulder as she led the way into the restaurant, hips swaying in tight white jeans and red-bottomed gold stilettos. A gold blouse, light and sheer, bared her flat belly.

"You know I'm all about the sweet spot," Sage said. She tried to smile but her joke felt flat.

"Uh huh..."

The hostess quickly seated them at a well-lit table on the second floor of the lofted style restaurant. The place was small, about the size of an actual lofted apartment with six small tables upstairs where they sat and twice that downstairs. The food smelled good but Sage wasn't in the mood to appreciate it.

Days had passed since she last saw Nuria at Errol's graduation. They'd talked about things, skimmed over the big elephant in the room of their friendship but hadn't arrived at a conclusion that satisfied them both.

With a wriggle of contentment, Nuria settled into her chair once the server brought her mojito and Sage's rum and coke.

"So what's going on with you, *macha*?" Nuria paused with the drink near her deep purple lips. "You look like shit."

"Thank you very much..." Sage muttered. She downed half her rum and coke in a few swallows.

"Obviously you own a mirror, so this can't be news."

"Well, I'm trying to act like everything is fine."

"That's never a good plan, I can tell you that from personal experience." Nuria sipped her mojito and licked a droplet of the drink from her bottom lip. "I like to match my inside with my outside as much as possible, and since I always look fabulous—" She spread her arms wide and leaned back in the chair so Sage could get a good look at all her fabulousness. "—I work a lot on making myself happy, no matter what the rest of the world trips me up with."

"Easy for you to say, baby love."

Little frown lines marred the smoothness of Nuria's mahogany skin. "You know that's not true..."

Yeah, Sage knew better. When all was said and done, Nuria didn't have it any easier than the rest of them did.

"Sorry."

"Don't be sorry," Nuria said. "Tell me what's up. Apart from what I already know, that is. You screwed up and kicked Phil out. You showed me your whole bi-phobic ass—" Sage sputtered in protest but Nuria kept going. "—and you've finally unstuck your head from up your own ass enough to see that your parents are better than you gave them credit for." She propped an elbow up on the table, balanced her pointy chin on top of her first. "What else?"

"I told you I'm not *bi-phobic* or—"

"Yeah, yeah. Skip over that. You need to get over whatever issues you have with my people. You're not there yet and because I love you, I'll be patient. But let's just be real with each other and move on from where we both are, okay?"

Sage released a deep breath and thought of the sea change that had taken place in her life over the last few days. "Okay."

The waitress popped up just then with their food, platters of ropa vieja, rice and beans, and tostones, in the middle of the table for them to share.

"Thanks, darling," Nuria said to the waitress then immediately reached for her empty plate to start serving herself. When she called to invite Sage out, she'd claimed to be *starving*.

Though Sage couldn't bring herself to eat yet, she put some of the food on her own plate. "This separation isn't as easy as I thought it would be," she said.

The tostones and shredded beef on Nuria's plate were fast disappearing into her mouth. But she was still able to talk just fine. "Oh, so you thought kicking out the woman who'd been in your heart for over a decade was gonna be like pissing out your morning tea?" Chewing slowly, she peered at Sage with a raised eyebrow like she was really waiting for an answer.

Of course, she wouldn't get it. "I can't be with somebody bi."

"*Somebody*," Nuria parroted with a sneer. "I wonder what the real reason is for you being so anti-bi? Because it can't be your fear of diseases. The way you carry on with these bitches like you can't get crabs or whatever else when you throw your mouth all over their pussies." She paused with a fork full of rice and beans pointed at Sage. "There's definitely something else here. And the way you're carrying on, I wonder if even *you* know what it is."

"Nope," Sage said with a quick shake of her head. "It's not any deep shit you may be thinking. I just don't like it."

To give her fingers something to do, she clumsily unwrapped her utensils from the paper napkin.

Nuria licked a few lingering rice grains from the corner of her mouth. "If that's true, you're an even bigger asshole than I thought." She snorted with disgust and looked away, her gaze wandering past the railing and downstairs.

Then she blinked.

"What?" Sage followed Nuria's gaze to see what had made her friend do that double take.

Her mouth dropped open. The fork she held between her fingers fell and clattered against the plate. What the actual fuck?

This time, she didn't make the same mistake. Yes, the long hair was thick and fell around slender shoulders, but the Adam's apple was obvious from this angle. This was Zachary Baxter, the *man* Phil had lusted after at the movie premiere. And right at that very moment, he was sitting at a table with Phil herself.

They were laughing. Their hands rested close on the table. They were drinking wine.

The rum and coke Sage drank earlier threatened to come right back up. She swallowed.

Downstairs, Phil and Zachary Baxter went on having a damn good time. It looked like they'd been sitting there for a little while. An empty plate with remnants of food sat in the middle of the small table between them and their drinks looked at least half-finished.

Without thinking, Sage pushed back from the table and jumped to her feet.

"Sit down, honey." Nuria put down her fork. "What Phil is doing here is none of your business. Not anymore."

But Sage couldn't accept that. A swimming red rage took her thudding down the stairs and up to the sun-lit table by the window. They didn't notice her at first. Baxter and Phil kept talking, their voices low and intimate.

The real burn of it was that they looked *good* together. Phil in her clinging black dress—like she was in mourning—with her hair straightened and curled under in sleek bob. Her face was so beautiful that it actually hurt to look at her dead on.

The guy wore black too. A dress shirt, slacks, and matte black

Italian loafers. His hair was loose down his back and he was obviously taller than Phil, even though she was wearing stilettos.

"Did you fuck him yet?" Sage growled.

Two pairs of eyes jerked up to look at her. It gave her a kind of savage joy to see the smiles disappear from their faces.

"If I did, it's none of your business," Phil said evenly. But she drew her hand away from his on the table.

"You must really hate her right now." The guy had the nerve to talk to Sage. His voice was deep and pretty enough if you were into that sort of thing, which obviously Phil was now. "You can't love someone and run up to embarrass them in public like this," he continued, his brown eyes hard and challenging. But he was smart enough to stay in this seat.

"Fuck off," Sage snarled at him.

"What do you want, Sage?" Phil asked, her voice infuriatingly calm.

"I want you to not be here with this asshole."

"Again, what I do isn't your business anymore," Phil said. "You made that very clear to me the other day."

Impotent anger ran rampant through Sage's veins, flushing her entire body with heat. "Phil, you can't do this!"

People were starting to stare, but she didn't give a damn.

Phil's chair abruptly scraped back from the table just as a server approached them.

"Is everything okay here?" the server asked looking from Sage to Phil with concern and bass in his voice.

"We're fine," Phil said from between clenched teeth. Standing up, she grabbed Sage's arm hard enough to hurt. "Even though it's not necessary, thanks for checking on us. My *friend* is just a little upset." She turned to Baxter with a tight smile of apology. "I'm sorry about this, Zachary." Then without waiting for a response from her date, she yanked Sage toward a narrow hallway and the sign that said "restrooms."

At least a dozen eyes watched them march quickly past.

As soon as the bathroom door swung shut behind them, Phil let go of Sage's arm like she had the plague. "I don't know what your problem is, but you better get over it *fast*," Phil hissed.

"My *problem* is you and this guy!" Sage shouted back. "What the fuck are you doing here with him?"

Phil eyes slitted with hurt and malice. "Living my life apart from you. That's what people do when they break up, even lesbians."

"No!" Sage's chest heaved. It felt like she had a locomotive rumbling through her breast, heading for a derailment. She stalked to the other side of the bathroom, her heavy footsteps taking her back and forth past each of the four empty bathroom stalls. "You can't...you just can't..."

The runaway train inside her rolled faster. She started to shake.

"I can't what? Get over you? Have a life?" Phil cursed and backed away from Sage, her high heels rapping loudly against the tile. "It doesn't work that way. You may not believe this, but there are actually people out there who like me just as I am. *All* of me. These are people I don't have to beg to be with me."

That wasn't right. Not just because of that man out there who'd probably had his dick and balls and hands all over Phil. It wasn't right that there was somebody out there who cherished and cared for Phil more than she did.

Is this the way you treat someone you love? A small voice whispered at the back of her mind.

The thought made her stumble back. Even if she didn't want to be with Phil like that, she still loved her. Right?

"Baby..." She reached out her hand.

Phil jerked back. "No!" For the first time, she lost her calm and her face crumpled like tissue paper. "No, Sage." She backed away. "You don't get to do this to me!"

But Sage kept reaching, kept moving forward.

Part of her knew Phil didn't deserve this, but she was a mess of want and craving and an unexplained jealousy that had no end. This man shouldn't have Phil. He wasn't worthy of her.

Sage dropped her hand but continued inching closer. "You haven't fucked him yet. I can see it on your face."

"Whether I have or haven't is none of your business." Phil's voice strengthened. But she kept backing away.

"You are my business." Moving snake-quick, Sage cupped Phil's her crotch through the thin black dress. "*This* is my business."

Phil's back hit the last stall and the door slammed open, pitching her into the bathroom. Sage followed, breathless, senseless, the locomotive in her chest rattling at a hundred miles an hour.

The stall door banged shut behind them and Sage just had the presence of mind to fumble for the flimsy little latch and lock them in.

"What do you think you're doing?" Phil demanded, her voice rough.

Sage dropped to her knees. "I don't know."

And honest to God, she didn't. Even though she should've expected it, seeing Phil with that guy just about broke her down. Her heart had lurched inside her chest then burst wide open, completely pulverized by the sight of them together.

"Get up," Phil snapped. "You're being ridiculous." But her voice was a little breathless.

They'd been in places like this before. And the sketchiness of it, the very idea of fucking in a handicapped stall while separated from other people by a flimsy excuse for a door that didn't even go all the way to the floor, made Sage's pussy flood with arousal.

Sage's breath shivered in her chest. Her clit felt suddenly too big in her shorts, fat and thick and aching for stimulation. Still on her knees, she clasped Phil's hips.

"Are you sure that's what you want me to do?" She dragged up the soft cotton of Phil's dress, over her knees, up her thighs. Phil wasn't wearing any panties.

Firm hands clamped down on Sage's shoulders. "Sage..."

"Yes?" If Phil told her no, she would let her go. Yes, she would shatter into a million pieces but she would get off her knees, and she would go back to her lunch and pretend none of this ever happened. Sage tried to show all that on her face.

A slow sigh leaked from Phil's open mouth. "Yes."

Thank God! Before Phil could change her mind, Sage shoved the soft thighs open and nuzzled gently between them.

Fingers gripped her hair and tightened. Dragged her head back so she had no choice but to look at Phil. "No," Phil said. She licked her lips, looking down at her with heavy-lidded eyes. The sleek mink of her hair swept down to frame her face in lustrous darkness. "Do it hard. Don't pretend this is more than it is."

Reaction clenched hard in Sage's belly.

The sensible thing for her to do was get up and walk out of the stall. Just walk away.

Phil's stare challenged her. *What do you want to do?*

With a deep groan, she yanked Phil's thighs wider and her woman's back thudded against the wall with an oddly erotic sound. Phil gasped. She was already dripping wet. The slick damp of her pussy greeted Sage's mouth. Slippery. Swollen. Hungry.

The heated smell of it pulled a long moan from Sage's very core.

Sage dove in, licking the loamy and soft flesh until juices dripped down her chin. Her fingers dug hard into Phil's thighs, feeding Phil the roughness she said she wanted. But the ravenous pussy under her tongue didn't want it hard. Didn't want it rough.

Sage had been making love to it long enough to know. The pink opened for her, wanting but with a hint of reluctance. It begged to be coaxed and tended to.

Above her, Phil bit her lip. She grabbed and squeezed her own breast through the thin dress, tugged a nipple. Squeezed it. Panting quietly, she rocked her pussy against Sage's mouth.

Good. So good.

Phil never took her eyes off Sage. The challenge was there in the swirling depths of her gaze. So was her pleasure.

Damn, she missed this...

Groaning and hungry, she distracted Phil with the pain of her fingers, gripping her soft skin hard enough to bruise while she licked into the familiar and salty flesh she'd called a home for twelve years. Hungry for every flavor, she sucked the pretty and tiny clit into her mouth, tonguing the underside with firm and sure movements. Wetness gushed into her open mouth and she groaned, drinking it all up. Her own pussy tightened in arousal and dripped its own pleasure. The clit piercing only heightened the sensation.

A soft breath of sound. The fingers in her hair tightened. Phil leaned back even more into the wall and lifted her thighs, one after the other, to drape them over Sage's shoulders.

Sage kept her eyes open, watching every shift and movement in her face.

With each stroke of her tongue, Phil's breath roughened. Her lashes fluttered down, fighting to stay open and watch Sage eat her out.

So damn beautiful.

Phil circled her pussy against her mouth, frantic and hard. But Sage made her touches gentle. Firm but soft. One moment passed, and then two. Phil's breath stuttered and she slowed down the wild bucking of her hips and surrendered to Sage's gentleness.

Just what Sage was waiting for.

She drew her mouth back. "Do you want this, baby?"

Phil's eyes snapped open and her lips parted, an obviously pissed off answer about to jump off on her tongue. Sage shoved two fingers deep into her slippery cunt and curled them, aiming for that spot she knew so well. Phil's back jerked off the wall just as her hands gripped Sage's shoulders. Her mouth flew open wider, her eyes. Pleasure twisted her face.

"Oh..."

That first thrust was just the beginning.

The next pushed another, softer noise from Phil. So soft, so delicious that if Sage hadn't been listening for it, she wouldn't have heard it.

A low bang sounded outside the bathroom. The sound of the door opening and someone coming in.

Sage kept licking.

"If you bitches are in here fucking, you better hurry up." Nuria's voice rang with amusement. "There's only so much small talk I can have with Zachary. He may be creaming his shorts imagining what you two are up to, but even he's not going to wait out there forever." Then the door banged open again. She was gone.

All through Nuria's brief visit, Sage never once stopped fucking Phil. She sucked that sweet clit to the rhythm of her finger's pounding thrusts, getting more and more into it with every uncontrolled glide of Phil's wetness against her face.

"Oh..." Phil's pussy quivered against her mouth.

Sage kept at it, stroking that spot inside Phil while sucking and licking her clit. That sweet sound came again and that perfect pussy clenched hard around her fingers, rippling, rippling...

A shudder of triumph kicked through Sage's belly.

That's it, baby. Come for me.

With a near-silent groan, Phil collapsed against the bathroom wall. Her breasts heaved under the black dress. Gently, Sage removed the trembling thighs from her shoulders and settled Phil on her feet. Inside her slacks, her pussy was raging to come. With trembling hands, she stroked the stiff peak of a nipple poking against Phil's dress, touching herself through the warm cotton of her slacks at the same time. Her pussy clenched hard and shudders of electric pleasure licked down her spine. She was so close. Just a little bit more...

"No." Phil batted Sage's hand away from her breast. She straightened her dress. Some of her lipstick was gone, bitten off while Sage had been snacking on her sweet cunt. "You don't get to come," she rasped, stepping around Sage. "Not with me."

Huh? Sage felt stupid with lust.

Her clit throbbed like an insistent heartbeat and the taste of Phil's pussy was like the sweetest of spices on her tongue. She *ached*.

But Phil wasn't about to give her any relief.

By the time she got it together and realized what was going on, Phil had unlocked the stall door and stood washing her hands at the sink. Water splashed all over the counter. The bright lights of the bathroom burned brightly over her dark head and bitten red lips, over the stiff nipples still trying to punch holes through her dress.

"Phil?"

Phil activated the paper towel dispenser with a wave of her hand and ripped off the brown paper it spat out. "We're done here, right?" After roughly wiping her hands, she dumped the piece of paper in the trash. "You already proved to yourself you can still pull my strings."

"That's not what this is about," Sage rushed to say. She squeezed her thighs together to get her pussy under control.

"Then what is it?" Phil crossed her arms, her lips tight as she waited. When Sage couldn't find anything else to say, she drew in a long breath. "That's what I thought. Because you found out I like dick every once in a while, you want to take me apart and play with the pieces you approve of then dump the rest."

"I'm *not* playing with you," Sage insisted, although she didn't have a clue what she was doing.

"Then what do you call this?" Phil made a rough noise and shook her head. The thick, black hair swung around her face. "You know what? Don't answer that question. I'm pretty sure I don't want to hear whatever it is you have to say."

Then she walked out of the bathroom without a second glance at what she was leaving behind.

CHAPTER TWENTY

Sage couldn't shake off the last conversation she'd had with Phil. Or the sex.

By the time she'd washed up in the bathroom and made it back into the restaurant, Phil and her date were gone. Nuria was still there, though. Her friend had finished off most of the food and sat at the table with a second mojito, exchanging nudes with some girl she'd met out in L.A. She was supremely unbothered by all the drama.

After Nuria finished laughing her ass off at what happened in the bathroom, Sage went home ready to apologize to Phil. But even though the yellow Corvette sat cold in their two-car garage, Phil was nowhere in sight.

In fact, she didn't come home for two days. On the third day, Sage got back from a long evening in the recording studio to see Phil's sleek shape stretched out on the sofa like nothing strange had happened between them.

"Where have you been?" she asked.

Phil looked up from the journal she was reading, thick-framed black glasses perched on her nose. "Sleeping with every hot man in Miami, you?"

Sage cursed under her breath and walked away.

In the guest bedroom where she'd been sleeping since her parents' visit, she put her phone to charge. Just as she plugged it in, the phone chirped with its monthly reminder about the plans she had that night with Phil, Rémi, and Dez.

Was that why Phil came back from wherever she'd run off to?

Cursing again, she yanked off her button-down shirt and tossed it in the laundry basket. With half an ear tuned to Phil and half her attention occupied with potential excuses for not going out to Shadow and Vine, she almost missed the sound of her phone ringing.

But she caught it on the last ring. "Hi, mother."

"Sage, how are things at home with you and Phillida?" her mother asked as soon as she was done with the usual pleasantries.

"Uh...she's fine." Sage rubbed her temples and wished she had a more truthful answer. Already a headache was throbbing behind her eyes and threatening to ruin her entire night.

"Is she really fine?" her mother asked.

"Yes. She's in the living room, probably reading one of the articles Daddy told her about."

Her mother made a disapproving noise. "Sounds like you didn't fix what's wrong between the two of you."

It was weird as hell to be talking to her mother about Phil after years of avoiding her as a topic of conversation.

"It's not so easy of a thing to fix, mother."

Another noise came at her through the phone, this one of doubt. Quickly, she changed the subject. By the time Sage got off the phone (she'd been passed from her mother to her dad then to Miss Opal) she was convinced her family was ready to adopt Phil despite the fact that they weren't together anymore.

What a difference a month made.

From out in the living room, she heard the faint sound of pages being turned.

She nudged herself to go wash her ass instead of listening for Phil's every movement like a creep. In the shower, she tried to keep her mind empty and her thoughts away from Phil and...anything else that mattered. Still, with the peaceful rhythm of water hitting the tile and splashing on her skin, the sadness rolled back and forth through her like seasickness.

After her shower, she felt clean and her headache was gone, but she was more twisted up inside than ever. Distracted. Roughly drying her hair with a towel, she left the bathroom and headed to the master bedroom where she still kept her clothes. The tiles felt cool and grounding under her bare feet.

Her thoughts a million miles away, she nearly bumped into Phil coming out of the bedroom. "Shit!"

Phil spared her a quick up and down glance, eyes lingering on the robe clinging to Sage's damp skin. "Excuse me," she said before continuing past and toward the front door.

In tight black jeans, purple heels, and a black shirt sheer enough for Sage to see her bra and the cleavage practically spilling out of it, she was dressed to fuck.

She didn't make the mistake of asking Phil where she was going. "You're not going to Shadow and Vine with us tonight?" she asked instead.

Phil didn't even turn around. "No. I have something else to do. Enjoy yourself, though." The keys to the Corvette jingled as she picked them up, then she was gone.

Seriously? This was what they were reduced to, living like roommates who could barely stand each other?

They couldn't keep going like this, sharing the house out of spite and hurting each other more every day. The sadness bubbled up inside her again, but she shoved it away.

If Phil wasn't going to the club, she'd made other plans her damn self.

Sage called up Hope and Candler.

"What are you up to tonight?" she asked with the phone balanced between her cheek and shoulder, the boy shorts snapping around her hips after she dragged them on.

Candler sounded like she was on the road, the sound of wind rushing past an open window coming through the phone. "Me and Hope are heading to Shadow and Vine."

These jokers were for real heading there too? Sage shoved aside the curtain and peered out into the backyard illuminated by the night time light, the pool a sparkling blue. On one of the chairs, a scrap of yellow drew her eye. The bottom to Phil's bathing suit they'd lost while messing around out there. Her fingers clenched in the curtains and she looked away from that small reminder of things she'd never have again.

"I was heading that way myself," Sage said. Shadow and Vine was a self-styled "sensuality cabaret" that catered mostly to women. It was the spot she and her friends usually went to on the monthly date they all showed up for unless there was some sort of an emergency.

But with everything happening in their lives, Sage doubted any of them would show.

"Cool! Come sit with us. Richelle and Marty will be there too. It's gonna be a nice group, like the old days."

The old days. Right.

Hope and Candler were die-hard studs she'd known when she was first coming out. She'd hung with them a couple of times, but their relationship didn't stick like it had with Rémi, Dez, Nuria, and even Phil. Even though she made time to hang with them at least a couple of times a month, there was something about them and their habits that didn't sit well with Sage. They didn't fuck as much as her Rémi and company, tended to be more vanilla despite their tough exteriors, and they talked a good game about monogamy and traditional values and shit. Which nearly everyone in her group was mostly into now.

She shook herself out of her uncomfortable mood and shrugged off her robe, reached for the bottle of lotion to start getting ready. "I'll meet you all there."

After a quick meal in her silent kitchen and a call to make sure her parents and Miss Opal were doing all right, she left the house. It was after eleven when she got to Shadows and Vine, just before the main features of the night started up. After paying the entrance fee, she waded into the bright front rooms of the club cum dungeon that Sage and her friends usually just treated like a strip club. The music was loud and thick with sex. Donna Summer's voice panting under the driving beat. Love to love you, baby.

Sometimes Nuria played, but more often than not, she would sit at their table and the bar with the rest of them, talking shit, drinking, and taking in at least one of the sex shows. A feeling of loss throbbed just under her breast. Sage breathed into it, acknowledged what it was, then ignored it. Nothing would come of her wallowing in that feeling tonight.

After texting to check on where they were, she easily found Candler and the gang. They must have come early and staked out one of the front tables in the massive room that was almost like dinner theater. But there was no dinner, just as much booze as your body could handle, private rooms to indulge and for others to watch you indulge, and a semi-circle of VIP balconies on the second level for people who liked to watch from afar and not get anything splashed on them from the stage.

"Sage!" Candler shouted out her name in the throb between a hard, bass driving song. Someone at the table held up the illuminated face of a cell phone, waving it in Sage's direction. The bass, slow and sensuous, gave the patrons ideas, and the beat loud enough to drown out the sounds of sex or whatever else was happening in dark corners of the club. A few people danced on the raised, circular dance floor under the DJ booth, but people were probably too sober for their hips to loosen up enough to dance. That would come much later.

Donna's endless song still played, her sensual moans tracking Sage's footsteps to the table that seated four people she hadn't seen in a few weeks.

"Good to see you, man." The table was small but had more than enough room for them all, and Sage reached over the grip the hand of the two she didn't know.

"Same," she said. "It's been a minute."

"True." Candler made a round of introductions then raised a flashing square card, signaling a waitress in the semi-dark room. "What do you want to drink?"

When the waiter came, muscle-bound and wearing pants tight enough to make him squeak, Sage ordered her usual rum and coke.

The stage was still dark, only vague shadows on its raised surface to give any hints about what the first show was supposed to be. While the place wasn't a strip club, the most popular part of the entertainment on offer at Shadows and Vine was its sex shows, sometimes amateur and fun, but most times a mixture of a strip show and Cirque du Soleil. Nuria liked to perform sometimes, just for fun, or to lure that night's fuck into her bed.

"So what you been up to?" Candler asked, pale skin flashing in the dim lights, her smile thin and knowing.

Although they weren't close, Candler knew her from way back. Or they knew of each other. She knew that Candler was a serial monogamist, liked her sex with a femme and a strap, while she thought she knew all about Sage. The smile on her face, a smirk really, was all about the assumption that Sage had been up to some kinky and crazy shit since they last saw each other. Which may or may not have been true.

The last few months, it had mostly been kinky shit with Phil —she felt that throb of loss again and she wrestled it back down— everything else she'd indulged in with other women had been pretty vanilla. Even the scenes she'd took part in, a little leather play here a there, some light spanking, demanding the girl call her daddy, were pretty tame.

"Just the usual," Sage settled for saying.

"I heard your friend Rémi hooked up for good with a bi chick. They're even getting married, right?"

"I heard it's Dez's mama!" Richelle crowed, throwing her head back. "That must have been a trip, right?"

"Shit..." One of the new girls looked both impressed and horrified. "If one of my friends came after my mama I'd beat that bitch with a bat."

Sage rolled her eyes. "That's their business and they're all fine with it now." She would never tell these people how Dez had struggled with it, had come to close to abandoning her friendship with Rémi and even turning her back on her own mother. "Grown folks' business," she said, injecting a note of finality in her voice. But the simple-minded people at the table apparently didn't hear it.

"Isn't Rémi scared this new piece will run back to her husband? I'm assuming she didn't turn lesbian all of a sudden. Not after having two kids and a whole life with a man. You can't trust those bi bitches, man."

"They're not really bi anyway. Most of them just want to keep one foot in the closet and keep their options open."

"Yeah, they don't want to come out and deal with the real shit we put up with every day."

The drink sat in front of Sage, the thin line of water on its surface spreading down into the rest of the rum and coke. Under the table, her fingers clawed into her thigh, the denim blunting the press of her nails. This shit wasn't really happening, was it?

"I don't see anything wrong with them," Marty said. And Sage felt herself starting to relax. Maybe they could have an actual discussion about this instead of blaming bi people for everything from AIDS to global warming. What they were saying wasn't far off from what she thought, but she didn't want these assholes talking shit about Claudia and Rémi. About Nuria. About Phil.

"Yeah," Marty went on. "I'd fuck a bi chick in a minute. I hear they're a bunch of freaks anyway, would do any damn thing you want, they'd probably even fuck a she-goat if you put a strap on it."

"Exactly," Richelle said like Marty had just admitted to partaking in satanic rituals. "That's just one reason not to fuck with them. They'd give you goat AIDS or some shit."

Marty scornfully sucked her teeth. "Whatever, man. I always use dental dams and shit. I ever wear a raincoat on my strap." She laughed long and hard like she'd made the biggest joke. "But I'd never do what Rémi did. I'd never marry a bi bitch. That's just fucking nasty." She gave a theatrical shudder.

The food Sage had eaten earlier turned over in her stomach. She knew a lot of lesbians didn't do the bi thing, but the way they talked about people in their own community... Nuria. Phil. She fisted her hand on top of her thigh to stop its tremor while at the same time, deep inside, she squirmed. Was this how she sounded when she'd talked to Nuria, and to Phil? No. No way. "You don't know how stupid you sound saying that shit."

"Yeah." Hope narrowed her eyes at Marty. "What's the difference? A night eating diseased pussy or a lifetime with it? Why would you risk your life like that? Condoms break all the time. Before you know it, you'll be pissing blood and have a fucking crab colony crawling around all in your shit."

Sage clenched her teeth so hard she swore her jaw creaked. "This is some old school shit you all are spouting right now. If anything, it's fucking all these lesbian broads back to back like you all do that will give you some shit to make your pussy fall out. Or even me. I love to fuck and I don't always use protection. Sure, I only fuck lesbians, but a lot of these chicks get around a lot just like I do."

"So, what? Are you defending that disgusting lifestyle now?"

Disgusting lifestyle? "Do you even hear yourself? You sound like those fucking straight bigots."

"Well, shit, you sound like you want to marry some bi-chick."

"Yeah. Is that what you want to do?"

It felt like the entire table turned to look at her and Sage just barely stopped herself from opening her mouth and popping out with some defensive, apologizing shit. "If I did, there's nothing wrong with it. We can't talk about wanting equality and respect when the next second we're talking shit about part of our own community and saying they don't deserve to get married and be happy like you just because they get off different from you. That's really fucked up."

A fist thudded on the table. "Chill, y'all. Damn!" Candler swung her head around to look at Sage. "I'm sure Richelle was just joking."

"I wasn't, and you know it. You've known me long enough to know what I think about that bisexual mess."

"Yeah. But you don't have to shout that shit from the rooftops. Especially not here."

The club prided itself on being inclusive. Not necessarily to straights but everybody who claimed to be part of the rainbow and wanted to watch some live sex. It was a policy they stamped on the door and on flyer invites to their parties. No biphobia, transphobia, or homophobia allowed. Sage didn't realize she'd memorized the policy until it popped into her brain.

"Y'all are a mess. You know those people carry more diseases than the rest of us and you still playing games." Richelle sucked her teeth, a true Jamaican in that moment. "Go ahead, fuck around and get gonorrhea of the throat." Cutting her eyes at everyone else at the table, she grabbed her drink and gulped down the entire glass.

This entire conversation was crazy. It didn't even seem real. Sage leaned toward Richelle, intent on asking her when she'd gotten her facts from. But the room suddenly plunged into a deeper darkness. A rainbow of strobe lights flashed then they were left in the dark again.

Sage blinked away the spots of light, after-image of the sudden brightness, and realized that while they'd been in the midst of their "discussion," movement happening on the stage. The lights in the main room dropped even more, covering them in complete darkness.

The waitresses and waiters were mostly gone, only the faint glow from their bowties gave away where they were, most lining the edges of the room. A spotlight dropped in the middle of the stage, surrounding a dark-clad figure who posed in silence for a few seconds, allowing time for anyone watching—and most of the club *was* watching—time to appreciate their outfit. The dick-hugging onesie, tight enough to show off the hard but supple body they were obviously proud of, was as tight as a figure skater's costume and just as dramatic with a V-neck low enough to show off curling chest hair and the lower part of their six-pack. It sparkled like it was made entirely of tiny crystals, winked outrageously in the spotlight and threw arcs of brightly colored light all over the stage. They did a slow turn and the audience obligingly let loose with a series of piercing wolf whistles.

"Ladies, gentlemen, darlings of all sorts and inclinations! Welcome to Friday Flight of Fancy." They preened again, moving around the stage with feline grace, the fire flash of the crystals accentuating every step. "We have a special treat—" A wink fluttered one wide fan of eyelashes and Sage realized then that the lashes were dotted in crystals, or at least glitter, too.

A song began to play.

Limit to Your Love by James Blake.

One of Phillida's favorites.

"I won't say too much more," the vision on the stage giggled. "I wouldn't want to spoil the surprise. Just welcome to the stage tonight's star, Silvia, Mistress of the Night." They flung up an arm, fingers pointed toward the ceiling and everyone looked up automatically.

A gasp of appreciation.

A woman hung, suspended in purple silks from the high ceiling, one leg twisted in the fabric, her body bare.

No, not bare. Sage blinked to get rid of the illusion of nakedness.

The woman actually wore a flesh-colored leotard with sparkling black sequins swirled over the shape of her breasts and her pussy. Her hair, thick and big and natural, was caught in a bun at the top of her head. She flashed bright teeth at the audience a moment before she made a motion and the fabric released her. She rolled, over and over, faster and faster, toward the floor.

She was going to fall!

But no. She stopped her lightning-fast descent barely a foot from the floor, lifted her bowed head and smiled at the audience again. Now that she was lower, Sage saw that she had very sharp teeth, actual fangs that looked deadly in the frame of her deep burgundy lips.

IS IT TRUTH OR DARE...

SLOWLY, gracefully, she released herself from the shimmering purple silks.

"Welcome, darlings," she purred to the audience, her voice clear and lush, despite the presence of the over-long teeth. "I am Silvia." Sage had expected to hear a lisp at the very least. "Thank you for coming." She turned, leaving her back to the audience, showing off the truly bare and slender length of her back, the flesh smooth with muscles moving beneath the pretty skin. "Tonight, I'd very much love to make one of you come." A rumble of excited interest rolled through the now crowded main room. "Any volunteers?"

Although she had other things on her mind, Sage couldn't make her way through the club in this darkness and she didn't want to be *that* asshole with her phone flashlight distracting everyone from what they came to see. But she also wanted to leave.

Lights flashed out onto the audience then, showing the dozens of hands flashing up to accept the challenge of volunteering for whatever Silvia, Mistress of the Night, had in mind. A hand near the front was way up, the woman standing and waving her gloved hand back and forth. The gloves looked like black leather, very soft and very expensive.

Silvia looked over the audience with a satisfied gleam and her eyes must have caught the same woman who had drawn Sage's eye. "You there, with the black glove on. Come, if you dare, be my tasty treat for the night."

A whimper of disappointment and frustrated longing came from a nearby table. Sage almost smiled. There were too many people at the show and interested in being played with for anyone to stand a real chance of being chosen. And she half suspected they had a plant in the audience ready to jump up when the call for volunteers came. Sometimes the games they played were far, far beyond what an amateur would be comfortable with.

Even before Silvia had finished announcing her choice, the gloved hand disappeared, a chair screeched loudly back and a slender woman was walking toward the stage. The spotlight followed her youthful, hip-swinging movements toward the toothy dominatrix. The little volunteer looked young. Almost too young. And there was something about her. Something...

Fuck no...

Crystal, and there was no doubt in Sage's mind that this was young-as-fuck Crystal, glided up to the stage, her movements stiff, her smile wide and full of false bravado.

"That chick looks crazy young," one of the assholes at her table muttered.

No shit. If Crystal's overprotective brothers and sister thought what Sage had done with Crystal was something to make threats over, then this was going to drive them straight into homicidal territory. What the hell was that girl thinking?

"Yeah. She must have a hell of a fake ID to even get in here."

"Her parents should kick the damn doorman's ass."

But the folks at the door of Shadows and Vine were diligent as hell. They didn't allow just anyone to stroll through their doors and up on the stage to get sliced up—or whatever—by a hot sadist.

Maybe Crystal knew somebody. Or maybe she'd fooled the woman at the door just like she'd fooled Sage. And the woman at the door only let her in the door, not fucked her on the couch of her little student apartment in some twisted idea of revenge.

Sage's cheeks burned. Yeah, she messed that one up. Big time.

On stage, the lights hugging Silvia's sleek and magnetic form slowly spread out. Gradually, they revealed some sort of medical tray, gloves, sterile looking instruments gleaming in the light, liquids in sealed bottled. A low leather chair waited near the small table of instruments. And next to the tray, a more comfortable looking leather chair with chrome armrests and a tall back.

What the fuck? Did Crystal even know what she was getting herself into here?

"Come, my dear," Silvia practically purred as she drew Crystal up to the stage and to the leather chair.

The leather chair sank slightly with Crystal's weight and Silvia smiled down at her, white teeth gleaming and predatory. Then she strapped Crystal's arms to the chrome armrests with a pair of thick leather cuffs.

Silvia looked ready to eat Crystal alive. With a negligent turn of a gloved hand, Silva slowly turned the chair Crystal sat on, showing off the girl to the audience. Her long neck and pretty face, the tight and high breasts under the deep V-neck of her blouse. The thick thighs and long legs wrapped up tight in leather pants.

The chair didn't so much as squeak. But the audience thrummed with excitement. To Sage, it seemed like it held its collective breath. Yeah, the women at her table talked about young Crystal was, but that didn't stop them from staring at her with appreciation. She was young, looked on the edge of maturity but still firmly there. The pulse in her long-bared neck thrummed fast. That much was obvious in the light shining on her.

Her lashes fluttered wildly against her cheeks and she licked her lips.

"Are you happy to be here, darling?" Silvia stroked a long finger down Crystal's neck, right along that runaway pulse.

"Y...yes."

"Hmmm." The fingers on Crystal's neck skimmed lower, down her chest, following the bared V of skin. "I guess I'll take that for now." Silvia pinched her nipple through the shirt and Crystal yelped. The audience tittered. Silvia hummed again.

With a few graceful and seductive motions, Silvia produced

disinfectant from somewhere—the smell of it was sudden and bright in the room—and wiped down the side of Crystal's neck.

The girl blinked at the audience, eyes looking furiously around.

Was she searching for somebody out there?

A needle appeared in Silvia's hand and, after raising an eyebrow at the audience and giving a wide-teethed grin, she slid the needle into Crystal's neck.

A slow gasp of pain poured out of her. Two drips of blood welled up on both sides of the needle, brilliant rubies on her sepia skin, and Silvia licked them away.

Sage sat up in her chair. This didn't feel right.

But Crystal didn't call out to put a stop to it. If anything, she slumped back in the chair. Her eyes still blinked widely though. Still searched the audience. When Silvia touched her neck again, she moaned, a broken sound that was nothing like the noises she made when she was turned on.

The tall woman's hands moved at Crystal's throat, slowly with an almost machine-like efficiency. When her hands moved away, Sage could see a piercing at Crystal's neck like a vampire had bitten her, leaving two pinpricks of light, diamonds, instead of rubies. Or blood.

The audience applauded. Shit. The sudden jewelry was as pretty as it was unexpected. Then Silvia took off Crystal's blouse.

Her small bare breasts. Nipples soft. The delicate weight of them vulnerable under the bright lights.

Silvia tilted Crystal back in the chair so everyone could see her. "Isn't she gorgeous?"

From the looks on the faces Sage could see in the dark, nobody disagreed. Crystal was young and cute, firm everywhere with a filthy innocence Sage knew from first-hand experience.

On the stage, Crystal slumped in the chair and Silvia turned her to her side was to the audience and to the camera broadcasting her every moan and whimper on the projected image big enough for everyone in the club to see.

Silvia's gloved hands produced another antiseptic wipe, and this time, she cleaned down Crystal's entire left side.

Wait a second... Was she going to puncture down the girl's entire side?

Crystal whimpered again and curled up in the chair.

Silvia leaned closer to her and the monitor showed her glowing eyes, the way they focused on the throbbing vein in Crystal's throat, the piercing she already put there, on the girl's obvious fear.

Sage knew vampires didn't exist. But in that moment, with the scene playing out on the stage, she could've sworn in front of a court, on an entire stack of bibles that Silvia was a real vampire and she was about to drain Crystal dry.

On the screen and in living color on stage, Silvia slid a green-handled needle into Crystal's side and the girl cried out, at the spike of pain looking more alert than before, her lower lip trembling, eyes darting back and forth between Silvia and the audience.

With that sound, a feeling of *wrong* twisted in Sage's gut. Crystal didn't want to be there. She was crying out for help with each twitch of her eyes although she wasn't saying a word. She only spoke with her tiny teeth bared and lips spread wide in a rictus of a grin. But her eyes were wide pools of sheer panic.

"I don't think that girl is really into that shit."

From the look on her face, Crystal looked one breath away from screaming her head off. At least she would if she had any sense of self-preservation. But from what Sage knew of her so far, she had a child's trust in the world, or maybe that was just naïveté.

Crystal whimpered then and turned her panicked eyes to the camera. She couldn't have screamed for help any louder.

Sage couldn't watch any more of this shit. She jumped up, ignoring the looks the other women at her table gave her, and rushed toward the stage, with the light of her phone, carefully navigating between the tables until she was at the stage, jumped up to the platform where Crystal lay obviously paralyzed with fear. The spotlights were hot on her neck, her back, instantly prickling up sweat along her hairline.

"She's done here." She bent down to undo the buckles strapping her arms to the chair. Despite the hot lights, Crystal's skin was cold to the touch. Was she in shock?

Silvia stood to her full and intimidating height. So close, she was over six feet in the high heels she'd put on once getting off the trapeze silks. Her intense gaze burned into Sage. "This is none of your business."

Sage wouldn't have been surprised if she'd ended that statement calling her "human." Yeah, this shit was too much.

The woman moved closer with her menacing height and snarling teeth. But Sage had never been one for being intimated by strangers she didn't know anything about. Being short all her life, she'd had to gauge threats and deal with them as they came, not allowing her height disadvantage to deprive her of anything she wanted. She ignored Silvia, finished unbuckling Crystal and pulled the girl gently to her feet. She whimpered and fell into Sage's arms, her own arms clutching Sage around the waist while her big eyes plead for something Sage didn't have to offer.

"She's scared," Sage muttered, shrugging off her thin jacket and wrapping it around Crystal's shoulders. "If you're too dumb to see that then maybe you shouldn't be doing this."

The dominatrix moved abruptly closer, her clawed hand reaching out and Sage doubted it was to give her a high five. The MC appeared out of nowhere, mic held behind their back. "Maybe you should let this one go, Silvia. We probably shouldn't have picked her anyway."

Silvia said something but Sage didn't wait around to see what it was. With a low grunt, she lifted Crystal into her arms and took her off the stage. She breathed a thankful sigh, grateful for the spotlight that followed her off the platform and guiding her toward the exit. A muttering of voices rose up, getting louder and louder with each step she walked through the crowded room.

"Is this for real?"

"I think it's part of the show."

"There's no way I'd let somebody snatch my sub out of a scene like that!"

Sage ignored it all and waded through the crowd, the nearly dead weight of Crystal, clinging and whimpering, getting heavier with each step. But she didn't stop. She didn't even want to take the chance of going into their bathroom. There was no telling what would happen in there.

Although she'd been coming to Shadows and Vine for years and trusted them as much as she trusted a place to serve her and her friends good drinks, the minute they'd allowed a sadist to start working on an obvious newbie, warm-up or not, was the moment they lost her as a customer.

With the show going on, the crowd was thin at the door but still with at least a dozen people making their way through the corridor and she turned sideways, bumping people out of the way as gently as she could with "excuse me" on her lips. Most moved quickly out of her way once they eyeballed the situation. The hostess at the door jumped to her feet behind the podium.

"Is she all right?" She moved toward Sage and Crystal but she swung the girl out of reach, holding her protectively against her chest.

"She just needs to get out of here," Sage said. Her arms burned from carrying the girl's weight but there was no way she was letting her go.

"Okay, okay." She pointed toward another door where only a

single bouncer, thick with muscle, stood with his gaze moving constantly and carefully around the club. "Through there."

And then they were out in the fresh air, Sage gulping in the more plentiful oxygen free of the scent of leather and antiseptic and arousal. After a quick scan of the parking lot, she found her SUV, headed for it with Crystal stirring and muttering into her chest.

"You came to get me." Crystal blinked up at Sage, her smile wobbly around the edges.

What? Before Sage could give a proper response, a shout drew her attention.

"Hey! Sage!"

Rémi and Dez, both dressed in dark jeans and summer leather jackets were practically running toward her. "What's going on?" Rémi was the one who spoke.

She jerked her head toward Crystal who still flopped in her arms but stared at the newcomers with no recognition in her face. Another pathetic sound left her throat. "She volunteered to be part of the show tonight. I don't think she knew what she was getting into."

Dez came closer, dark eyes quickly taking in the situation. "Does she need to go to the hospital?" She already had her phone out.

"I don't think so. Maybe a place to chill for a second. I was just going to put her in my car and clean her up with the first aid kit in my trunk." The single needle in her side bled sluggishly.

"Put her in the back seat of my truck," Rémi said, instantly taking charge. "I'll get your first aid kit and we'll get her someplace safe."

Dez grabbed the kit from Sage's trunk while Rémi opened her truck, yanked open the door to the back seat and stood back while Sage pulled the still mumbling girl carefully against the leather. Once Crystal was settled, resting on her side so there wasn't any pressure on the needles, Sage got in beside her. Nearby, she heard Rémi speaking, soft words she couldn't hear, into her cell phone.

"Here." Dez handed her the medical kit and stood back.

"You should probably take out those needles."

"Yeah." Carefully, she pulled it free, wiping the wound with antiseptic wipes before putting antibiotics on it, then put a band-aid on it. "She's good," Sage said.

"Cool."

Rémi slammed the back door shut an instant before did the same to the opposite door. They both climbed into the front seat, then they were on the way, carefully pulling out of the parking lot.

"What the fuck happened?" Rémi twisted to look back at Sage and Crystal. "I thought you weren't coming out tonight."

"Yeah. I..." What the hell had she been doing? What had she been thinking? It had all been guilt and helplessness, tangled feelings that everything to do with Phil. She'd wanted an outlet and got this instead. "Shit... I don't know what I was thinking."

"And the other thing?" Dez jerked her head toward Crystal while Rémi stayed ominously silent, only driving the truck toward whatever "safe place" she thought they needed.

"She volunteered to be part of the scene tonight. She wasn't ready."

"I thought they had plants in the audience," Rémi said, speaking for the first time.

"Yeah." Dez frowned probably thinking back, like Sage was, to all those times they'd watched similar scenes and the obviously prearranged bottoms went up on the stage, eager and obviously experienced.

"Shit, I thought so too. When they picked her, I thought she was just some woman they'd picked in advance." Until she saw Crystal's face and realized that no way did this goal know what she was about to in for. "She's tricky. She may look fucking innocent but she's tricky. I wouldn't be surprised if she managed to switch with the regular girl."

"Why would she do something so stupid?"

Sage clamped her mouth shut.

But without looking in the back seat, Rémi got it in one. "No fucking way..."

"What?" Dez looked confused.

"Is she that young chick you fucked the other day?" Rémi asked the question although she obviously already knew the answer. "Phil said something about her stalking you."

"She's not stalking me." But even Sage wasn't convinced by her weak-sounding defense.

Dez snorted. "I thought you weren't into the young ones. Isn't that what you said the other day?"

"Why does everybody keep throwing that shit in my face?"

"Then don't say shit that will come back to haunt you."

Sage felt Crystal's eyes on them the whole time, watching each of them as the accusations flew. "What were you doing at that place?" she asked, her voice low.

"I... I just felt like going out."

"In case anybody in this car feels like telling the truth, I'm sitting right here and ready to hear it," Rémi muttered something else Sage was too distracted to hear. Moments later, the SUV pulled into a quiet driveway. Rémi's house. Of course.

"Okay." Dez undid her seatbelt, climbed out of the car. "Let's put her in my old room."

"All right."

Right. This wasn't weird at all. Sage's teenaged fuck holed up in Dez's old room that happened to be in the house Rémi now shared with her hot lover, aka Dez's mom. Sage wiped a hand over her face, winced at the smell of antiseptic that clung to it despite the gloves she'd worn while seeing to Crystal.

While she talked Crystal into sitting up, Dez unlocked the front door and moments later, a slender shape in a thin nightgown and robe appeared in the doorway. Claudia. "Do you need any help, love?"

"I think we'll be okay." Rémi lowered her head to bury her face in Claudia's throat, muffling her next words. Then she pulled back. "Did you get the room ready?"

"Of course. I have some aspirin for her too is she needs it."

Together, they helped Crystal, unresisting and silent, into the house and down the quiet hallway to the room Sage had visited countless times as a kid. The sheets were already pulled back and she tucked Crystal under the sheets after taking off her shoes.

Claudia appeared on the other side of the bed with a small glass of orange. "Here's some juice. It'll help settle her nerves." Without being asked, she sat down on the bed. "Hi, sweetheart. Can you drink this for me?" She moved the glass toward Crystal's mouth but the girl turned her head away, whimpering.

"She'll take it if Sage gives it to her," Rémi said from behind Claudia.

Sage scowled at them both but took the juice from Claudia without saying a word, helped Crystal to sit up. "Drink this."

The room was loud with silent "I told you so's" as Crystal, propped up with Sage's hand behind her head, obediently opened her mouth and started to drink.

Sage felt her face heat, the warmth of Crystal's head into her palm only helping to singe her all the way through with embarrassment. Someone cleared their throat.

"Let's give them a little room." That was Claudia, ever practical.

Even though she wasn't looking up, Sage felt most of them leave, their mostly silent footsteps trooping out of the room until she was alone with Crystal and Dez sitting quietly in the chair on the other side of the room. Her friend didn't say anything.

With a soft sound and a movement of her head, Crystal signaled she was done drinking.

"Get her to take one of the pills mom left."

Sure enough, there was a bottle on the nearby bedside table, labeled as extra strength with Codeine. Should the girl be taking anything that strong? It was only what amounted to a demo piercing for fuck's sake.

"It'll also help her sleep," Dez said. "She might not be up for the embarrassment of facing all this," she gestured to the room and beyond. "—right now."

Yeah. That decided it. She put a tablet near Crystal's mouth. "Just one more sip to swallow this."

Once again, the girl obediently opened her mouth. Once the pill was down her throat with another swallow of the orange juice, Sage let her rest back into the pillows. Crystal looked up at her with gratitude, a trembling smile, a look on her face that Sage couldn't even begin to interpret. With a sigh, Crystal turned on her side and pulled the sheet even further up to her chin, but she only turned so far, tucking herself in bed to keep pressure off the punctures and, Sage noticed with a wince, keep Sage in her sight.

"You're such an idiot," Dez muttered.

She was afraid her friend was right. Letting loose another unavoidable sigh, she awkwardly patted Crystal's hand. "Get some rest, okay."

"Okay." Her reply was soft, already threaded with sleep.

Once her eyes closed, Sage stood up and felt Dez begin to follow her out. The house itself was silent though a low light blazed in the living room. From habit, she took the path through the comfortable room where she'd spent too many years with her friends and followed the well-worn path to the double doors leading outside and to the pool. Once she opened the door with a soft click, the sound of quiet conversation flowed toward her.

They were by the pool. Claudia and Rémi sat shoulder to

shoulder on the edge of the pool, their bare legs dangling in the water as they spoke, low-voiced. Rémi's half-boots lay discarded nearby, her slacks rolled up to the knees. Sage hesitated, as always, a little thrown by their intimacy. But Dez only came up from behind her, dropped into one of the lounge chairs, sprawled on her back and toed off her shoes.

"What the fuck, Sage?" The look Dez gave her should have incinerated her where she stood. But she ignored her friend and took one of the chairs on the opposite side of the pool.

"Did she manage to fall asleep?" Claudia asked, her voice threaded with concern.

"She did," Sage answered. "Thank you for the pills."

Although she'd stopped referring to her as "Mrs. Nichols" or "Mrs. N" a few years before, she'd never gotten out of the habit of paying the most careful respect to Claudia Nichols. Not only was she not "Mrs" anything, she was fully Rémi's woman now and had very little to do with the man who Dez and her twin called father.

"You're welcome." Claudia gave her a comforting smile although Sage didn't know why when it was Crystal who needed soothing, not her.

"You look twitchy, man." Rémi tipped slightly sideways, resting her cheek momentarily against Claudia's, and arched an eyebrow at Sage. "You okay."

"I'm cool."

A disbelieving grunt came from Dez's direction even though her eyes focused on her phone, thumbs flying on its surface as she texted somebody. Probably her wife. Claudia's low voice said something Sage couldn't hear and Rémi responded with a stroking hand down her girlfriend's back. Sage chewed the inside of her lip and looked away.

For so long, she'd thought that she and Phil had what her friends were missing out on. Perfect companionship. But with that notion completely fucked out of the water, it hurt to be in the house where so much love obviously lived.

A sharp ache radiated from under Sage's breastbone. "I should go," she muttered, stumbling to her feet and fully intending to leave and get a cab back to Shadows and Vine where she'd left her car.

"Go and do what, leave your jailbait here?" Rémi looked at her like she'd lost her mind. "Nope."

"Yeah, that's not smart, Sage."

Fuck smart. She didn't sign up for any of this. Not the pain, certainly not for some child to...to... Shit. Make a mistake that could easily have made at that age.

"Fine. You're right. Let me just figure out what to do and then—"

The patio doors slid open and Phil spilled through them, tall and narrow-eyed on her queen purple stilettos. "What's going on?"

"What are you doing here?" Sage stood up, heart suddenly hammering in her chest.

"You didn't answer my question." Phil left the door open and moved closer, her high heels clacking on the concrete.

Sage was just about to tell her to shut the door the way she'd found it when Nuria came up behind her and took in the scene with a single sweep of her thoroughly unamused gaze. They were together? She came back to the conversation just in time to hear Phil ask Dez the same question she'd asked of Sage.

Dez slid her phone back in her pants pocket. "You saw my text. The girl is passed out in the guest bedroom now."

Was everybody ganging up on her now? "You told her about this?" Sage stared at them both.

"What?" Dez looked bored of their conversation already. "Was I supposed to keep this stupidness a secret? From Phil? Naw, man."

From the corner of her eye, Sage saw Nuria slid off her shoes and join Rémi and Claudia at the pool's edge. She kissed both women on the cheek then sat down, feet in the water to watch it all like it was a telenovela.

"First of all, I thought *we* all had plans to go to Shadows and Vine together." Phil used a single finger to indicate everyone on the patio. "And second—"

"But you weren't there, you and Nuria were someplace else."

"Jealous, honey?" Nuria looked amused.

"Right." But it wasn't too far off. Although she didn't know who she was more...possessive of. Nuria who was supposed to be her best friend but was cozying up with Phil probably talking bisexuality together. Or Phil, who she still thought of, despite all the bullshit, as her better-than-a-best-friend. Someone she shared everything with, including all the fucked-up shit about herself.

"If you want to know what we talked about, all you have to do is ask." Phil stood over her, a hip cocked in challenge. Her posture was combative but her eyes were soft, a melancholy cloud obscuring their usual vivacity. But she'd be a self-deluding fool if she didn't know what that look was about or why it was even on Phil's face in the first place. "But wait, that's right, you don't really want to know everything about me. Just the things that you find acceptable."

"Girls, please." Claudia's voice cut through the warm night. But other than settling her gaze on them both, she did nothing else. Said, nothing else.

But Rémi didn't have any such reluctance. "You two get your shit together. That girl in there needs help, no matter how or why that came about. Deal with her, take her back where she belongs and deal with your shit. This has gone on for far too long."

"You can't tell everybody what to do, Rémi. This isn't your fucking playroom."

Rémi's green-flecked eyes turned ice cold. She looked at Nuria. "Deal with your friend."

Water splashed up as she took her feet out of the pool then stood up, reaching for Claudia's hand to help her to stand up. Moments later, the couple disappeared into the house, the slide and snap of the glass doors a final and loud sound in the silence.

"I'm going to check on this little girl," Phil said before she too left and went inside the house.

"How the hell do you manage to upset Rémi of all people?" Dez rolled her eyes then, getting to her feet with a grunt, dragged her phone back out to send what Sage assumed to be another text. "I'm heading home. Let me know if you need any help with this mess. Phil said her people wanted to kick your ass the other night. You know if they want to throw down, Rémi and I got your back."

Yeah, she knew that. But this situation felt even more ridiculous than usual.

"Thanks," she said. "I'll deal with all this. It's no big deal."

"Okay." Dez dragged out the word, filling it with all kinds of doubt. "You know how to reach me. I'm heading back home to the wife."

But in a split second, her look turned from annoyed to infatuated with the mention of Victoria. Hardly "the wife," and definitely the love of her life who'd pulled Dez from her whoring, self-destructive ways and given her the balance that none of them had even known she was looking for, least of all her.

"Cool," Dez said. "I'll call you later."

Then Sage was alone on the deck with Nuria, the pool sparkling turquoise and still rippling from the passage of Rémi and Claudia's feet. With the distance of feet separating them, Sage felt far indeed apart from her best friend. They hadn't been able to truly connect since that disastrous evening of Phil's revelation when Sage had proved herself to be even more of an asshole than she ever thought.

Sage cleared her throat. "So..." The awkwardness got even worse.

"So what?" Nuria gave her an unsympathetic look. "You want to ask what me and Phil talked about?"

"No. Not really. I can guess."

Nuria's low laugh wasn't the least bit amused. "I'm sure you'd be wrong though. Not everything revolves around you, honey-bunch."

"I wasn't thinking you all were talking about me!" she protested. "About the whole bi thing, sure."

"Which you'd turn into a whole thing about you. Poor betrayed, strictly clitly stud who wants nothing to do with real dicks and balls. Especially if they've been in her girlfriend's mouth."

Sage swore she nearly gagged. "Fuck! Stop. That's—"

"Gross?"

"Hell yes. But also unnecessary as fuck. I don't want to hear about any of that shit."

"From what Phil says, you don't want to hear about a lot of things. Have you always been such an asshole and I just never noticed it?"

Nuria's words had her stumbling back.

"What the hell is that supposed to mean?" Sage asked.

"If you need me to decipher that then I really can't help you." Nuria looked at her watch. "Anyway, let me get out of here. A little birdie told me you'll have your hands real full in the next few." Then she too was gone.

The loneliness of the evening pressed down on Sage. All her friends disappeared into the house and leaving her to her own twisting guilt. Then do something about it. That damn voice again. But what the hell could she do? It wasn't as if she could turn the clock back and make Phil not bisexual anymore. Even if she could pinpoint exactly when that change happened.

I'd never marry a bi bitch. That's just fucking nasty.

Was that what she'd become? Just another shitty stereotype of a narrow-minded stud? Marty's words stabbed her memory again, and her own reaction, not one strong enough to defend the women she loved against damn near strangers.

God, she was such a coward.

Moonlight shimmered over the pool's surface. Her rippling reflection. The water looked cool and inviting. At the very least it offered a moment's distraction from her thoughts, from everything. She imagined jumping into the water, boots and all, having the heaviness cover her mouth, her eyes, block out everything but the steady sound of her own heart beating. The tap of her boots against the concrete warned that she had moved closer to the edge. Her image wavered. The compact body, dark clothes, the misery eddying across her face.

"God..." This was not a good combination. She turned away from the water, hand reaching for her phone.

Phil stood in the open doorway leading to the house. She simply watched Sage's face, her own blank. Finally, she spoke. "I'm leaving."

"Okay."

She stood in the doorway for a moment longer, lips slightly parted like she had more to say. But then she just turned her back to Sage and went back into the house.

Silence again. The lure of the pool, the oblivion of the water. But no way. Sage took out her phone and called a cab. She'd just go back to the club, get her car then come back to pick up Crystal and take the girl back to her place. Hopefully, the coming of the morning would bring her back to her senses, her and Sage both.

But things didn't go quite as planned. When she came back with her car to get Crystal, the girl was already gone, taken someplace by Phil Rémi told her from the doorway, her growling voice betraying that she hadn't completely forgiven Sage for that crack about the playroom.

The surprise of it stayed with Sage long after she left Rémi and Claudia's house and arrived back to her own, found her way through the dark and into the guest room. She was too exhausted to stay up and worry. Sleep came quickly and thoroughly, sweeping away whatever lingering guilt and sadness that had nearly pushed her, fully clothed, into the pool.

Tomorrow. Everything would look better tomorrow.

CHAPTER TWENTY-ONE

She woke up to voices.

Low and soft. Two different tones rolling together in a harmony in the house she wasn't used to being separate from. Before falling into bed, she'd left the door open, certain there as no one in the house but her. Obviously, she'd been wrong.

Groaning quietly, Sage rolled over and buried her face in the pillow, the weight of her body pressing down into the sheets, her entire being feeling heavier than before, heavier than she remembered ever being in her life. Okay. She was ready for this to be over now.

She'd been fortunate. Her parents weren't poor. They never let her starve. She'd had the very best of friends who continued to stand by her through every fuckery and bad decision. But now, even with the uncertainty of her life with Phil and knowing now of the wasted years she could have had with her parents, she knew now that she'd had in damn good.

Laughter rang out through the house and slipped down the hallway and into the room she'd exiled herself in. She squinted at the watch still on her wrist. It was almost two in the afternoon. Past time for her to get up.

After shoving herself back into last night's clothes, she stumbled down the hallway, scrubbing a hand over her hair then rubbing her eyes. It was Phil's voice. She easily recognized the ringing bell of her laughter, the way it tapered off into giggles then a low and amused sigh. At the entrance to the living room, she nearly tripped over feet.

Wearing loose sleep pants and a tank top over bra-less breasts, Phil sat on the massive couch next to Crystal. A tray holding two small plates of food—breakfast made by Phil most likely—sat on the ottoman drawn close to their knees, and the smell of bacon and made-from-scratch biscuits trailed through the room from the kitchen.

Crystal looked almost happy, draped in one of Sage's faded button-down shirts she'd rolled up at the elbows. Her feet were bare, her hair in the usual ponytail as she sat curled up in the couch and talking with Phil.

They didn't notice her.

"What's up with your family? They're a little nuts, don't you think?" Phil asked Crystal.

"They're just overprotective. I'm the youngest and..." She shrugged like that explained everything.

Phil held a piece of bacon between two fingers. "They need to pump the brakes on that before somebody gets hurt." The bacon crunched loudly between her teeth.

"They wouldn't hurt anybody, especially not your girlfriend," Crystal said with a roll of her eyes. "Sage is your girlfriend, right?"

Phil made a doubtful noise. "Oh, okay." She slowly finished chewing the bacon in her mouth. "No, Sage isn't mine. Not anymore."

The pain from her words hit Sage sharp and low. This was her fault, but still...

Crystal pushed forward. "But you used to be?"

How did she know...? But before Sage could finish the thought, her eyes caught the Billboard Award trophy on its pedestal, the black and white portrait of her and Phil done barely two years before, Phil in a glittering evening dress, high-necked and obviously couture, sitting in the foreground, smoke rising from the cigar she held close to her unsmiling lips.

In the photo, Sage stood in the background wearing an A shirt, tattooed shoulders sleek with muscle, suspenders drooping down her thighs her arrogant face in profile. It was a portrait Phil had taken down when Sage's parents had come to visit. Even before they left town, she'd brought it back and put it where it belonged. Sage supposed that was only fair.

"Yes, we used to be." Phil plucked a piece of bacon from one of the two plates, bit into it while looking away from Crystal. In that quick movement, she noticed Sage. "Are you just going to lurk in the corner all morning or join us for breakfast?"

Her tone, joking and friendly, caught Sage off guard. Just last night, she looked like she wanted to rip Sage apart with her bare hands.

"I'm not sure," she said. But she slowly made her way into the living room anyway. "Is there coffee?"

"What's your nose telling you?"

Sage narrowed her eyes at Phil. So this was how it was going to be?

Scowling, she took a detour to the kitchen for coffee. The kitchen was an organized mess. A platter of bacon and eggs, carefully layered on top of paper towels that soaked up any remaining oil lay covered with a glass cake dome sat on the spotless kitchen island next to a basket of still warm biscuits.

Coffee waited, still fresh and smelling like a normal weekend afternoon in their house. Because she didn't eat pork, she knew the bacon was beef, because she didn't do white flour, the biscuits were wheat, and because flavored coffee was the devil, the Ethiopian Yirgacheffe was plain.

But when she grabbed the almond milk to pour into her mug, she found the hazelnut cream was dead center in the fridge. It always drove her crazy when Phil didn't put the condiments back in their proper compartment, the single thing in her life she was obsessively neat about. But she left it right where it was before closing the fridge.

When she got back into the living room, they were still sitting close, but Crystal had the tray on her lap and was devouring the sandwich she'd made from the biscuit, bacon, and scrambled eggs. Phil was doing most of the talking, but the young girl was nodding, making affirmative noises through her over-stuffed mouth.

"And it works for us," Phil was saying. "Or at least it did until recently."

Crystal muttered something that was obviously meant to be a question, but Sage didn't understand a word.

Apparently, Phil didn't either. "What did you say, honey?" Patiently nibbling on a sliver of bacon, she waited until Crystal swallowed her latest bite of the sandwich.

"What happened to change things?" Crystal asked.

Phil shrugged, then she looked up, pinning Sage with her eyes. "Things just happened."

"Right." Crystal went right back to eating her sandwich even after she noticed where Phil's attention had wandered. "So, you're not pissed that she fucked me?"

"I wouldn't say that." Phil's voice was desert dry. "We don't fuck for revenge, or at least we didn't. We fuck when or because we want to. Because it's fun. Not to get back at the other person."

"I get it. Your relationship is built on the love you have for each other, so the things you do even though they may seem like they're outside the relationship, they have to be somehow based on love too to keep the relationship together, even sacred in a way." A noise of understanding hummed from Crystal, a surprisingly mature noise from someone who Sage basically considered a kid. "So what Sage did must have been really messed up."

"I think so."

"Oh, jeez..." In that moment, Crystal sounded so much like a kid that Sage cringed. Had she really fucked this girl and thought it was okay?

The girl nibbled on her sandwich, obviously thinking too much.

"So would you...would you do it, too?" Hesitation laced Crystal's voice when she finally spokes, but she looked determined too.

Sage knew exactly what she was asking. She drew her breath in a sharp hiss, but the other two women in the room ignored her. This girl was so far past innocent. If only her rabid brothers and sister would get a damn clue.

"What are you talking about?" Phil asked with a frown.

Her girl wasn't being her usually sharp self, Sage thought with a surge of spite. "She wants to fuck you too," she said, acid spilling off her tongue.

Phil shifted her gaze to Crystal, the twitch at the corner of her mouth betraying her amusement. "Really, honey?" A clear, *it's never going to happen.*

"Well..." Crystal stammered and looked between Sage and Phil. "I mean you're in an open thing, right? And it's not that I'm asking you to revenge fuck me. You...you're being really nice to me."

"I didn't feed you so you'd owe me a fuck," Phil murmured. "I don't work that way, and if that's how you've been conducting your affairs you need to seriously evaluate some things."

"No!" Crystal put her sandwich down and sat up straight, twisting her fingers together in her lap like a child begging for candy. "It's not like that. I like you. Don't you like me?"

Sage rolled her eyes. God save them from needy kids. But when she settled her gaze on Phil, there was something soft in her face. Ah, she was probably remembering being a needy and gullible kid herself, always wanting to please. Bursting with hormones and longing.

"Honey, you don't owe me a thing." Phil regarded Crystal with the amount of patience Sage didn't have. "I'm...nice to you because it's the right thing to do, no matter how you came into my life."

But that didn't make Crystal back off. If anything, she came closer to Phil. "So what if I just want this? And I'm not saying you should fuck me because it's what I want, but..." She unbuttoned the shirt she wore and Sage winced because the damn girl hadn't even wiped the bacon grease from her hands. Then she wasn't thinking anymore because Crystal now sat on the couch with the shirt open all the way, her breasts bared and her tiny panties the only thing keeping her pussy covered. Then she pulled that off too. "Don't you want..." And it was almost laughable, the way she flashed her young body before Phil like Phil hadn't had fresh snatch before.

Phil sighed. She dipped her head to one side, the corners of her eyes pulling with sympathy, maybe even pity. "Cover yourself, honey."

"No!"

And Sage sat back, amazed, as Crystal climbed into Phil's lap, paused with their faces only inches away, then leaned in to tenderly kiss her on the mouth. That kiss was nothing like what she'd shared with Sage in her shabby little living room.

This was tender and curious, and aware. After only a few moments, she pulled back from the relatively chaste kiss, her mouth glistening with oil from their breakfast, and from Phil's mouth. Her face was painfully naked with want for Phil. For love.

"Okay, that's it," Sage said, standing up. Jealousy twisted in her stomach like a sickness. She didn't like the feeling. "Let me drive you home. This is getting out of control."

But Phil surprised them both when she shook her head. "It's okay." She draped her hands over Crystal's thighs, gripped them, then drew the girl closer until her crotch was flush against Phil's stomach. "Come here, honey."

Sometimes Sage forgot Phil didn't have the same hang-ups that she did. Or maybe she just wasn't a hypocrite. She'd never made any claims that girls—or *people* now, Sage supposed since she was all bisexual—under twenty-one were too young for her to fuck. Although before, she always said she was a lesbian, she'd never been stupid enough to say what or who she'd never do.

Phil tried something if she'd never had it, dismissed or embraced it as she was inclined and then moved on. She'd always been open to change, the lightning to Sage's steady earth. So it shouldn't have surprised Sage that Phil reached out to Crystal like a lover. But somehow it did.

Phil liked Sage, loved her, but they were not alike. It was easy to forget that sometimes.

As she watched, Phil drew Crystal in for another kiss. A slow press of her lips on one cheek, then the other, a more intimate European hello and goodbye. Whatever Crystal had expected, that wasn't it and she gasped, an unhappy sound.

"You're very sweet," Phil murmured once she drew back to take a long and thorough look at Crystal. A long finger stroked the girl's gently rounded cheek. "Which is why, I think, we should end the afternoon right here."

"Huh?" As Crystal realized what was happening, her eyes got big and round and sad. "But..."

Very gently, Phil moved the girl off her lap and onto the couch. "I was going to...to do something to prove a point. But I won't. I can't. I don't need to be cruel to you just because Sage was cruel to me."

Sage jerked where she sat. Cruel? No. That wasn't what Sage had done. Was it?

"But you're not being cruel! I want this." Crystal looked desperately at Phil who, Sage couldn't help but notice, was avoiding her eyes. "Please!"

"No, honey. Put your clothes back on. I let this little...whatever it is we're doing here, drag on for too long."

"Damn right," Sage muttered, although she second she spoke, she realized things would've been better off if she'd kept her mouth shut.

"Really?" Phil's eyebrow rose and she suddenly looked coldly furious. "So you're the only one who has the right to fuck her?"

Sage hissed out a breath. "That's not what I meant, and you know it."

"What did you mean then?" Phil snapped, instantly ready to defend herself against Sage's challenge. "Because I don't deal with double standards."

Aware of Crystal watching their fight while quickly yanking back on her panties and shirt, Sage squirmed. "Why don't you tell her what *you* did, Phil, instead of making me look like the bad guy."

"I'm not interested in making you look like the bad guy, honey." Phil sneered. You're doing a great job of that all on your own."

"What's the big deal then?" Crystal jumped in, eyes flicking between Sage and Phil. "Why can't you just say what happened?"

But Sage had had enough of her.

"Our relationship isn't here for your entertainment, Crystal," she snapped.

"We don't have a relationship." Phil arched an eyebrow. "Isn't that what you told me the other day at the beach?"

And there was the real knife in the ribs. A sharp pain, like an actual blade sinking into her side, pushing agony out of her chest and nearly up her throat, held Sage frozen, the breath locked in her chest. "That's not fair. If we didn't have a relationship, then why are you here in my house?"

"*Your* house?" Phil snarled. "You're such an asshole." The loose pants around her long legs fluttered when she stood up in a rush. "I don't know where Crystal lives and I thought it was better for her to sleep off whatever happened to her last night in the company of other people instead of being alone." She stalked out of the room. The sound of clanging came from the kitchen, the hard click of a mug on the marble island.

"You probably weren't together too long huh?" Crystal yawned and pushed her long hair out of her face. "You suck at relating to people. Even her. And she seems really nice."

She is nice, Sage wanted to say. But she clenched her teeth shut.

Moments later, Phil was back. "I'm going to head out," she said, barely looking at Sage. "I think you've got this under control now."

"What?" Sage jumped up then hissed when she spilled hot coffee all over her hand and thigh. She cursed, abandoned the mug on the side table and yanked the hot, wet cloth away from her skin. Fuck that hurt! "You're just going to leave her here?"

Phil's lips twisted with mockery. "What, are you afraid she's going to bite?"

"She already knows I'm not into that," Crystal called out, her voice on the edge of teasing.

Sage ignored her.

"You should stay, Phil." Suddenly, she didn't want Phil to go.

The thought of her leaving was unbearable. Now, with Phil in the house making coffee and lounging around in her pajamas like on a normal Saturday, it just seemed *right*. She took a step toward Phil but Phil stepped back and crossed her arms over her chest. Pain spasmed across her face.

"I'm leaving," she said and her voice was strong and unyielding. "And I'm taking your pretty piece of almost-jail bait with me." She raised her voice. "Come on, Crystal honey. I'm taking you home."

"What?!" Was she taking Crystal home to fuck her on the same couch that Sage had? That was too much, even for Phil.

Crystal's mind was obviously running along the same path as Sage's because she came running up to Phil, already dressed and grinning hard, in record time. "I'm ready!"

This was *not* okay. Sage opened her mouth. "Listen—"

Phil completely ignored Sage and just grabbed up her keys and stalked toward the door leading to the garage. Crystal practically plastered herself to her back.

"I can just put her in a cab, for fuck's sake!" Sage didn't embarrass herself by chasing them, but it was a close thing.

The sound of the garage door opening rattled her teeth and made her clench her fingers into the edges of the doorway way where she stood.

Don't go, she silently begged. *Please. Stay and fight with me. Anything but this.*

But Phil wasn't a mind reader and it wasn't long before her bright yellow Corvette backed out of the garage and the door rattled closed behind her.

After the last sounds of the garage door faded away, the emptiness of the house dropped down around her like an avalanche. Loud. Painful. Unbearable. Sage stood in the doorway, hands still clenched into the wood, waiting for...something.

But nothing came, and she eventually had to move.

The night came back to her. Crystal, needy and reaching out desperately for her. Phil, hurt and lashing out. While she just stood there, locked in her own uncertainty. In her fear.

Fuck.

Sage looked at her watch, then looked away. With nothing else to do, she cleaned up after the afternoon breakfast. Put the food away, washed the dishes. Wiped down the countertops and the kitchen island. An hour passed. Then two.

What the hell was she doing with Crystal for so long?

The same thing you did with her the other day, her stupid mind helpfully supplied. The unwanted images washed over her.

Phil pushing Crystal down into the couch. The two women entwined and naked. Pussies bared and grinding against each other. Phil cumming with a restrained shudder.

Would Crystal ask if she came? Would she even know what to do with a woman who didn't broadcast her orgasm to the world?

Another hour passed.

"I should leave," Sage said to the empty air.

But she didn't. Instead, in a fit of desperation, she called Dez. "Hey, what are you up to?"

"The usual." Dez's voice rumbled deep and content through the phone. "Just chillin' at home. Sorry I didn't call to check in on your situation this morning, by the way. Victoria and I got into something and..." Dez chuckled. "You know how it is."

Yeah, she did know how it is. Or she used to. She and Phil spent many a lazy Saturday morning having slow and sun-drenched sex before dragging their asses out of bed too late in the day to do anything useful.

"Yeah..." Sage said anyway. "That sounds pretty good." She scraped cold fingers through the thick curls at her crown.

"But *you* don't, though." Dez's voice lost some of its soft edges like she'd sat up wherever she was. "What's up? Did Phil make actual fish bait out of your little piece from last night?"

Her friends always knew to spear to the heart of things. "No, she...she took her home."

"Oh, really?" Dez's tone rang with all the suspicions Sage had had when Phil and Crystal left together.

"Yeah, but it's cool." Sage forced the words out.

"Because you two are done?"

"Something like that."

"Shit..." Dez drew out the curse word. "You're being such an idiot right now. How the fuck you can throw away twelve years on some bullshit is beyond me."

It *was* mostly bullshit. Even Sage had to admit that now. "I just don't know what the hell to do."

"Easy. Just grovel. Say you fucked up and prove that you want to change and stop being an actual asshole for a change. You know, we're too old to be doing this kind of crap."

Too old, too tired, too...everything.

"You know that's easier said than done, right?"

"Most things are. Doesn't mean we don't do them." The sound of movement and rustling cloth came at Sage through the phone. "When I fell for Ruben back in college, I was shocked." Ruben. The guy Dez ran off with after years of declaring herself a lesbian. "It felt like my whole world changed. My whole identity. That was partly why I ran away with him instead of staying here in Miami. I wouldn't have been able to take it if my friends rejected me because of who I was fucking." Dez sighed through the phone. "So I ran. When I came back to Miami for my mom, finding my way back to you guys was one of the hardest things I've ever done. I never told anybody, but I was so damn grateful for your acceptance. I don't know what I would've done if you'd turned me away. You didn't make a big deal out of who I'd been fucking—at least not to my face—and we carried on with our lives." Dez paused. "If you love Phil like you say you do, why can't you do the same thing for her?"

Thick emotion slithered down Sage's throat. "I do love her. Fuck...so much. But—" The sound of the garage door cut off the rest of what she wanted to say. She swallowed. "Listen, I gotta go. Phil is back."

That fact alone made her want to do cartwheels.

"Okay..." Dez's sigh blew harshly against the phone receiver and into Sage's ear. "Just be good to Phil. If you don't want her, let her go find happiness with somebody else."

Somebody else? The very idea twisted the rusty knife of jealousy already buried in Sage's gut. Then she thought about Zachary Baxter and his hand on Phil's that day in the restaurant. Her queasiness got worse.

"I gotta go." Despite the burn of tears, she managed to see enough of the phone screen to end the call.

What the hell was she turning into?

"That a private conversation?" Phil stepped into the living room, still in the sleep clothes she'd left the house in. She looked tired. "Is that why you ended the call so fast?"

She came close enough for Sage to smell her. No scent of sex. No cheap floral soap from Crystal's bathroom. The relief almost made Sage lightheaded.

"Nothing private. At least not in the way you're probably thinking," she said, although she wasn't entirely sure what Phil was thinking at this point. "It was just Dez."

Phil slid her a look laced with suspicion then hummed a noncommittal response as she walked through the living room and to the kitchen. Out of sight, Sage still tracked her movements through sound. The fridge door opening and closing, a glass clicking against the countertop. The gurgle of juice of being poured. She came into the living room with a glass of pineapple juice, no ice, and sank into the couch. There, she leaned her head back and closed her eyes on a sigh.

What happened out there with her and Crystal?

"So..."

Phil opened one eye but said nothing. She just waited.

Despite what her nose told her, the question spilled out anyway. "Did you and Crystal...?"

Slowly, Phil straightened in the couch. "What if I did?"

"Well, if you did, it would be okay. It's only fair." Sage carefully weighed her next words, wondering how exactly to phrase them.

Phil made an impatient noise. "Why don't you just ask the question that's really on your mind and stop dancing around it."

Fine. "Did you sleep with Baxter?" There, the question was out now.

"If I said yes, does that mean you're done with me?"

Weeks ago, the answer to that question would have been "hell yeah," but now Sage wasn't so clear. Other reasons for her anger, real reasons, were crowding into her consciousness and she just couldn't ignore them.

Still...

"I just don't want things to change between us," she said. As she spoke, she remembered Dez's words from before, about change being necessary. But she refused to believe that, not about her and Phil. "Before you...confessed, our life was perfect."

"Your life maybe, but not mine." Phil's soft words echoed dully for a moment.

But they cut like the sharpest of knives.

"That's so not true. You were happy. Just forget about that whole dick thing and stay with me. We're good together, you *know* that." Sage was so close to begging, she felt pathetic. But she was finally accepting that, no matter what Phil wanted, she was the woman she wanted. Phil just had to...stay.

Phil shoved the untouched glass of pineapple juice on the coffee table. "I can see why you kept yourself in the closet all these years. It wasn't because of your parents at all. You live in fear and expect everyone else to do the same. I won't do it anymore. I can't."

Sage stiffened. "I'm not afraid of anything. *You're* the one who's suddenly afraid of being a lesbian now. You just want to be straight and leave all this gay shit behind—"

"What?" Phil jumped to her feet, her eyes wide with anger and disappointment. "I— You know what? *Fuck* you." Phil spun and stalked down the hallway to the master bedroom, her voice burning a trail behind her. "I'm over this narrow-minded, selfish shit you have going on. I thought if I waited, if I didn't move out yet, if I showed you what we have... But no. I'm obviously the idiot Rémi accused me of being."

Not ready to let her out of her sight, Sage followed, slamming the bedroom door shut behind them. She wrenched on a light. "What do you mean? Phil come on. I just..." But she couldn't go on.

"You just want? Want to fuck that girl and eat me too, then claim all bisexuals fuck you up so you can carry on being the motherfuckin' martyr you've been acting like the last few weeks? No. I'm completely *done*." Phil's breath came quickly, the fury obvious in the spastic motions of her body, in the way she jerked Sage's clothes off her like they hurt. The tank top. The pants. Leaving her completely naked and striding toward the chair where her clothes from the night before lay neatly folded.

"Baby, wait..."

"No! You don't get to 'baby' me. Not now. Not ever. I'm through letting you fuck with me, with pretending none of this hurts me while you go through your crisis." She sneered the last word, yanking the black jeans over her legs one after the other. "Go find some pure fucking lesbian to put up with all your shit, and when she doesn't conform to your ideas of how people should behave and not change I'm sure you'll just dump her too and pretend the fault is all hers. Have a nice god damn life!" Her hands were trembling as she wrestled the buttons of her jeans closed then grabbed her blouse.

Sage grabbed her arm. "You know it's not like that!"

"All I know is what you told me, and what you showed me." Phil pulled the shirt over her head or at least tried to, but Sage yanked it away so she could see her face. Phil yanked it back with a low hiss. "I can't be someone else, Sage. Not even for you."

Phil jerked her shirt on and smoothed out her hair.

How the hell had they come to this?

Desperation rolled in Sage's chest, the truth clawing its way up her throat despite how many times she swallowed.

"I can't give you the damn kid you want!" Sage froze, her eyes wide, heart pounding like a war drum. "Can't you see that I can't do this? I can't watch you walk away from me with a man, knowing only a dick can give you what you've wanted for so long."

Silence echoed in the room. Then Phil drew a deep and trembling breath that pulled her body up tall and straight. She swallowed a few times before she spoke again. "I would never leave you. I thought you knew that."

Never was a long time when you wanted a kid and had no ready source of jizz to give it to you. She'd seen it enough in couples within the community.

"Phillida, don't make promises you can't keep," she said tiredly.

They stared at each other, no more words between them.

Phil finally spoke. "So this really has nothing to do with me being bisexual?"

"I didn't say that. It has everything to do with it. At least with the non-detachable dicks you want all of a sudden."

Turning away from her, Phil crossed her arms over her chest, looked out the large window splattering with the beginnings of rain. Darkness outside, artificial light and their chilly silence inside.

"I never asked for this, you know that," Phil said after a long time. Her narrow shoulders were stiff, her posture defensive like she was ready only for Sage to hurt her.

Sage didn't want to hurt her, not really. But she didn't know how to handle this. "But you want a kid. That's the thing you've been wanting for months now. Isn't it?"

Phil's shoulders rose and fell with her harsh breath. "Yes."

They'd danced around the issue, even half-way planned to make it happened, but like most things that happened with them, they didn't discuss, only assumed and moved forward.

"You know I can't give you that." Saying it felt like such a failure. So stupid.

"Yes, you can. You know you can. We've seen it happen." A few of Phil's tangential friends had either adopted or had kids through artificial insemination. It was the new lesbian "it thing" to do, she'd joked before. Her tone implying she wanted none of that.

"But how convenient is it that after that, you tell me you want some dick in your life? Too fucking coincidental, and you know that."

A bolt of lightning illuminated the pain on Phil's face and thunder shook the house. The rain came down harder, tapping an urgent SOS on the roof.

"If I'd wanted to skip the insemination clinic and get some dude to shove his dick into me just to get a baby, I would've said that. My being bi has nothing to do with that."

Sage shook her head. "I just don't want to lose you," she finally choked out.

"And that's why you just threw me away?"

"I didn't—"

"Yes, you did." Phil's voice vibrated with pain.

She didn't have to say anything else. The fucked-up details of the last few days streamed behind Sage's eyelids in vivid High-Definition. Hurt after hurt. Rejection after rejection. In the midst of it all, she'd felt justified, victimized even. But now, with distance and time and the woman she loved stoic and hard-eyed in front of her, she had no choice but to see the wreckage her actions had left behind.

"I'm sorry," Sage said.

"I know. But sometimes that's just not good enough." The sadness in Phil's voice twisted the knife of regret in Sage's chest.

The corners of Phil's eyes tightened. "I'm leaving for real this time. I stayed too long as it is." Her movements disjointed and stiff, she pulled on her high heels and grabbed her purse from the dresser. "I guess we'll talk later."

"Where are you going, anyway?" They'd talked a lot about Phil leaving but not a word about where she would go.

"I'm not sure yet, but I'll figure something out," Phil said, not breaking her stride.

Sage followed her from the bedroom. Other words crowded behind her lips, ready to tumble free and somehow convince Phil that...that she *was* sorry. She didn't pray very often, or at all, but she squeezed her hands into fists and prayed to every deity she'd ever heard of for Phil to stay and at least begin to forgive her.

Lightning flashed again, the rumble of thunder quick on its heels, and Sage felt the vibration of the thunder through her whole body. Then the world went dark. She almost bumped into Phil who stopped suddenly, both of them frozen in the sudden and absolute dark.

"Seriously? This is happening right now?" Phil, who already had her hand on the door to the garage, turned the doorknob and peered inside.

Everything was dark, the hulking shape of both their cars hidden in layers of shadow.

"Why did you park in there anyway?" Sage asked. "You could've just left your car in the driveway."

"Well, I didn't, okay?" Phil muttered, clearly annoyed.

"And now you're stuck here."

As butch as she claimed to be, Sage never bothered to find out how to open the garage door without electricity. Assuming there *was* a way.

"Well, my car may be stuck here, but I'm not. I'll just grab a cab for now and come get it later." Phil pulled her phone out of her purse. "Shit." She frowned down at the dark screen like it had done her wrong. "It's dead." The disgust, whether at the phone or at herself for not charging it, came through loud and clear.

"You can use mine," Sage said. They didn't have a house phone.

They went back into the bedroom to get Sage's phone, only to find it dark and dead, too. Another nine-hundred-dollar paperweight.

"You're fucking kidding me," Phil muttered.

Quick heat rushed into Sage's face but she refused to act like she was the one who had fucked up. She stepped back with crossed arms and peered up at Phil.

"Shit." Phil had the grace to look embarrassed. After all, she was the one who'd shown up at the house with a phone nearly dead. At least Sage had the excuse of being at home, a place where she regularly forgot to charge her phone unless Phil reminded her.

Phil turned away with a hiss of frustration and left the bedroom with a rapid click of high heels against the tile floors.

Shit. What were they going to do now?

Sage followed, carefully navigating her way through the darkened house and out the front door. The scent of the rainy evening rushed into Sage's nose. She breathed it in, caught up with and matched Phil's footsteps across the small verandah. With a quiet click, she opened the umbrella she'd grabbed from the stand on the way out and lifted it over Phil's head.

Phil smiled briefly at her in thanks.

The solar lamps along the walkway blushed in the dark, guiding their slow steps to the edge of the empty circular driveway. Rain, neither heavy nor light, tapped the umbrella over their heads. Rainwater eddied around Sage's bare feet.

The entire neighborhood was covered in gloom.

Warm evening airbrushed over Sage's bare shoulders and throat. She tilted her head back to look at the stars. They winked down at her from their place in the immense darkness like they had a secret to tell. But she had a feeling no secrets would be shared tonight. Not by the stars, not by anyone.

"Whose idea was it *not* to get a home phone again?"

"Yours," Sage answered, now watching the endless shadow that had become their neighborhood. Where did they even keep their flashlights? Did they even have batteries?

"We better go back inside," Phil said. "No use standing out there looking like targets in The Purge."

Sage rolled her eyes. "The first motherfucker who comes in here trying to Purge will get a bullet straight between their fucking eyeballs."

"You don't even know where we keep the gun," Phil said with a soft laugh.

"True."

Guided by the solar lamps, Sage made her way back into the house with Phil close by her side and still under the wide umbrella.

"So...now what?" Phil closed the door after Sage shook out the umbrella and slid it back into its low stand.

Details of her form were shrouded in shadow, but Sage could

clearly make out the confrontational lift of her shoulders.

Well, if it was one thing Sage wasn't in the mood for was more confrontation. She'd had enough of that for the day, thank you very much. She

"I don't know about you, but I could use a drink," she said. But first thing was first.

She lit the candles in the living room, nearly two dozen of them, with the silver lighter they kept easily accessible on the bookshelf. Candlelight flickered golden and soft around the room, lending the large space an intimacy, a softness it hadn't had in a long time. Raindrops drummed steadily on the roof, a sound like music. With the rain and candlelight, the gentle shadows hugging the room, it was easy to pretend the last few weeks hadn't happened.

A dangerous illusion.

Denim whispered against leather as Phil sank into the couch and lay back. "God... What did people do before electricity?"

"They went to bed early and got up with the sun. Maybe play board games?" Get drunk? Sage shrugged off her mild irritation and went for the bar where she fully intended to make herself a very large drink. "Thank God for progress and modern inventions."

"I'm sure kids today feel the same way about the internet and free porn."

"We've come so far..." She made two drinks, a rum and coke for herself and an extra dirty martini for Phil and walked them to the couch.

Phil murmured her thanks and sat up, reaching for the martini. A sip, then a low sigh left her mouth. "You haven't lost your touch," she said with a pointed purse of her lips. *You still know me,* her gaze said. *I haven't changed. Not really.*

"Maybe not that, but I lost my mind. Just a little."

And the divide between them came back sharply into focus.

"Did you find it again?" Phil sat with the martini glass tilted next to her mouth, her pose on the couch one of complete relaxation. Shoes off, long legs stretched out in the dark jeans, her shoulders back. But Sage knew her well enough to feel the tension practically vibrating from her. It tightened her mouth into a plush line.

"I'm trying to," Sage said.

She spoke softly, matching Phil's low tones. Maybe it was the candlelight. Maybe it was because tonight was the first time since being at Shadow and Vine with those other women, so-called friends, that she could see herself for what she'd become. What she'd done.

Darkness often changed things. It brought with it a clarity often missing during the day, a womblike space that nurtured the things that daylight obliterated.

Her father's words came back to her.

You're acting like the bigot you thought your mother was.

It hurt, but it also was true. Sage tried to lick the nervousness from her lips.

"I love you, Phil. I can't pretend anymore that I don't. And it hurt me, all this bad shit going on between us." She held up her hand when Phil opened mouth. "I know. This isn't about me. I know that. That's why I'm asking you, honestly, what do you want me to do with what you told me?"

It was a question she'd never asked, not really.

Phil's lashes fluttered down to hide her expression as she sipped her martini. All Sage could see was the wide fan of her lashes against her cheeks.

"What do you need, Phillida?" she asked again.

The glass in Phil's hand shook and quiet tears slid down her face and plopped, one by one, into the barely touched martini.

Phil looked up, her eyes big and wet. "I need us to stay us. I need the life that we planned together."

The lump in Sage's throat got bigger. "I'm scared—," She choked out the words. "—that I can't give you the kind of life you want now. I'm scared you'll find it with someone else."

"I'll never leave you," Phil said softly. She cradled the martini in her lap while fingers plucking at the stem of the glass. She met Sage's eyes as she spoke. "I told you that. Not for any woman, any man. Or even any kid that ends up in my belly. We swore this to each other. Remember?"

Sage nodded. Of course, she remembered. Even though she was the one who'd broken that promise.

If she so easily broke her word, what would stop Phil from doing the same thing?

But she knew Phil was would never do that. Her girl kept her word even about the smallest things. Appointments. Threats. Buying shit on their grocery list. Sage was the one who fucked up constantly. Hell, even the friction with her parents was her own damn fault. At some point, she had to start cleaning up her messes. Ice rattled in her glass as she put down the drink she'd barely touched.

"I've been an idiot, I know that, but I—"

A loud barrage of knocks at the front door cut off the rest of her words. The sound of voices rang out, too muffled for her to understand.

Sage spun toward the door. "What the fuck is that?"

Rain still pounded hard on the roof and the window panes blurred with lines of falling water. Who was out there at this time of night in this shit weather?

Their phones were dead. What if someone was trying to reach them?

What if something was wrong?

The flickering light from the candles showed the same questions on Phil's face. She and Phil rushed at the same time toward the front door.

"Who is it?" Phil asked just as Sage unlocked the door and yanked it open.

Someone could need help.

But no.

The lightning flashed again, illuminating the figure on their doorstep. A nameless terror seized Sage's chest and she almost slammed the door. It wasn't some masked boogeyman with a knife. It was Zachary Baxter.

The man was soaking wet, his hair plastered to his face and shoulders, clothes dripping water and stuck to his body from the steady rain.

Didn't this guy have to be in Hollywood someplace?

"What do you want?" she demanded.

Despite the drenching rain, he looked as comfortable as if he were standing on the deck of a yacht taking in some sun.

"I'm here to see Phillida," he said.

Nobody calls her that but me. The ineffectual words rattled around in Sage's brain.

"Zach." Phil came up from behind her, a hand on Sage's shoulder. "This is a surprise." She gave Sage a look, then pushed the door open wider. "Come out of the rain. There's no point in you standing there like a drowned rat."

"Thank you." He smiled faintly and stepped around Sage who was frozen in the entranceway. This guy was in her house. What was going on? What did this mean?

Baxter was steadily dripping rainwater in their foyer and for that alone, Sage was ready to shove him back out into the rain and say "good luck, bitch." But moments later, Phillida appeared with a large towel.

"Dry yourself, please." She looked at Sage again, "I promise she won't bite."

To make Phil into a liar, Sage growled.

The guy didn't look the least bit intimidated, though.

"Thanks for the towel but I'm only here for a few minutes." He took the towel and briskly ran it over his face and throat. "I'm heading out of town tonight and wanted to make sure I put this back in your hands."

"What...?"

He reached into his jeans pocket, pulled out an envelope, and gave it to Phil. "I know how special this is to you."

Phil opened the envelope and gasped. An echo of the sound that left Sage's throat.

A platinum chain with an infinity symbol glittered in Phil's palm. The belly chain Sage had given her years ago that she rarely took off.

"Oh my God, thank you!" Phil clenched her hand around it and gave Baxter a grateful smile. She moved forward like she was about to hug him but stopped herself at the last minute. A faint smile hitched up Baxter's mouth at her obvious hesitation. "I really appreciate that," Phil said. "I've been looking for it everywhere."

"I can imagine how frantic you were." He tipped his head Sage's way. "You're a very lucky woman, by the way."

Phil bit her lip, an unfamiliar look of indecision on her face. "You're a good man, Zach. Thank you!" Then she darted forward and gave Baxter a quick hug before stepping back. She stumbled into Sage who caught her easily, holding on for dear life.

"Don't get worked up, Sage," Baxter said. "For some reason, the only person she wants is you. If she'd given me half a chance, I'd be flying her to LA with me tonight or hell, maybe hanging around Miami for a while. But I guess it's true what they say, the good ones are always taken." He brushed gentle fingers across Phil's cheek. "Maybe I'll see you around," he said, then turned and walked back into the rain.

The door closed firmly behind him, leaving them in the loud silence.

Finally, Sage couldn't take it anymore. "What...what was that about?"

Phil licked her lips and brought her clenched fist, the one with the belly chain, to her chest. Her soft sigh whispered between them. In the darkness of the foyer with only the candles from the living room to give the faintest of light, she looked like a ghost, an ephemeral creature who was in Sage's home by illusion alone.

The thought suddenly struck Sage that if she blinked too long, Phil would disappear.

"You were there," Phil murmured in response to her question, then she headed back into the living room. "He returned something that belonged to me."

"How did he have it?"

"How do you think?"

"You had sex with him." It wasn't a question.

"Yes."

"And...?"

"Maybe I should ask you that question." Candlelight flickered over Phil's face as she made her way to the chair she'd been sitting in before Zachary Baxter came to the door. "Now you know I slept with a man. What does that mean for you, for us?"

It was all rocketing through Sage's brain at a thousand miles an hour. Baxter and his pretty face. His offer to take Phil to LA or to stay here. This was a man who made a living as an actor, who cared about Sage's woman enough to bring her back something that...

"You told him I gave that to you?" Sage nodded her head toward the belly chain.

"Yes," Phil said. "I told him about us before we did anything. I let him know I wasn't available for more than a fling...I just wanted to see what it was like." She'd never been with a man before.

"And?"

"It was good. He's a very intuitive lover and cares about his partner. He learns fast. Like you." Phil flashed a brief smile tinged with nervousness. "But he's not you. You're who I want as my partner."

Images flashed behind Sage's eyelids. Her woman with this man. But she pushed them away. No matter how good it had been between Phil and Baxter, that was just sex. In the end, it was nothing.

A weight that had been sitting on Sage's chest since she saw the actor at her door slowly eased away. "So, you're not leaving me for him?"

"You never listen when I talk, do you? I told you, I'm not leaving. You kicked me out and I'm still here, doesn't that say something?"

Yeah. It said that Sage had been a complete asshole. She'd almost thrown her happiness out the car window and backed up over it.

"Shit..." She collapsed into the couch at Phil's side.

The leather whispered faintly as Phil turned to look at her. "Yeah."

Sighing, she twined her fingers with Phil's and slid close enough to feel each exhale from her love's parted lips. The tenderness for her woman took over and left her stripped bare.

She'd never believed in things like guilt or penance. Weren't these concepts all just tied up in religion anyway? But now, she felt that terrifying sense of shame for what she'd done to Phil. To her love. Baby batter-filled dick or no, Zachary Baxter was no more a threat to her happy home than their casual female lovers had been. Sage was an idiot. The heretic in the sacred temple of their love.

Now, she needed to do penance.

"Saying I'm sorry isn't enough," Sage rasped through the tears clogging her throat. "I know that now."

Phil squeezed her fingers. "Do you?"

"Yes. I do. Tell me, how can I fix this?"

"Fix? I...I don't think anything was really broken," Phil said softly. "But this can't happen again."

"It won't." Sage knew she was talking about the craziness with Crystal, their stupid and unnecessary breakup, and everything else Sage had thrown in the way of them being happy. "I promise," she said.

Over the last few weeks, she'd crawled so far up into her own ass that she didn't realize the fucked-up shit she had been doing. Yes, Phil was bi. Yes, this was a big ass change. It wasn't going to be easy. But she couldn't leave her woman to struggle alone just because she was...struggling.

No judge or minister had given them a blessing, but their thing was for better or for worse. For as long as they both lived.

She promised Phil this years ago and, if necessary, she'd renew that promise.

She loved her woman. If nothing else, the thing with her parents showed that she was a coward. Nothing she didn't know before but, shit it was a hard lesson to learn in real life.

Because of this cowardice, she'd thrown away years of being close with her parents. She almost threw away the twelve years she'd with Phil and their chance of many more.

They lay on the couch together, their hands clasped together, and the night's shadows draped securely around them like a lovers' blanket. The silence between them was a tender absolution and she drifted peacefully toward sleep.

"I love you," Sage whispered just before she tumbled over its edge.

"I know." The soft words brushed her lips like a kiss.

In the darkness, she smiled.

EPILOGUE

The ocean stretched out on both sides of the highway and shimmered a brilliant turquoise blue under the late afternoon sun. Sage drove her SUV down Highway 1 toward the Key West, the steering wheel held lightly between her fingers.

She felt so happy it was a little disgusting.

In the passenger seat, Phil, wearing a bright blue bathing suit top and a sunshine yellow skirt, looked completely relaxed. She lay back in the seat with her bare feet up on the dashboard, her toes bright with blue polish. Watching the pretty, if monotonous, scenery pass by, Phil lolled her head against the backrest and hummed along to the Halsey song throbbing from the speakers.

In mid-hum, Phil lazily turned her head from the window. "Like what you see?"

"Always."

Her woman tipped her head in a sexy "come fuck me" look and Sage perked up in her pants. What was Phil up to now?

She kept her hands on the steering wheel, half of her attention on the road, the other firmly on Phillida.

They'd come a long way since that crazy night at the movie

premiere all those months ago, but there was still work left to do. Their problems hadn't been magically solved. Sage was still worried about the whole bisexuality thing. Still jealous. But she knew she wanted to keep Phil by her side for as long as possible. Maybe forever.

With her gorgeous mouth titled in a teasing smile, Phil slowly pulled something out of her skirt pocket. It was small, purple, and shaped vaguely like a wave. If waves buzzed and looked like something beamed from outer space.

Distracted, Sage frowned. She knew where she'd seen that thing before. And how much it cost.

"I can't believe you bought that thing," Sage muttered.

She turned her attention fully back to the road for a moment, just to make sure she wasn't about to run into somebody's bumper. But the road ahead of the truck was clear for at least a half mile.

"Why can't you believe it?" Phil asked.

"That thing was at least a hundred plus dollars." Maybe more. Sage had been looking over Phil's shoulder while her woman clicked through the sex shop's weekly newsletter like a kid in a digital candy store.

"Correct." Phil nodded like Sage was the dunce here. "Which means it's a damn good vibrator." She squeezed the toy in question like it was already her favorite. It was only as big as the palm of her hand.

Sage eyed the toy doubtfully. It didn't look powerful enough for the kind of vibration her woman usually liked. "That's a big assumption to make."

"I didn't doubt you when you dropped almost two grand on that creepy ass, realistic skin monster dick made in some German pervert's basement."

"But you did though." Sage clearly remembered Phil saying "no way!" and laughing when she took out the toy. But the laughter had turned into loud moans and screams of pleasure once Sage had the tentacles buzzing, one buried in Phil's ass, the other in her dripping pussy.

"True," Phil said, "but let's not live in the past." She rolled the little purple vibe between her fingers. "This is pretty, isn't it?"

"Pretty isn't what counts, babe," Sage murmured with a superior grin, practically daring Phil to use the toy. But why else did she take it unless she intended to use it?

"Trust me, it's more than a pretty face." Phil dimpled. "Kinda like me." She flipped a hidden switch on the toy and the thing buzzed to life.

Sage kept both hands on the wheel, her eyes straight ahead. Well, maybe a little bit to the right to make sure she wasn't ignoring her woman. Trying not to be too obviously eager, she squirmed only a little in her seat. "So...um...you already tried it out?"

"Of course." The toy jumped across Phil's palm, its elongated nose nuzzling the base of her fingers. It looked like a small hunting animal with one thing on its mind.

Sage licked her lips, eager now to get the show on the road, so to speak. "You going to show me what your little expensive new purchase is all about?"

"Do you really want to see?" Phil playfully stroked the head of the vibrator with her thumb.

Shit. Sage shifted again in the leather seat and already felt about two seconds from begging Phil to just play with herself already.

"Only if you want me to, baby," she said. But the breathless hitch in her voice ruined any attempt at nonchalance.

But, Phil, the little tease already had her hand at the hem of her skirt. Slowly, she pulled up the gauzy yellow material.

Her toy buzzed.

Sage swallowed thickly.

Phil slowly tugged on the skirt. The hem slithered up her long legs and thick thighs, baring her beautiful skin to the sunlight. Sage's mouth watered. Her pussy too.

Finally, finally, the skirt moved that last couple of inches. Phil's neatly trimmed V of pubic hair came into view. Then her pretty pussy.

Sage released a sigh and squeezed the steering wheel hard enough for it to hurt. "You couldn't wait until we got to the cottage to do this to me?"

"Everybody else is already there, remember?"

How could she forget? About a week after she and Phil got back together, Dez started singing "*Reunited and it feels so good*" whenever she saw them. Then finally, when Sage was ready to stuff anything down her throat to shut her up, Dez said she got them a house, all three couples, on the canal on Key West. A long weekend to reconnect and rejuvenate. A couple's get-away.

"What about Nuria?" Sage had asked, being a smart ass.

Dez shrugged. "She's in San Diego or Hollywood someplace with her newly employed ass. Who the hell knows?"

And so, the trip was a go. At nearly one in the afternoon and a half hour until their destination, Dez, Rémi and their women were already waiting for them in a big three-bedroom cottage in Key West.

But back to what was really important...

Watching Phil, Sage bit her lip and squirmed some more. Yeah, they were only half an hour away from where they were heading, but she couldn't wait a second longer.

"Show me what your little toy can do, baby."

Phil's wet smile was the very definition of sin. "My pleasure."

Keeping her bare feet on the dashboard, she slowly parted her legs, then slid her fingers between her thighs. She combed through her silky bush to open up the lips that were already glistening and wet.

Sage's tongue ran wet with the need to taste the slick of her woman's desire. Fuck...

"You should just use your fingers," she said, eyes trained on Phil's dripping pink opening while she curled her hips and ass in the seat, hunting for stimulation against her clit. "You're already halfway there."

"Fingers aren't what I want right now, baby." Phil's voice was getting lost in her lust. It rumbled low, getting deeper the more turned on she got. Stretching sleek as a panther, she tipped her hips up, leaning back in the seat to bare herself even further to Sage.

With another flick of her tongue over her already damp lips, Phil slid the buzzing toy between her legs. The eager little vibe nudged her clit right away, and she cried out.

"Oh!" She jerked in the seat and Sage swore she felt the same jolt of pleasure in her own lap.

Phil gripped the edge of her seat with one hand and opened her legs wider. "It's *so* good. And this is the lowest setting."

Damn.

Sage moved her ass in the seat, rubbing back and forth against the leather. A moan rose up from deep inside her chest. God... She had been about to give this up? Shit.

"You like what you see, baby?" Phil gasped out the question.

All Sage could do was nod. Then toss a quick glance toward the road to make sure they weren't about to get into a wreck.

Then she went back to paying attention to what was really important.

Phil's clit, swollen and wet, jumped under the toy. It looked like a hell of a vibration. The little purple vibe dipped down between the butterfly wings of her damp pussy lips then floated back up, shiny wet, to dance on top of Phil's clit again.

Her woman was moaning steadily now, the sound of her pleasure creating a buzzing in Sage's own pussy. She swallowed past her dry throat, tried desperately to say some of what she felt.

"I love what I see, sweetheart." Sage threw another distracted glance through the windshield. "And I love the fuck out of you."

"Yeah...?" Soft panting breaths. Phil's delicious hips sliding back and forth in the seat to meet the toy she held between her fingers in a death grip. Already, Sage could see she was close to coming. "How much do you love me, baby?" Phil panted.

That was easy. "All the way. No limits. Forever."

"No matter what?"

"No matter what." Sage had been an idiot before, but that was over. They still had a lot to talk about. She was nowhere ready to share her woman with a man, but she wasn't ready to write off her love because of a hypothetical encounter with a dick. If Phil came to her with her desire to sleep with a man, they'd talk about it. They'd do the whole lesbian thing (for Sage's sake anyway) and process the shit out of it, but she'd never leave her woman. Not now. Not ever.

"Sage!"

Phil began to shiver, hips bucking wildly, her teeth clamping hard down on her lower lip. Her eyes fluttered shut and she reached blindly across the seat and clutched at Sage's breast, pinched a nipple through the thin material of her tank top.

It was a rough squeeze, just enough to ramp up the lust tearing through Sage at the sight of her lover jilling off in the leather seat, her juices dripping down into the leather, the smell of her pussy, salty and mouthwatering, yanking her closer to something good.

Another moan wavered its way from Sage's lips. Fuck, her love looked good. The rub of Sage's jeans against her clit was another kind of good. Hell, it was fucking *great*.

"I love you so much, baby!" she gasped.

"I want to ask Errol to be our sperm donor!" Phil cried out, her hips bucking more.

"What...?" The seam of Sage's jeans rubbed her harder, pressing firm and the wet and the electric all together in her pants. Breathing hard enough to dry out her lips, she dug her short nails into the steering wheel. That slight additional sensation fired her clit and completely disengaged her mind. "Whatever you want, baby..."

"Yeah?" Phil panted, her legs trembling and stiff and her nipples like rock candy under the flimsy bikini top.

"Yeah!"

"Sage...my baby...my heart. I love you so much." She gasped out one last time, then wailed, her pussy gushing and splattering the seat and the floor of the truck with the thin liquid stream of her cum.

The sounds, the sight of her wide open and throbbing pink, dragged Sage over the edge too. At the last, she couldn't stop it. Couldn't help it. She squeezed her eyes tightly shut and dug her fingernails into the leather steering wheel.

The symphony of their panting, the music of shared pleasure, filled the car for long, throbbing moments and Sage, with her eyes still closed, trembled from it.

"Baby, baby!" Phil's voice threaded with panic pulled Sage back to where she actually was.

In the car. Speeding along the highway to Key West.

Shit!

Speed was the keyword. Sage abruptly eased up on the gas. "Sorry, baby..." She licked her lips and said a quick and thankful prayer that nobody had been close to them on the road.

Still lust-drunk, she wriggled in the seat, the cooling cum in her pants fast on its way to being uncomfortable. But that was secondary to what flashed through her mind.

Sperm donor?

"Did you just completely play me?" She slid a look toward her woman.

"Do you feel played?" Phil sighed and stretched out in the seat, body on sleek display, face damp with sweat, her eyes satisfied. Her fingers brushed over Sage's still hard nipple through the tank top.

Hell, yeah she felt played.

But she also felt good enough to melt all over this car and drip with pleasure all over Phil's delectable body. Despite the cool wetness slathered all over her underwear, a deep and satisfying breath trembled through her.

"So, you didn't say anything." Phil took her feet off the dashboard and arranged the long sunlight-colored skirts around her thighs like a queen settling into her throne. Her fingers plucked at the material of her skirt, betraying her nerves. She was so damn cute. "What do you think about me asking Errol to be our donor?" she asked finally.

Sage almost laughed but held back. The last time Errol had been to their house for dinner, she'd thought about asking him the same thing. She decided to wait though, not sure if Phil was ready for that important step. But apparently, her woman was more than ready.

"Sure, baby." Sage squeezed Phil's thigh through the pretty skirt. "Whatever you want." And she meant that.

"Good, because he already said he would do it." A thread of nervousness ran through Phil's breathless confession.

"Why did you bother asking me then?" Sage muttered.

"Don't be like that, baby. I just—" For the first time since her orgasm, she met Sage's eyes and obviously saw the humor there. "You bitch! You're making me squirm on purpose!" She slapped Sage's thigh, a sharp and loud sound. Relief twitched up the corners of her mouth.

"Hey, that hurt!" But Sage couldn't hold back her laughter anymore. Her relief.

They were back on the same page again and it felt so incredibly good. Like how it should be.

"You are such an ass sometimes..." Phil muttered, but her smile was as bright as the late afternoon sun.

"That's part of why you love me, baby."

Phil grunted. "Not really."

The song changed to something moody and sensual, and the sound of it mingled with the light sound of the SUV's tired rushing over the highway. Following the beat of the music, Sage tapped her fingers on the steering while. Her face hurt, she was smiling so hard.

"So we're really going to do this, huh?" she asked.

Phil bit her lip through a smile of her own, looking both excited and nervous. "I guess so."

Music and the sound of tires against the road ticked between them for a few breaths.

They spent the rest of the drive talking about what it meant for them to have a kid. To change their lives. By the time they pulled up to the two-story bungalow they were supposed to share with Dez, Victoria, Rémi, and Claudia for the next three days, they'd moved on to picking names for their hypothetical baby.

"It's about time you all got here." Dez strolled down the drive to meet them, relaxed and casually sexy in linen pants rolled up at the ankles and a tank top that showed off her sleek muscles. The front door hung open behind her and loud, feminine laughter poured out. "We've been waiting."

Through the wide windows of the lime green and white house, Sage could see the other three women gathered around the coffee table. Sage couldn't tell if they were playing cards or calling bullshit on one of Rémi's many ridiculous stories.

"Now you don't have to wait anymore," Phil said, jumping

out of the truck. "Here we are." Twirling in a skirt-swinging circle, she smiled wide like she was auditioning for *The Sound of Music*. Happiness looked good on her.

Sage tried not to be jealous when Dez swept Phil up high in a big hug, leaving bare feet dangling inches off the ground.

"I missed this look on your face." Dez grinned up at Phil who, in her bright yellow skirts and thick hair loose around her face, looked just like a piece of sunlight.

Although she knew all was forgiven, Sage flinched. It was a gut reaction. Yeah, she was an idiot. Because of her, for months, Phil's smile had taken off for parts unknown.

But Sage was done with the fuckery. This woman made her happier than any other. She would do whatever it took to keep her around.

"You guys going in or you going to make kissy faces at each other all afternoon?" she muttered at them, only joking a little.

Dez looked at her around the gorgeous explosion of Phil's hair. "Now that you mention it..." She loudly kissed Phil on both cheeks and Phil, laughing like a wild thing with her head thrown back and her hair blowing in the salt-laced breeze, allowed her to.

Then she looked over at Sage whose heart squeezed tight at the look in her woman's eyes. Phil threw out her hand, her fingers spread wide and wiggling playfully.

"Come on, baby," she invited with a grin. The edges of that grin were soft, asking for promises Sage was eager to keep.

I'm yours. You're mine. That's it.

With an answering smile and gladness warm in her chest, Sage grabbed her woman's hand. She allowed Phil to pull her along, up the driveway and at their friend's side, toward the rest of whatever their lives together would bring.

THANK YOU

Thank you so much for reading INSATIABLE APPETITES, book 3 of the How Sweet It Is series! If you enjoyed it, please take the time to write a starred review online – it doesn't have to be a long one – and share your experience with a friend or three.

To keep up with the latest releases and get free reads, subscribe to my newsletter here: http://eepurl.com/bjpDDr

To find me on the interwebs, go to my website www.fionazedde.com, my Facebook, Twitter, and/or Tumblr pages. You can even use old-fashioned email: f.zedde@gmail.com.

ALSO BY THE AUTHOR

Bliss
Broken in Soft Places
Dangerous Pleasures
Les Tales (novella collection with Skyy and Nikki Rashan)
Nightshade (novella)
Rise of the Rain Queen
The Power of Mercy
To Italy with Love (novella and stories)
When She Says Yes (stories)

Every Dark Desire (Vampire Desire #1)
Desire at Dawn (Vampire Desire #2)

A Taste of Sin (How Sweet It Is #1)
Hungry for It (How Sweet It Is #2)
Return to Me (How Sweet It Is #2.5

ABOUT THE AUTHOR

Jamaican-born Fiona Zedde is the author of several novels, including the Lambda Literary Award finalists, Bliss and Every Dark Desire. Her novel, Dangerous Pleasures, received a Publishers Weekly starred review and was winner of an About.com Readers' Choice Award for Best Lesbian Novel or Memoir. Her latest work, *The Power of Mercy*, is available now.

AN EXCERPT FROM THE POWER OF MERCY

The Power of Mercy is the second in Ylva Publishing's Super-Heroine Collection and features meta-human, Mai, a woman as strong as she is vulnerable. For her, jumping into burning buildings is easy, it's the women in her life that make things truly dangerous.

An Excerpt from *The Power of Mercy*

Mai stood on the roof of the twenty-story building, naked except for the cloak of her restlessness. Faint pain throbbed in her back—scratches from the anonymous woman she'd taken to bed barely two hours before—her thighs ached from the work she'd put into bringing them both pleasure, and the muscles in her arms still burned. The city of Atlanta, studded in starlight above and in bright lights below, hummed its particular late-night songs. A whisper of street traffic. A distant chopper. The thumping baseline from a rap song as a car cruised past.

The woman she'd gone home with still slept peacefully in her bed one flight below, but that same peace escaped Mai. Earlier that night, a familiar restlessness had pushed her into her favorite local bar, a place dark enough for private pleasures yet with a wide-open patio for fresh air and a bar well-stocked enough to drown even the deepest of sorrows. But she didn't go there for sorrow or for fresh air.

The woman she found wasn't exactly what she craved, but in that moment, with familiar demons pulling at her, the lush form with a head full of springy coils had been enough. She tasted like forgetfulness, pain subsumed, pleasure without the consequence of a tomorrow. Starved for what the stranger had offered, Mai had devoured her—the wet flesh between her thighs, her mouth gasping and plush, her breasts like summer-ripe mangoes.

But afterward, Mai was still keyed up. Tight. The big muscles in her arms and thighs jumped just under her skin, ticking away the moments toward an implosion she didn't want to happen. She rolled her shoulders and stretched her neck, spread out her senses to feel what was going on in the city below. It all rushed up to her in a wave of sound and color:

Couples whispering intimately to each other while their bedsheets beneath them rustled to the rhythm of their lovemaking. A police car roaring down the city streets with sirens screaming and blue lights ablaze. Even young children were awake and playing in a nearby courtyard, which was odd for the early fall, when schools were in session. And it was more and more of the same, in a rolling tide of awareness of murder, sex, cruelty, and laughter. The tapestry of a large city.

Mai felt it all, the ceaseless movement of Atlanta—a wild organism in constant flux that could not be tamed. All these things unfolding below her were too far away or too late for her to change. Other things... Mai tilted her head toward the sound of screams pulsing beneath her conscious hearing.

Screams of terror. A fire. Mai's breath hitched, and her body unconsciously swayed toward

that blast of heat barely two miles away. She narrowed her gaze toward the fire, sharpening her hearing. No sirens headed toward it. Not yet. She wasted a moment wishing for the phone she'd left in the pocket of her discarded jacket somewhere on the stranger's floor. Then she jumped.

Air rushed up to meet her, a gust over her face and bare body, both cooling and heating her as the adrenaline turned her body temperature all the way up to scalding. Everything was loud. Screams rang like church bells, and her body throbbed to the heat radiating from the out-of-control fire.

Falling, Mai grabbed for the stone façade of the next building as it surged up to meet her, bare inches from slamming into her if she miscalculated her headlong rush. She was far from invulnerable, but sometimes it was that vulnerability to death that made these risks worth it.

Closer to the fire, her body tingled, a flush of heat and excitement. She sprinted across a flat roof. Jumped to another. She flew past a couple pressed together on a blanket, the girl's blouse off, her pert breasts showing, her lover intent on mouthing between her spread thighs.

"Jesus! Did you see that?"

"What?" Her lover emerged, face wet, eyes only for the woman beneath her.

"A naked chick. She just ran past us."

Naked. Right. Mai shifted, felt her skin ripple, hardening and stretching in places. It was only a surface change. She still felt the wind as it brushed her bare skin. Contrary to the illusion she crafted, her hands were gloveless as she grabbed the next rooftop and slung herself over an angled flagpole. There was no sleek catsuit covering her from neck to toe. No high boots. And no mask over the top half of her face, hiding everything but the tight line of her mouth. Any potential witnesses would see what she wanted them to see, not a naked woman streaking across the Atlanta skyline, treating it like her personal sorority house.

Instead, she was Mercy. Face masked. Body covered. No secrets exposed. She ran on toward the fire, sliding down into back alleys and

darkened side streets when she ran out of roofs, the curse of living in a city with such a jagged and unpredictable skyline. Soon she was close enough to feel the flames, like invisible tongues lapping at her skin. The building was a new construction. Tall and flammable, tempting for any pyromaniac. She could smell the deliberately set fire. Probably someone who was just curious, then shocked when it all went wrong so quickly. She smelled the accelerant and the melting plastic from a disposable lighter, their scents overlaid with panicked sweat and regret.

The building was glorious. Yellow and amber flames swirled in its corners and crevices, holding it tight like a too-ardent lover. Mai took it in all in an instant—the shouts of panic and ringing alarm bells, people hanging out of the smoking mouths of open windows, their whispered or shouted prayers for deliverance.

She listened, dropped to the ground, and ran, her feet pounding the pavement, then leaped UP! Heat lashed her skin, and it was hard not to let it touch her and do what it wanted. The outer wall of the building was hot under her hands and feet.

"Mercy!" someone cried from below. Then a chant rose up—a sound of relief, a sigh, and praise. Just as with the flames, she had to pull herself away from the seduction of the name they had given her. The lure of their raised voices.

A child perched on a window ledge, eyes wide with terror but more afraid of falling the seven stories than of the fire eating his room, bit by relentless bit. Outside the room and screaming in terror, a woman—his mother, Mai guessed—was trying to break down the door. The woman rammed it with a wooden chair already on fire, trying to get to the boy. Smoke choked the woman and the entire apartment. Already she was weakening, nearly passed out from the smoke.

Mai jumped through a nearby window and fought her way into the apartment. She grabbed the woman.

"No! My son!" She whirled at Mai, fighting to stay in the fire, her fist slamming into Mai's face. Mai winced but bore the pain. A whip of flame lashed against her back, and she hissed, protecting the woman from the fire even as her own skin burned. The pain of it was oddly sweet.

Mai grabbed the woman's arms and pinned them behind her back. "I'll get him next if you calm down." She didn't shout. "If you don't stop fighting me, I won't be able to get him."

The woman stilled at once, and Mai threw her over her shoulder, covered her head with a wet towel she'd grabbed from the bathroom on the way in, and sprinted the way she'd come, with the woman's weight bouncing halfway down her back.

She rushed through the fire and out the window and dropped the woman across the street among the gathered crowd.

"Ty! Get my son!" The woman stumbled back toward the building, but her neighbors grabbed her.

Mai quickly assessed the fire, listened for the signs of life still in the building. A woman on a higher floor was in danger of suffocating in her closet. An older couple clung together even higher up and fading fast. Mai ran toward a nearby building miraculously free of the blaze, scaled its outer wall, and leapt from it to the flame- enshrouded condo complex.

She quickly found the woman in the closet, unconscious and clutching a Bible with burned hands. Up and over her shoulder. Mai did the same thing five more times, the smoke overwhelming her a little more with each rescue, the fire both weakening and strengthening her as she made her way through the building, grabbing limp bodies, resisting bodies, alive bodies. Like an assembly line, one after the other. She left the dead ones to their rest.

"Mercy! Mercy!"

"My son! You said you'd save my son!" The woman still struggled in the arms of her neighbors, her thin nightgown dark with smoke and falling off her narrow shoulders. Her teeth were sharp and fierce in her face, stripped down to the basic drive of a mother wanting to protect her child. It wasn't something Mai was familiar with, but she'd seen it in documentaries.

A blush of shame rushed through her. Up and up, perched at the top, the boy huddled frozen in terror. All he had to do was jump, but it was not going to happen. He was too scared.

Shit. She'd gotten distracted. Firefighters were coming. But they wouldn't get to the boy in time.

"Jump!" the woman screamed to her son. "Ty! Please, just jump!"

More people gathered below the window despite the flames spouting from the top of the building, encouraging him to jump with the outstretched protection of their arms. Not the most brilliant idea.

Mai cursed again, then ran back into the building. Coughing. Choking. Her lungs were already tight and scorched from pulling in too

little oxygen. Her senses swam. It was too late. She knew it when she reached through the fire, clambering up the superheated bricks that lit up the palms of her bare hands with pain. She'd screwed up and left the boy waiting too long.

His room door was cinders now. The flames flew across the carpet of his bedroom, devouring everything it could. Bedsheets. Toys. Posters of cars. His flesh teased the fire. It, too, would easily burn. All of him would burn.

The window felt even farther than before, its ledge practically glowing with heat. How could the boy sit in a heat so intense? When she finally got to him, she knew how. He was a statue of flesh transformed by terror into a panting but otherwise frozen thing.

"It's okay." She said the words even though she barely believed them. She wrapped the boy's body with her own and jumped, a quick breath up and out the window just as a fireball exploded in the room and blasted them out into the cool air.

Mai clutched the boy, whimpering now, as they flew through the air. She heard a rising tide of gasps below and controlled her own exhalation, used the momentum of the blast, and turned them in the air, keeping as much of her own body as possible wrapped around him. Something hard slammed into her back, drove the breath from her lungs. The side of the nearby building. She held on to enough presence of mind to roll down and cushion their fall with her body, leaving the boy untouched.

Mai felt rather than heard the people flooding toward them in concern. She stood, cursing her own stupidity, and lifted the boy, barely any weight at all, as she looked through the crush of people for his mother.

"Thank God!" The woman screamed her son's name and reached for him, the tendons of her neck etched in stark relief. Her nails scraped Mai's hands as she clutched her son.

Mai stood still long enough to make sure the woman easily bore the burden of the boy, then she spun away, ignoring the cries of the crowd shouting her name to finally pay attention to her body's aches and wounds. One alley, then two. Her arms stretched and burned as she reached up to lever herself higher and higher. By the time she reached a tenth-story rooftop, she felt better. The boy was alive. Traumatized, but she'd blame that on the fire instead of her own carelessness.

Before long, she was back where she started. A rooftop downtown.

In the aftermath of the fire, her breath heaved and her

muscles were loose and warm. Pleasure sang through her veins. This was what she had needed. This combination of usefulness and danger. Accelerated heartbeat and eased fears.

Going home to her own bed would be another pleasure. But only after she shared a different kind of pleasure with the stranger downstairs. She imagined waking to the softness of the woman's body, a moaning greeting, and then an explosive climax in the heat of her lover's embrace. A perfect bookend to the night.

Mai quickly descended to the woman's room. As quietly as she could, she showered the stink of adrenaline and smoke from her skin and slipped between the sheets, curling the length of her body around the resting woman. Sleep came as easily as the next breath.

BONUS CONTENT

"The Magical Femme"
A Short Story

I don't do femmes.

That's what I tell myself the whole time she's giving me the eye across the crowded restaurant. Tall and pretty in that average Atlanta way—meaning she'd be a dime in any other city. She's working her tongue on the edge of a half-full martini glass. The pink liquid in the glass sloshes dangerously, but she doesn't look away from me. From the prop of her hip against the chair she's leaning on, it's obvious she knows she looks good in that tight ass skirt, blue and high-waisted, clinging to her decent curves in a way that tells the open secret of her G-string underwear.

I can't do thong panties. The idea of something rubbing in my sweaty crack all day makes me shudder, and not in a good way. Though the fleeting thought of her panties, the thin string snuggled between the firm mounds of ass cheeks, inexplicably makes my mouth dry. I look away from the femme and take a quick gulp of my own drink.

The drink is cold and strong, just about the only good thing about the evening so far.

Coming to the restaurant was a bad idea. But my friend, Pauline, called me on the way from work, saying she was hungry, had a Groupon, and would love to take me out. Meaning she wanted me to drive us someplace so she could get drunk.

So I picked her up from her place and we made our way out into Atlanta nightlife on a Friday night, not thinking of where the place would be—Edgewood, the latest Atlanta *it* neighborhood—and what it would mean.

What it means is the restaurant that's normally a good place to unwind over a drink and good conversation is loud from the DJ playing the latest trap music—or top 40, sometimes it all sounds the same—while couples and groups of friends lean on square high tables trying to seem fuckable to anybody who wants to look.

Pauline takes in the whole restaurant, her eyes squinting in annoyance. Her solid body overflows the spindly chair while her Friday evening outfit of cargo shorts and Hawaiian shirt don't do much to blend her with the high heels and oiled beard crowd.

"This was a fucking mistake." She snaps a look at the DJ as if she could magically destroy both him and the music with the power of her eyes alone.

"Yeah." I look up from stirring my Moscow mule with the limp straw, my eyes instantly colliding with the bold browns of the brassy femme in the middle of the restaurant.

The friend she's with, equally femme, which could also mean straight as hell, is bouncing her ass to the music and shouting something in the femme's ear while looking toward the bar. There, a guy in dick-hugging sweatpants is scoping out the restaurant. He's standing near other bored looking twenty-some-things draped over the bar and shouting in vain to be heard above the too-loud music. His gaze doesn't linger on the femme's friend, but that doesn't stop the chick from stripping him naked with her eyes.

The femme looks at the guy, shouts something back to her friend, then goes back to looking at me. I look away quickly but not before she catches me checking her out. A smile curves up the corner of her very red mouth.

"You wanna leave?" Pauline's shout vibrates my ear drums.

I shake my head. This is the second place we've been to in the name of trying to use one of her thousand and one Groupons. She's addicted to those things. The first restaurant told us and our Groupon to fuck off, and that was *after* we paid for parking. I'd skipped lunch at work so now I'm just hungry enough to deal with restaurant number two's stupidly loud music and the femme trying to visually crawl into my non-existent cleavage.

"Okay," Pauline says. "Then let's order."

When the waitress comes back around, we order and the cute little thing in black leather shorts flirts with Pauline like her job depended on it.

Once we order, Pauline and I sit back to watch the crowd since talking is out of the question. I'm not really in the mood for conversation so this is good enough for me.

The healthcare company I work for was just bought by a larger and more aggressive competitor. After months of waiting, the news everybody in the office had been waiting for finally came down. They're slashing half our department and getting rid of the analysts, me included. I'm not in the mood to look for another job, but I sure as hell am not ready to live in a cardboard box since the new place I just bought comes with a mortgage that matches the well-paying gig I'm about to get laid off from.

Fuck my life.

I suck down the last of my cocktail and signal the waitress for another.

"Slow down. You don't have to drink me under the table." Pauline flicks her fingers at my empty cup although she's already two shots of honey whiskey into the evening. We have my car in the expensive ass parking lot around the block but the meter is for twenty-four hours so I have no problem calling an Uber to come get us if we both ended up too sloppy drunk to drive.

"Don't worry about me," I tell Pauline just as a shadow falls over our table.

I think it's the waitress with my fresh drink and look up with a thanks on the tip of my tongue. But it's the tight skirt femme. I dart a glance at the table where she was sitting before but it's empty now and her friend is at the bar, still shaking her ass to the questionable music but this time she's draped across Sweatpants Dick and he looks just as interested in her as she is in him.

"I'm leaving," the femme shouts down to me from her sky-high heels, skipping the introductions. "—but I want to get your number before I go. I want to take you out."

I blink at her like she's speaking Croatian, a language I don't know a word of, by the way. Pauline is grinning like a fool. Before I can do or say anything, my ex-friend grabs a pen out of my purse and scribbles my number and name on a napkin and hands it to the femme. I glower at her. She *knows* I don't mess with other femmes.

The femme takes the napkin with a nod of thanks to Pauline, but looks at me, eyebrow raised as if making sure I'm okay with this egregious breach of friendship protocol. I nod and she gives me a smile full of red lips and white teeth. Then she slides a business card under my empty cup.

"So you'll know who's calling you," is what I think she says, but the music is so damn loud she could have been reciting her ABC's for all I know.

I nod again, then she's gone.

Pauline looks pleased with herself as she watches the femme go. "Nice," she says, and I can easily read the word on her lips because that's her favorite word in the English language next to "fuck."

I roll my eyes and go back to searching the restaurant for our waitress. I'm getting hungrier—and thirstier—by the minute. Once the food comes, I can start thinking of excuses to get out of the date with the femme if she calls.

She doesn't call me that night. In my bed after a shower and with my head still spinning from the three drinks and teeth-rattling music, I spare the femme's fearless approach far too much thought before falling into the quick sleep of the thoroughly drunk.

The next day comes with the expected hangover and, after OD'ing on aspirin and coffee, I leave my house for brunch with some sad soon to be ex-coworkers. I pretty much forget about the bad night of Grouponing until I get a call from an unfamiliar number on the way home from the restaurant.

"Do you remember me?" Again she skips the usual greeting. And it's because of this more than the sound of her voice that I remember who she is.

But this doesn't mean I know how to respond. "What?"

"Oh, you don't remember. That's too bad." Her voice comes out low and amused, not at all insulted. "Are you free tonight? I'd like the chance to stimulate your memory."

Stopped at a traffic light, I stare down at the phone with my mouth open. Is this chick for real?

"How do you even know I'm gay?" I ask, knowing what she was going to say before she says it.

"That big stud you were with gave me a clue," she says,

confirming my assumption. "Mostly when she gave up your number so quickly." Her low laugh rolls over me through the phone. "So, are you free or will I have to duel with your stud for a few hours of your company?"

"I..."

"I'm Scottie, by the way, just in case you haven't looked at the card I gave you."

I'm still speechless and feel a little overwhelmed. Not even the most aggressive stud I dated in the past was ever this...determined. But the butterflies winging through my stomach tell me I'm not completely uninterested.

Strange.

A car horn bleats behind me, startling me away from my contemplation of this odd piece of business. As a formality, I stick my middle finger out the car window before putting my foot on the gas to glide through the green light.

"So, does tonight work for you?" Scottie asks.

Tonight? "No, not really." My only plans are to sit in front of the TV in my sweats and have a pending unemployment pity party for one. But that's not anything to share with a stranger.

"That's too bad," Scottie says, and she doesn't do a thing to hide her disappointment, although it sounds like she's laughing at me too. "I'd love to have a weekend to spoil you. Since I'm assuming you work, and I do too, how about next Saturday evening? I'll drop by your place to pick you up."

"No!" My denial is automatic. First of all, I'm not about to invite a stranger over to my place, and two... Just no.

"Why not? I'm not a mass murderer or anything."

"You could be a single murderer for all I know." The words spring to my lips, probably confirming for her that I had no real reason to say no to the date.

"I'll send you my LinkedIn profile once we get off the phone, and my Pinterest so you can see my hobbies in case you want to buy me a present later." She obviously manages to amuse herself. "Let's say eight next Saturday night. Text me your address sometime this week. I'll make a reservation someplace convenient for both of us."

"Are you for real?"

"Absolutely, gorgeous. Although I should be the one to ask that. When I saw you at that stupid restaurant looking so damn good and probably bi or lesbian too, my clit did a little happy dance."

I almost bite my tongue in half. She's talking about clits already? "Listen—"

"I know, too much too soon, right? It's okay. I know I can be a bit extra for some, but I'm hoping I'm just right for you." A low murmur comes through the phone, words I can't make out but are urgent sounding. "Listen, I have to run, honey. But I'll call you later."

"Wait!" And something happens low in my stomach when I don't immediately hear dead air, a sign Scottie's a listener, not just a talker and is interested in what I have to say. "Do you even know my name."

"Nailah."

The way she says my name jerks my foot on the gas pedal and it's a miracle I don't rear-end the car in front of me. I swallow. "Okay. I... I'll talk with you later then."

"That's a promise." She hangs up.

I'm surprised but shouldn't have been when she calls me the next night. It's Sunday and I can barely face the reality of going into work the next morning knowing my last day is coming soon. Curled up in my bed, reading, but not really paying attention to the words on the page, I jump and nearly hit myself in the face with the book when the phone rings. I lunge for my cell like a life line, not even looking to see who's calling.

"Hello?"

"You haven't saved me into your contacts yet? Shame on you. Do I have to punish you for that when I see you next weekend?"

I blink at my cat perched on the foot of my bed. From the nest he'd made of my cashmere sweater and a few pairs of socks, Osiris lifts his dark head to peer at me with his glowing yellow eyes, blinking back at me before resting his head once more on his paws to contemplate the mysteries of his small universe.

"Was that too much," Scottie asks into the resulting silence. But the amusement in her voice lets me know she's not even a little embarrassed, or deterred. "We can talk about that kind of stuff if you want. What your kinks are, if you have any." A rustling comes through the phone, like she's in bed too and rolling around in her sheets. "By the way, I hope I'm not calling you too late." It's just past ten, at least two hours away from my bedtime but this latest bombshell from my company has me seeking the comfort of my bed and books much earlier than usual.

"Would you hang up if I told you it *was* too late?"

"Not really, but I'd call you earlier tomorrow night. I know it's a work night. Or a school night." She paused. "Do you have kids to put to bed?"

I almost laugh. "No, no kids. And I live alone."

Way to invite a potential killer to drop by and murder me in my sleep. But as I think that, I remember the LinkedIn profile she'd sent me along with the Pinterest boards filled with Moorish architecture and Japanese bondage techniques; the photos of her pretty craftsman style house in East Point with her standing in front of and inside it. All proof that she had no other intentions than to take me to a nice dinner and possibly fuck me afterward.

I'm not quite sure I'm on board for the last bit, but something in me responds all too well to her commanding presence on my phone, the way she fearlessly approached me in the restaurant.

"Oh, good," she says with a throaty laugh after I basically told her she can come to my condo and murder me without interruption if she ever felt like it. "Now, even though I'm a pushy bitch, I'm not completely inconsiderate. Tell me a bit about yourself, something I can't find out from stalking you on Facebook, then I'll let you get your beauty sleep."

We end up talking for a long time, letting midnight pass with us still on the phone and playfully discussing the things we liked about our past lovers, what she wanted from me, what I could expect from her if we went any further than this. Whatever *this* was.

I find out she's bisexual and just as aggressive with her men as she was being with me. That she likes ice cream and always gets it in waffle cones, doesn't like sports but loves to watch rugby and women's volleyball for the hot and sweaty bodies on display. And that she's absolutely dominating in nearly every aspect of her relationships.

"And I want to seduce you," she says just before she hangs up the phone. "I know I'm not your usual type, Nailah. But give me the chance to show you that different can be nice."

I bite my lip, my hand digging hard into the mattress through my sheets, searching desperately for something stable to hold onto since her words threaten to sweep me away.

Suffering through a two-year long dry spell, mostly caused by my workaholic tendencies, I am now at the very least willing to go out with her, have a woman wine and dine me, one who thinks I'm worth pursuing. Scottie's boldness and wicked sense of humor are intoxicating, even though I pretty much already know by the time we sit down to dinner face to face and start to really get to know each other, her lack of swagger and proper set of muscles will kill any of my bourgeoning desire and with it any illusions I have that we can go any further.

"Okay," I tell her. "I'll give different a chance." Although I've never done that before.

"Okay," she echoes. Her voice falls into silence and I hear her breath through the phone. "Sleep well, Nailah," Scottie says finally. "We'll talk again soon."

She waits for me to wish her a restful sleep too before she hangs up the phone.

What the hell am I doing?

Still at the foot of my bed, Osiris has given up his regal cat pose to sprawl on his back, paws spread wide and snoring softly. Easy for him when he still has a job—to keep looking cute—and doesn't have a domineering and dangerously attractive pussy intent on eating his ass up one day soon.

*

We end up talking just about every day up until our Saturday evening date. Mostly around eight each evening after we'd both done our after-work gym penance, had dinner, and settled in for the night. The only exception was my friend date with Pauline. The whole time at the bar, though, Pauline kept asking what's going on between me and "the hot femme." Since I don't even know, I had nothing to tell her.

Scottie told me to be ready by eight o' clock, and everything I know of her so far tells me she won't be late. I time my evening down to the half hour, taking a shower an hour before she's supposed to arrive, putting aside thirty minutes to get dressed and another thirty to put on my makeup.

What does she expect me to wear, though?

In the past, when I went out with studs, that question was easy to answer: light make-up and perfume, high heels and easy to remove dresses in case the date ended with sex.

But Scottie confuses me. At least I think the twisting in my stomach is confusion. She'll undoubtedly wear heels and another tight outfit showing off her pretty shape. Does that mean I should wear pants and a strap-on?

So I settle for slim-fitting sailor slacks in black, a sheer white blouse over a red bra, and high heels. I remember Scottie's stilettos from the night we met. She's tall in them, a lot taller than me which is easy enough to be since I'm only five feet four.

I'm in the bedroom, fastening the buttons of my slacks when the doorbell rings, startling my fingers that are already damp with nerves.

Calm down, damn!

But easier said than done.

Is it her, though? My phone tells me it's just past seven, and it's one thing to be a little early for a date, fifteen minutes seems okay but a full hour? Maybe it was my neighbor, a cute gay boy who was forever locking himself out of his condo and finally just ended up leaving one of his spare keys with me. I check the clock again.

Yeah, it's about time for him to come home from the gym and get ready for his usual Saturday evening pre-date drinks with his friends. That makes sense.

I open the door with a smile, Derrick's key in my hand. "Right on time—" But it's not him.

Fuck.

Scottie stands in the doorway with a smile of her own. "Is this how you answer the door?" Her gaze sweeps my body from head to toe, taking in my full-coverage vintage bra, the few inches of my stomach on display before moving down to the high-waisted black slacks and my bare feet with the toes painted red. The look she gives me makes me feel naked and soft around the edges. Vulnerable and just a little horny.

How the hell did she do that?

I feel the blush rising, a wave of heat rushing up my neck, cheeks, my whole face.

The thick waves of her straightened hair are in an elegant French twist with wispy curls that frame her gorgeous face. Her simple outfit of a wrap-around silk dress and peep-toe high heels, both in black, leaves me tongue-tied. Did she wear such an easy to remove outfit on purpose? Was she planning on being the femme tonight?

"You're early." I clutch the edge of the door so tight my fingers hurt. "I thought you were someone else."

"Now, I'm *really* intrigued." Scottie doesn't wait for me to invite her in.

She moves closer until I retreat into my condo under the not-so-subtle shepherding of her tall body and massive personality. She closes the door behind her, locks it, takes a quick look around before bringing her gaze right back to me. "Nice."

And I know she's not talking about my little condo. The urge to stammer out something stupid is strong but I strangle it back and sweep out my arm. "Come in. I only need a few more minutes to put on my makeup and finish getting ready." Just her presence in my little place is causing chaos all through my body. Had I really been stupid enough to think she had no effect on me, that we had no chemistry? With just one look from her, I was ready to combust. "Would you like a drink while you wait? I have..." What the hell is in my kitchen? "...uh mineral water and orange juice. Coffee." My Brita water filter is thankfully full and cold in the fridge. I want to satisfy her, this simple need, even if this dinner we have tonight goes nowhere beyond the restaurant.

"I don't want anything to drink, just go get ready." She steps even closer, showing her white teeth in a smile that's probably dropped dozens of panties over the years. Hundreds maybe.

Since mine threaten to be next to hit the floor, I immediately turn to do what she says. "Okay, just give me a few minutes."

My heart is beating wild and fast, so fast it scares me but I swallow and rush into the bedroom, the blush still high in my face. I'm not dark-skinned enough for it to blend in and I wonder if she thinks I'm some clueless virgin to blush at the drop of a hat. Or the ring of a doorbell.

In the bedroom, I quickly run my fingers through my hair, grateful that the curly dreadlocks already fall in a decently attractive way around my face and shoulders.

"Don't rush, honey."

I gasp like the first chick to die in a horror movie at the sound of Scottie's voice right behind me. She'd followed me in on high heels silenced by the soft-enough-to-sleep-on heather gray carpet in my bedroom. Another cool glance around her, around me, and she smiles again.

"Yes, very nice." She moves closer until her front is only inches from my back.

I stare at the reflection of us in the full length mirror, at the way she towers over me, devours me with her eyes. Goose bumps rush over my skin.

"God, you're even prettier than I remember." Her gravely voice thrums over my senses. Standing behind me, she clasps her cool hands around my upper arms and I shiver. "How is that even possible?" And she leans closer, sniffs my hair, nudges aside the thick fall of dreadlocks with her chin and buries her nose in that tender spot between my ear and shoulder. "Delicious."

Jesus...

Suddenly I'm so wet I could probably float all the way to the damn restaurant. Again, why did I think I wouldn't be attracted to her once I saw her again? Sometimes I'm such an idiot.

I feel her smile against my skin and I'm absolutely frozen still, held captive between the light manacles of her hands on my shoulders and the press of her lips against my skin. My belly rocks with lust and I shift my thighs to ease the ache, then choke out a gasp when she playfully bites my neck.

Okay, so maybe Scottie being as big of a femme as me doesn't matter as much.

"You're so responsive." She presses her teeth into my skin, once, twice, and I can't help my whorish sigh, the fall of my head to the side to give her unrestricted access to my throat, my collarbone, anyplace she wants. Her tongue traces the line of my neck and I shiver.

I'm wet. And hot, and confused as hell. The crotch of my panties feels almost uncomfortably tight.

What is it about this woman? Why her?

"Come back to me, love. Don't escape into your mind. I want you here with me." Her hands slide slowly down my arms, stirring more goose bumps. "You didn't put on any makeup yet." I open my mouth to defend my choice, to tell her it's in the bathroom and ready for me to apply but her finger on my cheek, floating down to my naked lips, stops me. "That's convenient, isn't it?"

"I don't..."

I don't what? My mind spins in useless circles. Am I going to tell her I don't fuck before the first date? That she has the wrong girl? That I wasn't going to put on any makeup anyway? Whatever was poised to leave my mouth has already left my brain. Her fingers nudge my lips apart.

"Your mouth is so pretty." She strokes my mouth and I can only stand in her grip like I'm hypnotized, watching in the mirror as she parts my lips with her long and blue-tipped fingers. I smell the new lacquer of a fresh manicure on her nails, taste the faint bitterness.

My heart is beating fast. My panties are *soaking*. My lips tingle under the slow and firm caress of her fingers, a caress I feel an echo of between my legs. As much as I love kissing, my lips are not this sensitive. Not usually. I know I'm breathing fast but I can't stop myself, can't stop the flick of my tongue that wets her fingers. I feel her quick intake of breath against my back, her chest quickly rising and falling.

"I'm so glad you came to that club last week." She slips her fingers more deeply into my mouth. "Suck, baby..." And I suck.

Her fingers are slightly salty, bitter and smooth from the fresh nail polish. She strokes my lips and it feels even more like a touch on my lower lips, steady and hypnotic. Heady. I moan around the slide of her fingers. What's she doing? If her plan is to get them wet so she can finger me, she doesn't have to bother. I'm so wet she could shove her entire fist in me and it would slide in as smooth as a cherry through whipped cream. And I would love it.

God, I would fucking love it.

If how I'm responding to just her fingers in my mouth is any clue about other things...

Now, I'm moaning like I'm getting paid for it, squeezing my thighs together and silently begging her to touch me down low. She grips my hip and pulls me back against her then her fingers move down to smooth along the cotton of my slacks, tracing me from the top edge of the pants, down my hip bone, along my thigh, and down to my knee. She's not even touching skin and I'm ready to explode.

"Suck my fingers a little more, baby. Get them nice and wet."

I suck until I'm drooling around her fingers, spit dripping between them, and when they're wet enough to her satisfaction, she pulls them free of my mouth with an obscene pop, tugs my bra down and swipes her wet fingers over my already hard nipple. One graze. My knees buckle and she grips me effortlessly, bites my ear. Her teeth flash against her red, red lipstick and she smiles.

"Next time..." Her breath traces my ear. "Next time when I come over before you put on your makeup, I'll have you on your knees." Her wet fingers tug at my nipple, circle it, press into it. "Would you like that?"

God. Fucking. Damn.

The pleasure zips through me, intense and overwhelming. "Yes. I'd love—" A pinch on my nipple cuts off my words in a sharp cry. Her name rushes from my mouth and in this moment I'm willing to give her anything as long as she delivers on the promise of her hands on my breast. I moan her name again and she smiles at me in the mirror, licks around the shell of my ear.

"Oh, sweetheart..." She bites my ear again. "If you get any more perfect, I'm going to have to take you home to my mama."

Her hand touches my bare belly and my skin clenches in shocked arousal. When did she unzip...? My thoughts fall away again with the determined slide of her hands into my pants, over the black lace underwear. The cloth blunts her touch and I sob in frustration, even as a part of me is shocked at how needy and desperate I sound. For another femme.

Sweet Jesus...

Her fingers finally slide over my aching clit that already feels exposed and needy through the black lace.

"I love how wet you are." Her fingers stroke me through the lace, tracing the bulge of my swollen clit. "Is all this for me?"

Yes. The word hovers somewhere just out of reach and I can only nod, body limp yet electrified, all of me desperately wanting her touch. Her fingers are magic. Hot and firm, they press my clit through the underwear and I'm so wet it's embarrassing. Even through the cloth, I can hear the liquid slide of my lips, so swollen, so tender, begging for more of her touch.

I'm moaning louder now. And I should feel ashamed, but in the mirror she looks pleased, her lips parted in pleasure, her eyelashes dropping low over passion-dark eyes.

Then her fingers are *under* the lace. A light touch over my clit that feels as powerful as the long and firm stroke of a tongue. I buck and cry out.

She hums in satisfaction. "Fuck, you're perfect."

Her fingers light me up with sensation, all pleasure, a thumb stroking my clit, fingers firm inside me. Her spit-wet but drying fingers still tugging on my nipple to the rhythm of her thumb on my clit. My legs are shaking. My world is tilting off its axis.

God, already I'm so damn close.

My ass cheeks clench tight. I'm on my tip toes, pushing back into her, moaning loud enough to call the cops, my entire body singing with lust, a tight and aching bow of *almost-there* bliss. Her nails rake over my nipples, one after the other, then squeeze. The pain is sharp and so damn good. I cry out again, but maybe I never stopped.

In the mirror, we look like a pornographer's photograph. Scottie behind me with her red lips at my ear, one hand shoved in my red bra, the other buried in the black lace of my panties, fingers stroking. My face is slack with mindless lust, mouth damp and open, my belly heaving from the come that's racing toward me like a bullet to deliver my little death.

"Come for me, baby." She whispers the words soft and low at my ear. "Just like that. I want to bury my face in your pussy and smear my lipstick all over your cunt and feel your thighs tremble around my ears. I want *all* that." Her fingers pluck my clit like a mandolin. "But I'll settle for this, for now." She bites my ear and the red imprint of her lipstick there weakens my knees even more. "But next time, I'll come and it doesn't matter what I'm wearing or how much makeup I have on, I'll push you on your back and fuck this hot cunt of yours with my tongue..."

Her name howls past my lips as I come. My core gushing wetness, tightening and tingling, my senses all blanking out in one moment. Only to come back online in one overwhelming rush.

My breath heaving.

Heart drumming in my ears.

Skin damp with sweat.

Lips dry under the helpless swipe of my tongue.

"...until you scream my name just like that."

In the mirror, a half-moon of sweat gleams above Scottie's top lip, the edges of her elegant up-do are damp, and she looks as undone as I feel.

I'm a mess. My thighs tremble like I just finished running a marathon and I'm breathless, able to do nothing but lean back against her and gasp, grateful for her support. Slowly, I stand on my own shaking legs and reach for her, ready to show her as much pleasure as she showed me. But she takes my hands in hers.

"Later, baby." Her lips quirk up in that smile I'm becoming familiar with. "I don't want to smudge my lipstick."

I lick my lips. "I'm not offering anything that would involve those lips." And I go limp, preparing to slide to my knees in front of her, the image her hot words conjured burning inside me. I want to make her come, the desperation for it surprising me with its intensity.

"Baby, as much as I'd love to take advantage of your generous nature, we have reservations." She looks at her watch, mouth tilting up even more, and I realize she is exactly on time for what she had planned. A peek at her watch shows me it's a few minutes to eight. Just enough time for me to clean myself up, throw on my blouse, and do my makeup.

"You don't want me?"

The needy tone of my voice makes me cringe and I look away before I can seem too desperate. I just met the woman for fuck's sake. And she's not even my type. But Scottie takes my chin in hand.

"I want you, very, very badly." She takes my hand and puts it under her dress and I hiss in surprised pleasure at her lack of underwear, then another emotion entirely floods through me when I feel the drenched hairs and swollen lower lips. "I'd love nothing better than to push you back on this bed and ride your face until I come. But..." And she gently pulls my fingers away from her flesh, fingers that had automatically begun a slow stroke. "I want this to be something more than a pre-date finger bang and face fuck. I want to fuck you slow and in a bed. I want this—" She gestures between us. "—to last. If you're open to it, that is."

God...am I ever open. And all from one orgasm and a few nights of good conversation. This is one magical femme.

But even my cynicism can't hide how much I want this to go well—the date, the promised slow sex, everything Scottie has to offer.

"Okay," I say. Then, making sure she watches me, I lick the salty slick of her pussy from my fingers. She takes a single step toward me, then abruptly stops herself, a growl vibrating her throat. "Rain check then?" I ask, smiling.

"Rain check." Her voice is rough. She clears her throat. "Get ready, Nailah." And she looks at her watch again. "Dinner is set for eight thirty and I'm starving."

The mischievous smile she tips my way lights a fire low in my belly, and I want nothing more than to reach for her again and convince her to stay in and have a date night here. But now, I want what she wants. Something that burns hot and long and deep.

"In that case, we better get going," I tell her. "I wouldn't want you to go hungry tonight."

Scottie hums, a low and sexy sound that vibrates between my legs. "I'm sure all my hungers will get satisfied," she says. "If not tonight, then very soon."

Blushing, I turn away and rush to the bathroom to make short work of putting on my makeup. When I come back into the bedroom, she's standing before the mirror and reapplying the already perfect red to her lips. She sees me and caps the lipstick then slips it into a clutch purse I didn't notice earlier.

Her long-lashed eyes sweep my entire body in naked approval and make my stomach flutter like mad. "Are you ready?"

With my purse tucked under my arm, I lick the corner of my mouth, easily imagining the sweaty and satiated end to our evening. I smile and walk ahead of her out of the bedroom, my hips rocking even more than usual because of my high heels.

"For you?" I glance at her over my shoulder. "Absolutely."

Made in the USA
Columbia, SC
03 March 2018